Until the
End of Time

By Danielle Steel

THE RANCH • SILENT HONOR • MALICE
FIVE DAYS IN PARIS • LIGHTNING • WINGS
THE GIFT • ACCIDENT • VANISHED
MIXED BLESSINGS • JEWELS
NO GREATER LOVE • HEARTBEAT
MESSAGE FROM NAM • DADDY • STAR
ZOYA • KALEIDOSCOPE • FINE THINGS
WANDERLUST • SECRETS • FAMILY ALBUM
FULL CIRCLE • CHANGES
THURSTON HOUSE • CROSSINGS
ONCE IN A LIFETIME
A PERFECT STRANGER • REMEMBRANCE
PALOMINO • LOVE: *POEMS* • THE RING
LOVING • TO LOVE AGAIN
SUMMER'S END • SEASON OF PASSION
THE PROMISE • NOW AND FOREVER
PASSION'S PROMISE • GOING HOME

Nonfiction

A GIFT OF HOPE: *HELPING THE HOMELESS*
HIS BRIGHT LIGHT: *THE STORY OF
NICK TRAINA*

DANIELLE STEEL

Until the
End of Time

A Novel

DOUBLEDAY LARGE PRINT HOME LIBRARY EDITION

Delacorte Press New York

Published in the United States by Delacorte Press, an imprint of The Random House Publishing Group, a division of Random House, Inc., New York.

DELACORTE PRESS is a registered trademark of Random House, Inc., and the colophon is a trademark of Random House, Inc.

ISBN 978-1-62090-947-8

Printed in the United States of America

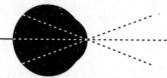

This Large Print Book carries the
Seal of Approval of N.A.V.H.

To my wonderful, beloved children, Beatrix, Trevor, Todd, Nick, Sam, Victoria, Vanessa, Maxx, and Zara, whom I love until the end of time, and beyond.

With all my love,
Mom

Love
　　is a shooting star
　　　　　　that lands
　　　　　　in your heart,
　　　　　　　　and lives
　　　　　　　　　forever.

Until the
End of Time

Bill and Jenny

1975

Chapter 1

The atmosphere in a room off the ballroom of the Hotel Pierre in midtown New
York was fraught with tension as forty-
five tall, rail-thin, bare-breasted models
were getting their hair and makeup done,
while simultaneously trying on shoes,
and dresses for last-second alterations.
David Fieldston was looking them over
carefully, while a cameraman filmed him
for a documentary on Fashion Week,
and he explained the inspiration for his
winter line. He was a stylish-looking man
in his late forties, with gray hair, and he
had been an important name in the

fashion world for twenty years. Two years earlier he had been on the verge of bankruptcy, and the fashion press said his designs lacked energy, his work was all déjà vu, and he was out of steam.

And now, thanks to a dynamo named Jenny Arden, he was back on the map. His last season had been his best one ever. His designs had taken off again, and his career with them. Every collection he'd done since Jenny Arden had begun advising him was vibrant, full of new, fresh ideas, and alive. He had taken off into the stratosphere and was better than ever, and privately he credited it all to her, and had told his closest friends and associates that she was a genius. Jenny was more modest about it, since she didn't do the actual designing, but she did research for him and came up with fresh inspiration for his line that made the collections exciting and really work. She met with him several times a week between seasons, and she was on hand, watching everything, when he presented the collection. And he paid her handsomely to do it. He wasn't

Jenny's only client, but he was her most impressive success so far.

Jenny came by her love for fashion honestly, and had followed it since she was a small child. Her French grandmother had been a première in the haute couture ateliers in Paris, and her mother was a dedicated seamstress. They had had a small but respected business in Philadelphia while Jenny was growing up, where they had diligently copied the finest designs and gowns from the couture houses in Paris. And at eighteen, after watching them all her life, Jenny had gone to Parsons School of Design in New York hoping to become a designer. She had found the classes tedious to the point of agonizing, discovered she had no talent herself for the mechanics of draping and wrestling with fabrics, and no patience to do so. She was much more interested in the trends and the direction that fashion was going.

Her clients in recent years liked to say that she was psychic, and could smell a fashion before it happened. Jenny *made* it happen, and knew just what to do when it did. She was a style director, and a muse for the designers she worked for, and no detail was too small for her meticulous attention. Accessories, and the way a fashion was worn, were everything, she insisted. It wasn't enough to design a dress, a coat, or a hat—you had to turn it into a living thing, she insisted, that breathed on its own and was not just an object. She was passionate about what she did, and she infused her vision and energy into her clients, and that turned up on the runway when they showed their clothes, just as it was about to happen when David Fieldston showed his new line to the fashion press and store buyers during Fashion Week in New York. The crowd was waiting breathlessly for the show to start. And while David was being interviewed, Jenny was doing her job, threading her way through the models, watching the hair and makeup with a keen eye, tugging a dress as it was put on, lifting the collar of a jacket, snapping a bracelet on a wrist, changing a shoe at the last minute.

"No, no, no!" she said, frowning, as

dressers put clothes on a model as though she were a doll. "The necklace is on backward, and she has the belt upside down." She rapidly made the necessary changes, nodded, and sped across the room to a model who was being sewn into a see-through lace dress. They hadn't had time to put the zipper in before the show. It happened all the time. And Jenny knew the dress would be a showstopper, you could see the model's naked breasts and most of her body except what was concealed by a flesh-colored G-string, which kept the model relatively decent. David had been nervous about it, and Jenny had assured him that it was 1975 and the country was ready to see breasts, at least on the runway, if nowhere else. Rudi Gernreich had come to the same conclusion, and his bold designs were sensational and had been well received. *Vogue* magazine had been showing breasts for a dozen years, since Diana Vreeland introduced them when she was editor in chief in 1963.

Diana Vreeland was Jenny's role model and goddess. Having realized that she didn't want to work on Seventh Avenue and be a designer to earn a living, Jenny had started out as an errand girl at *Vogue* when she graduated from Parsons eleven years before. She had eventually become the keeper of "The Closet," during Mrs. Vreeland's regime as editor in chief. Diana Vreeland had started at *Vogue* four years before Jenny got there. The Closet was where all the fabulous clothes were kept, and for a young girl inebriated by fashion, and in love with it since her earliest memories, it was sheer heaven. She got to see and touch all the beautiful things going in and out, and how they were put together for every photo shoot. Jenny soon caught the attention of the illustrious Mrs. Vreeland, and worshipped at her feet and became her senior assistant.

Then Jenny decided to leave the magazine five years after she'd arrived. Everyone said she was crazy, she had the perfect job. But she wanted to start her own fashion consulting business, to advise designers and style photo shoots on her own. And remarkably, the only support she got for her project was from

Mrs. Vreeland, who secretly told her she was doing the right thing. And much to Jenny's amazement, Diana Vreeland left *Vogue* at almost the same time. She had become a consultant to the Costume Institute at the Metropolitan Museum of Art, and she was in the audience at the Pierre, waiting to see David Fieldston's show that day. She had been incredibly good to Jenny, who was unfailingly loyal to her in exchange. Jenny had easily recognized the senior editor's genius when she worked for her every day, and had learned much from her, although she had her own distinctive style.

Like a good puppeteer, so nobody would notice her as she worked the strings from backstage, she was wearing black from head to foot, as Mrs. Vreeland had. Jenny's long, shining dark hair swept her shoulders in a straight blunt cut, she wore very little makeup, and her huge blue eyes took in the entire scene. The models were almost dressed by then, and she was still watching them like a hawk, thinking of nothing else. And seconds later she could hear the ballroom go quiet and the music come on. They were opening with a Beatles song, to keep the mood light. The clothes they were showing were for the following fall season, seven months away, so store buyers could order them now. And no one in the ballroom cared that it was the beginning of February and snowing outside. Orders had to be placed months in advance.

Jenny continued to watch the models, as they lined up and got ready to walk the runway. She was almost as tall as they were, minus the high heels. She was long and lean and beautiful herself, but she loved being invisible in this dazzling fashion world, always behind the scenes, making things happen. The producer of the runway show gave her a nod, and she signaled the first girl.

"Go!" she said, as their most beautiful model stepped through black velvet curtains onto the runway that ran the length of the ballroom and had taken two days to set up. It was made of copper, and Jenny had reminded the girls to be careful not to slip—no mean feat in six- and seven-inch-high heels. The shoes were only samples, usually made in only one size, as prototypes, pre-production, and often didn't fit. And they had to make it look effortless as they crossed one leg over the other and sauntered down the runway. And if one of them fell on the slippery surface in the awkward shoes, it wouldn't be the first time. Whatever happened, they had to keep going.

"Go!" Jenny signaled to each girl, making tiny corrections before they went out, as the first girls came back into the dressing room, and dressers stripped them and dressed them again. David Fieldston was watching from a slight distance, and looked as anxious as he always did, but Jenny could tell from the applause in the ballroom that the show was going well. And he had designed a spectacular fall line, with Jenny's help. She had vetoed several things he loved, and suggested others, and luckily it all worked, and he always forgave her for her interference and sometimes-offbeat suggestions. It was what he paid her for, and her advice had been flawless so far.

Jenny stood back with a smile as David rushed past her and kissed her cheek on his way to take a bow, with the last model in a brilliant green velvet evening gown, at the end of the show.

"You did it again!" he whispered with a grin, and then ran out to the runway to join the models. The applause was deafening. Jenny had spun him into an icon in two short years, and turned his career around. And he was grateful to her for all of it. He took nothing she did for granted. And the best part about it for Jenny was that she loved her job. This was what she had always dreamed of doing, making fashion work. Not just designing pretty dresses, but actually creating fashion and making it make sense, memorable, and something every woman wanted to own.

Fashion had been her passion ever since she could remember, and now she got to create it every day. She could think of nothing better, as she put little pouches of safety pins and double-sided tape into her bag, put on her coat, and literally ran out the door. Her next show, for a brand-new client, was in two hours, in a theater downtown. Fashion

Week was insane, and she loved every minute of it. She had done a show for one of her clients the day before, and had two more the next day. Designers rented restaurants, lofts, and theaters all over the city, or ballrooms like David Fieldston at the Pierre, to show their lines for the next season. And for someone like Jenny, it was a race to get there. Her new young designer, Pablo Charles, would be waiting for her breathlessly in an off-off-Broadway theater he had rented for his show.

Jenny ran across the lobby of the Hotel Pierre, carrying her heavy bag, as a tall, good-looking man ran behind her to catch up. He was even taller than she was, and snatched her bag out of her hand, as she turned to smile at him. It was her husband Bill, who had come to see the show. He tried to see them all, and he was always proud of what she did.

"What do you keep in here? Rocks to throw at the press?" he teased her, as he followed her through the door of the hotel onto the street. He was as fair as she was dark, and very aristocratic looking, and he had been in love with her since the day they met. He had always said it had been fate, and she had finally come to believe him. It felt that way to her now too. There was a town car and driver waiting for her at the curb to get to the next show, and Bill slipped into the car beside her. He had taken the afternoon off so he could see both shows. He was her biggest fan. "Great show, Jen. I loved the dresses at the end. So did the crowd. Suzy Menkes was smiling from ear to ear." She was the most important fashion journalist of all. And Bill had noticed Mrs. Vreeland there too, as a gesture of affection for Jenny. She always came.

Jenny looked pleased at her husband's comments as he leaned over to kiss her. For a man who hadn't known one designer from another when she met him, she had turned him into a fashion aficionado, and he thoroughly enjoyed what she did, and all the excitement around it. Although it was total insanity for her, he loved all the hype and chaos around Fashion Week. It felt like carnival time to him, when the circus came to town. And he had learned to appreciate the talent and expertise of what she did. He had great respect for her, particularly knowing how hard she'd worked to get there, and she had done it all herself. No one had ever made life easy for her until he came along. It was all he wanted to do for her, and she had been just as good to him. They had been married for five years. And their bond to each other had strengthened with each passing year.

Jenny came from humble beginnings, which was something he respected about her, and particularly her mother, who hadn't had an easy time. Jenny's mother Helene had come to the States to try and find opportunities she couldn't in France in the turbulent days before the Second World War. She had arrived in New York in the spring of 1939, a penniless seamstress, hoping to find a job, which turned out to be not as easy as she thought. She was nineteen years old, spoke no English, and wound up working in a sweatshop on the Lower East Side, sewing beads on sweaters for pennies, barely making enough to eat and pay rent. Her own mother was a trained seamstress at the house of Chanel, working in haute couture after an apprenticeship of twelve years. Helene always said her mother was an artist, and readily admitted she didn't have her skill.

Life in New York had been harder than she thought. She had been almost ready to give up and go home when the war broke out in Europe in September, and her mother told her to stay where she was. Life was even more arduous in France at the time, so Helene stuck it out at the sweatshop for three years, and then met a handsome young soldier on leave, at a party at the USO that a friend took her to in 1942. In the heat of passion and young love, and knowing he was shipping out, they married a week later, and Helene spent the rest of the war waiting for him to come home. Jenny had been born on a kitchen table on the Lower East Side in 1943. Her father came home two years later, and took his baby and war bride home to Pennsylvania. He had suggested to Helene several times while she waited for him that she live with his mother there, but she didn't want to go without him, and be among strangers. And by then she had friends in New York.

Nothing had prepared Helene for life in his hometown of Pittston, Pennsylvania, when Jack Arden came home. His family had been coal miners for generations, which he had told her, but she had had no idea what that meant, after growing up in Paris with genteel middle-class parents. Her father had been an art restorer and worked at the Louvre, her mother a talented seamstress who worked for Chanel. And Jack was a kind, loving man who adored Helene and treated her like a jewel. But they had no money, and his life was hard. He went back to his job in the coal mines where he had worked before the war, along with his four brothers and several cousins. Both his uncle and father had died in mining accidents years before, and his mother was a thin, sad woman who worried about her sons and cried all the time. And whenever there were strikes at the mine, Jack and Helene had no money at all. The weather was brutal, and sometimes all they had for dinner was bread and mayonnaise. Nothing he had said to her had warned her of the hardships of their life. But she never complained. She loved him too much to do so. What she remembered most about those years, when she talked about it afterward, was never having enough to eat, and never getting warm. Her mother-in-law had died the year they got there, and Helene couldn't get a job and leave Jenny alone.

Helene spent all her time taking care of her daughter and waiting for Jack to come home from the mine at night. They were both still very young. They wanted another child, but she miscarried several times, and they couldn't have afforded another child anyway. She missed France and longed to see her parents, but they had no money for her to go home. It was a miserable life, and the only thing that brightened it for her was her love for Jack, his tenderness with her, and the joy they derived from Jenny. Jenny remembered her father as a big man who played with her and carried her on his shoulders and told her bedtime stories. She looked a great deal like him, judging from photographs when he was young. Her mother was small and fair and looked very French.

They had been in Pittston for three years after the war, when there was an explosion in the anthracite coal mine where he was working, and Jack was one of five men killed that day. He had been greatly respected and well liked, and the head of the mining company came to tell Helene. They gave her a small settlement, but it was enough to make a difference to her, along with a surprisingly decent life insurance policy Jack had taken out for her in case something happened to him. It was more than most of the men had to leave their wives. The two amounts together allowed Helene to move to Philadelphia with Jenny.

Helene's father had died two months earlier in Paris, shortly before Jack, and her mother was sad, living alone. She tried to get Helene to return to Paris, but jobs were scarce after the war, and she had been in the States for nine years by then, and didn't want to go back, and convinced her mother to join them in

Philadelphia. Jenny was only five years old then, but she remembered moving from Pittston with her mother, and her grandmother arriving in the States to live with them.

The two women started a seamstress shop in Philadelphia after Thérèse, Helene's mother, arrived from Paris. Jenny had called her "Mamie," in the French tradition, and learned to speak French from her. The shop did well, and once one of the Main Line socialites discovered them, they became all the society ladies' "best little secret," copying Paris gowns for them. Thérèse's skill was remarkable, and Helene did the simpler work, lacking her mother's training. They made some beautiful dresses and earned a good income, which eventually sent Jenny to Parsons, where her own career began.

Jenny's first internship one summer, while still at school, was working for Oleg Cassini, during the time when he was making dresses for Jackie Kennedy when she was First Lady, and Jenny saw her there a few times, selecting designs for important occasions. Her

mother and grandmother had been excited to hear of it, and proud when Jenny
graduated, and landed the job at *Vogue*.

The two women were always excited
to hear about what Jenny was doing.
They subscribed to *Women's Wear Daily*
just so they could read about her. Their
little couture shop and the money
Jenny's father had left them had served
them well. Bill had been incredibly impressed by Jenny when he met her, and
even more so when he learned her history and met her mother and grandmother. He thought they were three remarkable women, and his wife most of
all. The five years of their marriage had
flown by, and he loved her more than
ever. His life had been improved by her
immeasurably, and Jenny insisted that
hers had been too. He was supportive
of everything she did. She was still at
Vogue when he saw her first, on a snowy
day in New York, when she was running
a shoot outside the Plaza, and in spite
of the weather, he had stopped to watch.

Jenny had been running around the
models like a shepherd dog, herding
them back to their places, as the snow

fell. She was wearing a huge fur hat herself, which she later told him was a po-
liceman's hat she had bought on the
black market in Moscow, while on another shoot. And she was wearing jeans,
boots, and a big down man's coat. Everyone on the set looked frozen, and
Jenny was moving too fast to care, as
she watched the photographer and
models, and made constant adjust-
ments to their clothing or their hair. Bill
had noticed them, as he hurried past on
his way to a meeting, and something
made him stop. He liked to say that it
was fate. He looked at Jenny and stood
there for so long in the falling snow
watching her that she turned and
glanced at him, and he smiled at her.
She smiled back as the snow landed on
her lashes and the Russian fur hat. He
just kept standing there, mesmerized by
her, feeling foolish. He had just graduated from law school the year before
and was working for his family law firm
with his father and brothers, but he was
bored by what he was doing, and everything about Jenny exuded joy.

He continued watching the photo

shoot in front of the Plaza, getting soaked himself by the snow, and during a break he approached her, and could have kicked himself afterward for what he said. He felt like a moron, but he didn't know what else to say. He walked toward her and extended his card to her, and burbled the words.

"If you ever need a lawyer . . . ," he said, as she grinned.

"I hope not," she answered, pocketing his card politely, and he had the distinct impression she would throw it away as soon as he left. Why would she need a lawyer? He didn't dare tell her how beautiful she was, or how mesmerized he was by her. His business card was the only thing that had come to mind as a way of telling her his name and how to reach him, not that she would. She was watching the photographer out of the corner of her eye, as she talked to Bill for a minute, and then nodded and told Bill she had to go back to work. As he walked away, feeling desolate, he could hear her talking to the photographer in French. He was certain he would never see her again. And she hadn't told him her name or how he could reach her. She was concentrating on her shoot, and Bill was sure she thought he was an idiot, with his ridiculous comment when he gave her the business card. He was haunted by her for days and thought she was the most beautiful woman he had ever seen. She was full of life, and when he had looked into her eyes, he felt like he could see her soul.

He had his secretary call several magazines to see if any of them had had photo shoots in front of the Plaza that day, and he eventually found out that it was *Vogue.* A very unfriendly voice at the magazine said that if he left a message they would give it to her but they wouldn't give him her name. Feeling even more stupid and awkward than the first time, he asked the girl to say that "Bill Sweet had called to say hello" and left his number. He was sure he'd never hear from her. And after that, he put Jenny out of his mind and went back to work. He was doing estate work for a client, and the prospect of doing that for the rest of his life was not a cheering one. But that was what the men in his family did. None of them seemed to mind it, and his brothers, both of whom were older than he was, actually liked their work, as partners of the firm. It was one of the most respected law firms in New York, and had been founded by his great-grandfather. They were blue bloods serving other blue bloods, just as they had for generations. It had never dawned on Bill to do anything else.

A week later, he was driving to Boston to meet with one of their clients, about setting up trusts for his grandchildren, when he stopped to get gas halfway there. It was March, it had been a long, bitter-cold winter, and it was snowing again. He got out of his car, while the attendant filled his tank, when a rental truck lumbered in, and a woman jumped out impatiently waiting for service. He watched her for a minute, and as she turned toward him, squinting in the snow, he saw the Russian fur hat again. And this time he was absolutely certain that their meeting was fated. How could he run into the same woman twice? He had thought he'd never see her again. He was smiling when he walked toward her, and she looked up at him in surprise. He acted as though they'd already met.

"I left you a message," he said, looking at her cautiously, "but I don't suppose you got it." He was smiling down at her, like a kid at Christmas, and feeling foolish again. He felt fourteen years old, while she looked so cool and poised.

"I think I did." She smiled back at him. "You're a lawyer, right? I haven't gotten into any trouble yet." She still had his card somewhere in a coat pocket or on her desk. She remembered that his name was Bill Sweet. For some reason, it had stuck in her mind.

"What's with the truck?" he teased her. "Are you driving away from a bank robbery, or moving furniture for a friend?"

"I'm doing a shoot in Massachusetts." It was a story about an important socialite, being shot by a famous French photographer. "For *Vogue*," she added for good measure.

"I tried to get in touch with you after I saw you at the Plaza. They wouldn't tell me your name, which makes sense. I probably sounded like a stalker." She

laughed at what he said, and the earnest look in his eyes. He looked like a
nice guy, and she could see he was nervous talking to her, which touched her.
Most of the men she met were sophisticated and blasé.

"They're used to stalkers where I
work. Most of the time they're after the
models, not the assistants," she said
with a wry look. Her fur hat was covered with snow again, just like the first
time. He couldn't believe he'd actually
run into her again. It was the best luck
he'd had in years, possibly ever.

"Their mistake," he answered her
comment, as the attendant serviced her
car. "When are you going back to New
York?" he asked her, feeling breathless.
What if she said it was none of his business? He was a stranger, after all. It was
a Thursday afternoon, and he was going back the following night, for the
weekend. He had a date on Saturday
with a girl he'd been seeing for a month,
had nothing in common with, and didn't
really like, but she was the younger sister of his brother's wife, and Bill had
nothing else to do. He knew a thousand

girls just like her, but not one like Jenny.
He could already tell. Everything about
her was exciting and different.

"It depends when we finish the shoot,"
she said vaguely. "Saturday or Sunday.
I'm driving all the props up to dress the
set. I'll be the last one to leave." He was
sorry he couldn't offer to drive with her.
He had a feeling he would have enjoyed
it. She looked like she laughed a lot.
There was a twinkle in her eyes.

"Would you like to get together next
week?" he asked bravely.

"I would, but I've got three shoots
back to back. That's what I do. I style
for the magazine, which means I'm in
charge of a lot of their photo shoots, for
the back of the book, the fashion sec-
tion." He nodded, trying to pretend he
knew what she meant, but he didn't.
And he could hardly concentrate when
he looked at her. All he could see were
her beautiful big blue eyes, her smile,
and her sensual lips. And he couldn't
tell if she was brushing him off or was
as busy as she said.

"Do you get a day off?" he asked,
looking hopeful.

"Once in a while. Not very often. It's kind of like being married to your job." She looked as if she didn't mind it, which made him curious about her.

"Do you like what you do?"

"I love it." She looked happy as she said it. "This is what I've always wanted to do."

"Drive a truck, delivering furniture?" he joked, and she laughed.

"Yeah, something like that. You can come to one of the shoots if you want. We're doing two in a studio next week, and one on location in Harlem, at a nightclub called Small's Paradise. We rented it for the night. I'll probably get a dinner break around ten P.M. You can meet me there, and we can do KFC, or a funny Chinese place we eat at sometimes when we're uptown. It's a dive, but the food is terrific. I can't take long though. I've got four big models that night, they're flying in from London and Milan." It sounded like fun to him. And he would have agreed to meet her on a subway platform, with or without food.

"Sounds good," he confirmed, and she told him where to meet her on

Thursday night, and said she'd call if anything changed. And then he thought of something he needed to know urgently. "What's your name?"

"Jenny Arden. You can call me at *Vogue* if anything changes. I have a pager, but I only use it for work." She never gave the number out.

"I won't call, Jenny Arden. See you Thursday night. Have fun on your shoot this weekend."

They both paid for their gas, and she opened the door to the truck and got in. "It's kind of funny we should meet like this," she said thoughtfully as she looked at him, and he wanted to say it was something to tell their grandchildren, but he didn't dare.

"No big deal. I've just been following you for two months," he said with a boyish grin, and she laughed.

"See you Thursday," she said, and waved at him as she drove away in the snow. Bill was smiling all the way to Boston, and he could hardly wait to see her again. He felt like destiny had been very, very kind.

* * *

Their date the following week was typical of Jenny's life while she worked for *Vogue.* Everything was moving slowly on the shoot. One of the models was sick, and the photographer had a temper tantrum. She didn't get a dinner break till after midnight, and by then the Chinese restaurant was closed. Bill stood by patiently, and they went to Burger King for twenty minutes instead. He was fascinated by what she did, and stuck around for another hour, watching what happened on the set. He was impressed by how efficient she was. She had everything in control. He left around one-thirty in the morning, and when he called her the next day, to see how it went, she said they'd been there till four A.M. She said they worked all night sometimes, and as she and Bill got to know each other better, she explained that it accounted for the fact that she had no life except her work, but she didn't seem to mind.

They dated haphazardly for the next few months, and they had a great time together. All other women paled by comparison, and he found he was learning everything he had never needed to know about the fashion world. But she made it interesting for him. And eventually, he admitted to her how little he enjoyed his own work.

"Isn't there something you can do related to the law that would be more fun?" she asked sympathetically.

"Not in my father's firm. They're the best tax lawyers in New York. I thought I'd like to be a litigator at one point, or do criminal law, but my father would never forgive me if I left the firm. And it must be me—my brothers love what they do. I do as much pro bono work as I can, with the indigent, and the ACLU, and through the courts, but my father isn't too thrilled with that either." Bill was two years older than Jenny, but she seemed so sure about what she wanted to do, and was on her path. Most of the time he felt lost in the woods and off course. It embarrassed him to be so much less certain than she. She loved everything about her work, even the long hours and crazy situations she handled every day. None of it bothered her, and she enjoyed the challenge.

They'd been dating for two months, when he decided to take a theology class at Columbia. It was something he had always wanted to do. He didn't tell his father or brothers, but he told Jenny, and she thought it was a great idea. She was always encouraging and open to new ideas, and he admired that about her. In fact, he was crazy about her, and six months after they started dating, he was head over heels in love, and she admitted she was too. They had no plans to do anything about it—they just reveled in the time they spent together. And when he finished the theology class, he signed up for three more. He was taking them at night, so they didn't interfere with his work. But he was having much more fun at school at night than at his father's firm. By now he hated everything he did there. He had tried to question his brothers about it several times, but they both insisted they were satisfied and happy with what they did. They were both married, and their wives looked like all the girls they had grown up with. They were blond, blue-eyed debutantes, whose families had known their own for years. His older brother Tom's mother-in-law had gone to Vassar with their mother. And neither of Bill's sisters-in-law worked. And they'd each had two children. To Bill, they seemed like cookie-cutter lives, predictable from birth to the grave.

Jenny was so much more interesting and came from a totally different world. Her early years in a mining town, with a coal miner father, only made her more intriguing to him, and he was impressed by her success. She had come a long way from Pittston, Pennsylvania. And he thought her mother and grandmother were lovely women who were dignified and brave. He had gone to Philadelphia with Jenny and met them both, and they had been warm and welcoming to him, unlike his own family, who couldn't have been worse when they met Jenny. With considerable trepidation, he had taken Jenny to meet his parents at their Connecticut weekend home, over the Labor Day weekend, six months after they started dating.

His father was jovial with her at first, but Bill knew him better and saw something cold in his eyes. And his mother conducted the interrogation about where she had grown up, where she had graduated from college, and if she'd gone to boarding school. Jenny was open and honest and ingenuous with them. She told them about her father, and moving to Philadelphia. She said she had gone to public school there, then to Parsons, and she told them about her job at *Vogue.* To anyone else, it would have been a success story, and they would have been impressed. To his parents, her entire history was a crime, and dating their son made it even worse. His brothers looked at her strangely, and their wives had been incredibly rude to her and ignored her completely. As far as they were concerned, a coal miner's daughter did not belong in their midst. If they had thrown rocks at her, their message wouldn't have been clearer. Bill was furious and humiliated by the time they left after dinner, and he apologized to Jenny profusely on the way back to New York.

"Don't be silly. They probably didn't know what to expect, and they don't meet people out of their own milieu very often. I deal with people like that all the time." Some of the socialites they shot for *Vogue* were truly nasty to her and treated her like a slave. Her feelings were a little hurt this time, but Bill was so upset about it that she felt sorry for him. Clearly, she was not welcome with his family—they had made that clear—which was embarrassing for him. "Don't worry about it," she reassured him as they drove home. "They were probably terrified you would say you're going to marry me," she laughed. Bill pulled the car over and turned to look at her.

"Jenny, that's exactly what I have in mind," he said in a gentle voice. "I don't deserve you, and my family sure as hell doesn't. I don't care what they think, I want to spend the rest of my life with you. I love you. Will you marry me?" Jenny stared at him with wide eyes. She knew they loved each other, but she had had no idea that that was what he was thinking. She knew the world he came from, and there was no way she could fit in. They would never accept her, and she was afraid that they would punish Bill if he married her.

"What about your parents? They'd be heartbroken if you married me," she said sincerely with sad eyes. She didn't want to destroy his life, but she loved him just as much.

"I'd be heartbroken if you didn't marry me." He was being honest. He had intended to ask her by the end of the year, maybe at Christmas. But he loved her so much, and wanted her to know how serious he was about her. His family's shoddy treatment of her had made him want to speak up now. He kissed her then, even before she answered, and she looked at him solemnly.

"Do you mean that?" she asked him in a whisper.

"Yes, I do." His eyes never left hers. "Jenny Arden, will you marry me? If you do, I will love you until the end of time." She smiled when he said it. He was so earnest, and such a good man. She had known from the very beginning that he was the one for her. And he had finally convinced her that it was destiny that

they'd met. They were perfect for each
other, they got along, and the fact that
their paths had crossed twice seemed
like more than just happenstance or
blind luck. They felt made for each other,
whatever his parents thought.

"Yes," she said in a tiny voice, with
tears in her eyes. "Your parents will kill
you, though. I didn't go to boarding
school, or Vassar. I was never a debutante, and I'm not blond." She was teasing him a little, but she had them nailed.

"I don't give a damn," he said, smiling, as he kissed her again. He was ecstatic, and she was smiling too. They
were engaged! "I'm twenty-nine years
old, and they're not going to stop me
from marrying the woman I love. And
besides, they may have been rude today, but they have no right to interfere
with us."

As it turned out, he underestimated
them. His father was outraged and discussed it with Bill in an icy tone. His
mother had nearly fainted when he told
them. "Are you *insane*? A *coal miner's*
daughter? Are you on drugs?" And his
brothers had begged him not to break

their parents' hearts. They said that Jenny seemed like a nice girl, but not someone he should marry. They told him he'd get over it, and when he assured them he was serious, his brother Peter had stormed out of the room and slammed the door, after telling him he had been a weirdo all his life, and now it was obvious he was nuts. Tom was more restrained, but clearly felt the same way. They acted as though he had told them he was planning to join a monastery or cut off his head. No one in the family had ever married someone who wasn't in the Social Register, and hadn't been a blue blood for countless generations. Bill didn't tell Jenny how bad it got or how rude they were, and their appalling behavior convinced him even more that he was right, and he didn't want to wait.

On Thanksgiving, he told them that he and Jenny were going to be married in January, in a small ceremony. They had decided to get married in New York, in a tiny church they loved. Her grandmother and mother were going to come, and there would be a lunch afterward.

Bill's mother burst into tears, and Bill was grateful that Jenny wasn't there to hear it. She had gone to Philadelphia while he told them on his own. It was a painful weekend for Bill. They didn't sway him, but they made it as hard for him as they could. By Sunday, his parents said they would give a luncheon for them at their home after the wedding, providing they kept it small. They didn't want to lose him by boycotting the event, but Bill had the feeling they would have planned his funeral with less despair. All of them were treating his marriage to Jenny as a tragedy. He was exhausted when he went home that night, and he spared Jenny the details of the weekend. He told her about the luncheon his parents were giving for them after the wedding. She had spent the weekend designing her wedding gown with her mother and grandmother. She wanted something very simple, but spectacularly beautiful for their big day. It was going to be absolutely exquisite, covered with incredibly delicate embroideries and tiny pearls, encrusted on antique lace. It was a gown that would have cost a fortune in Paris and would look magnificent on Jenny.

The wedding went off as expected. Bill and Jenny were radiant in the tiny church with a few friends. Her mother and grandmother were happy for her, though concerned about her unpleasant in-laws. And Bill's family was as chilly as possible to Jenny and her family and gave restrained toasts at the luncheon, that made their disapproval clear. Bill and Jenny were both relieved when it was over, and they went to the Bahamas for a week and had a wonderful time, although the atmosphere in the office was painful when he returned to work. They treated him like an outcast and never mentioned his wife, as though she didn't exist. And they wished she didn't.

It made Bill's next decision easier, when he completed the three theology classes he'd been taking. And as he did with everything, he told Jenny first. He wanted her approval before taking such a major step. He hoped to enter the seminary, get a master's of divinity, and become an Episcopal minister when he graduated. He had already explored the possibility, and he could do his course-work at Columbia. It would take three years, or four or even five if he stretched it out. He wanted to leave his father's law firm and go to school full time. It was a huge decision and a complete change of course. He had no idea how Jenny would feel about it, but he was sure now that it was right for him.

"I think I have a vocation," he said, looking embarrassed. "That sounds so holier-than-thou. But I've loved every-thing I studied for the past year. I thought about it a lot, and it feels so right. But I don't know what you think about being married to a minister." He looked wor-ried, but she smiled tenderly at him.

"Will you still love me when you're a minister?" she asked gently.

"More than ever," he said, and kissed her.

"Will you object to my working in something as superficial as fashion?" She looked concerned, and Bill seemed startled by the question.

"Of course not, silly. I'm proud of what you do. I'm not going to turn into some righteous prig if I become a minister. I just want to do some good in the world, and I think that's the right way for me."

"I think so too," she said gently, "and I'm proud of you too. I think it's a wonderful idea, if that's what you want to do and it makes you happy. I'm behind you a thousand percent." She always was, which meant the world to him. He told her then that he was planning to quit the family law firm, and she was worried for him about the explosion it was likely to cause, and possibly a serious rift with his father and brothers.

"I'm ready for it," he said calmly, looking wise and mature. Making the decision to do what he wanted had already grounded him. And he looked more peaceful and sure of himself than she had ever seen him. It was obvious to both of them that it was the right thing for him to do.

The ensuing explosion, when he told his father and brothers that he was leaving, was entirely predictable. He told them that he believed he had a vocation, which they brushed off as immature and irresponsible. No man in the Sweet family had ever not become an attorney or quit the law firm, and none had ever joined the church. His brother Peter told him he was psychotic, and Tom just looked pained. And for good measure, they all blamed Jenny.

Bill left the law firm in February, and began his coursework at Columbia in March, toward his master's of divinity, and he had never looked back after that, or regretted it for a moment, although his family still acted as though he was doing something truly crazy, and even dishonorable. Bill stayed on his path, with Jenny's support, and stretched his studies to the full five years.

As they headed downtown to the second fashion show she was doing that night, he was five months away from graduation. He was going to be a minister. Jenny had encouraged him all along the way, just as he had done for her when she left *Vogue* and began consulting. And if anything, he had become more tolerant and compassionate over time. He had discovered that his strength was in the Arts of Ministry, which integrated psychiatry and psychology into the counseling he did. His gift was working with people in a religious context, rather than the drier areas of theology, church history, or Bible studies, although he enjoyed them as well. But his real forte was in reaching out and offering comfort. Jenny was proud of how much he had grown in the past five years, and their marriage had never been better. All was well in their world.

Her grandmother had died two years after they were married, which had been a great sorrow to Jenny, and she still missed her. She thought of her while she was planning to give Bill a lunch when he graduated from Columbia in June, and wished Thérèse could have been there. Her mother was coming from Philadelphia. Helene still made dresses for her clients, though far less elaborate ones than Thérèse had made. But she made a good living at it and led a comfortable life.

They were going to invite his parents

to the graduation, and Jenny was determined not to let them ruin it for them
this time, as they had tried to do with
their wedding. This was going to be Bill's
big day, and she wanted everything to
be perfect for him. She had been planning it for months.

He got out of the car with her, when
they reached the theater that Pablo
Charles had rented for his show. She
had been there, planning the production
with him until two in the morning the
night before, and everything had been
under control. It was organized chaos
when Bill followed her backstage to
where the models were putting on their
clothes. Half of them were naked, and
Bill no longer even noticed. He was so
used to it, it seemed commonplace to
him, and they were so emaciated, and
most of them were so young, they didn't
even look like women to him. Most of
the girls they used as runway models
were between fifteen and seventeen.
  Pablo was frantically sewing a high
embroidered collar onto a dress when

they walked in, and he looked at Jenny in panic.

"The fucking thing just arrived from the embroiderer ten minutes ago. How do they expect me to get it on in time for the show?" He was desperate as Jenny told him she'd take care of it, and signaled to one of the women doing last-minute alterations and showed her how to put the collar in. She left her struggling with it on the model, and then sewed it quickly and expertly, as Jenny went to check on everything else. It was all in order, and even though Pablo was a bundle of nerves, she could see that his show was going to be a hit. He was a young Puerto Rican man with enormous talent, who had emerged as a major star in the past two years, in great part with Jenny's help.

"Hang in," she told him when she saw him again. "It's almost over, and the show is going to be fabulous. Trust me."

Bill watched her as she raced around backstage solving problems, amazed, as he always was, at what she did. She was a magician, and she pulled rabbits out of the hat every time.

Bill kissed her before he went to the auditorium to take his seat. He was happy to be there with her, and give her the support she gave him. "See you after the show. Knock 'em dead!" he whispered to her, and then went to find his place among the buyers and the press. He recognized most of them now, and enjoyed talking to some of them. It was a world he found interesting at times, and he loved seeing how respected Jenny was in her field. It was richly deserved. She was a talented woman, and she worked hard. She had climbed the mountain all by herself, under her own steam. The coal miner's daughter from Pittston, Pennsylvania, had become a star in the fashion world. It had taken her eleven years to get where she was today, and three before that at Parsons. It had been a long, hard, dedicated climb to success.

As he sat down in the audience, squeezed on either side by buyers from the Midwest, he was thinking about Jenny and smiled to himself. He was a happy man, deeply in love with his wife, and they were both pursuing careers they loved. You couldn't ask for more than that, except for a family of their own one day. They talked about it a lot. But for now, the blessings they shared seemed abundant to them.

Chapter 2

The day after the last fashion show of February Fashion Week, most of the designers started working on their next collection, which was resort. There was no breathing space in the fashion business, no downtime. The minute you finished one collection and one season, you moved on to the next. And the weeks after the shows were always a busy time for Jenny, meeting with each of the designers she worked with and advised, talking about the next season. It was a time to throw out new ideas. Many of the designers did historical research, digging back into the archives, even to find designers who were no longer remembered but had been important at one time. The weeks after Fashion Week were all about inspiration, and Jenny was part of that process. More than one designer called her their muse. And she had fun discussing their research with them. She also enjoyed working with designers who were entirely different from each other and unique. The clean, more classic look of David Fieldston contrasted with the wild, edgy young spirit of Pablo Charles and the half dozen other designers she worked with. It was a little schizophrenic collaborating with such different people, but it made the process more exciting for her. And she had two assistants now, who helped her keep all the balls in the air. They took care of appointments and logistics, but she did all the design consulting herself. That was what her clients hired her for.

One of her assistants, Nelson Wu, was a young Chinese boy from Hong Kong originally, who wanted to become a designer one day himself. He made clothes in his loft in the Village. He worked for Jenny occasionally to help her out, and was more passionate about his own designs. But he enjoyed his time with her, and she was grateful for it when she was overwhelmed.

Her other assistant was with her full time. She had dropped out of Parsons, when she had discovered that design-ing wasn't for her. She was an excellent illustrator and photographer, and did a little freelance photography at night or on the weekends. Jenny had discovered that most people in the fashion industry, if they were truly creative, wore many hats, just as she did herself. And Azaya Jackson was a beautiful girl, whose mother was Ethiopian and had been a famous model. Azaya had grown up with fashion, and also did some model-ing on the side. She took a real interest in Jenny's clients and had great admira-tion for her. They had met when Azaya modeled for a shoot when Jenny was at *Vogue,* and she had turned up again when Jenny was looking for an assis-tant once she had gone out on her own. She was twenty-five years old, very bright, and excited to be working with Jenny. She was willing to do any task and hungry to learn the business side of fashion.

And just as Jenny had been until she met Bill, Azaya was so busy with so many projects, she never had time for a social life. She was in the office all the time, and Jenny always urged her to go out and have some fun.

"Just like you, right?" Azaya teased her. "When was the last time you and Bill went out? You work late every night."

"That's different." Jenny smiled at her. "I'm married, and I'm older than you are. Besides, Bill has exams." He was wrapping up all his final classes, finishing his term papers, and completing his thesis for his master's. By the time Jenny was deep into the resort collection with her designer clients, in mid-March, Bill was three months from graduation, and struggling to get everything done. He was grateful that Jenny was busy too, and happy not to go out. They planned to celebrate in June and take a vacation. But until then, neither had time for fun. And they were happy with what they

were doing, so it didn't matter. And they
knew it was only temporary. After Bill
graduated, they'd have more time.

He was in the process of applying to
churches at the moment. He had written to dozens of Episcopal churches in
the city and nearby suburbs, hoping to
find one that needed a young minister
freshly out of school. He didn't want to
commute for many hours a day, and
where he worked had to be close to the
city for Jenny's career. She was too
busy and had too many clients and projects to commute. And everything she
did was based in New York. She ran
from one meeting to the next all day,
looking at new designs, consulting with
her clients about fabrics, discussing the
direction they were taking with the next
collection, and new trends. Bill knew he
couldn't consider a job that was too far
away. But so far, no one had offered him
one. He had recently listed himself with
a service that sent out inquiries about
positions in churches all over the United
States, but he had been very clear that
he had to stay in New York. And every
place he had applied to in the city had

turned him down. They had no openings and the same was true in the suburbs closest to New York. He wasn't discouraged yet, he was sure that something would turn up. He had applied to a few churches in Connecticut and New Jersey, but nothing had panned out there yet either. He had feelers out all over the place.

He was working on his thesis one afternoon when his brother Tom called and invited him to lunch the next day. Bill rarely enjoyed contact with his family, but he didn't want to alienate them any further, and he tried to see them whenever he could. Tom was usually more reasonable than Peter or his father, although he didn't pretend to understand the choices his younger brother had made—neither his choice of wife, nor his decision to become a minister. It seemed like a terrible waste of a bright legal mind and an excellent legal education and the social connections he had. And they needed him at the firm. Bill's radical break with family tradition was incomprehensible to Tom.

In an effort to keep the channels of

communication open, Tom and Bill met
for lunch at "21" the next day. It was
familiar turf for both of them, and a restaurant they both liked and had enjoyed
going to since they were boys.

"So what are you up to these days?"
Tom asked, sounding cordial, after they
both ordered a glass of wine. The two
brothers were ten years apart. Tom had
just turned forty-four, and it always
shocked Bill now to realize that his
brother was middle-aged, and even Peter would be turning forty in a few
months. And each of his brothers had
two children, while he and Jenny had
none. Their lives and focus seemed very
different. And even more shocking to
Bill, Tom's younger son was in high
school, and his older boy had just started
college. Bill told Jenny that it made him
feel old, even though he was only thirty-
four. At least his brother Peter's children
were considerably younger.

"I'm working on my thesis," Bill said
in answer to his brother's question. "It's
taking me forever."

"Have you found a job yet?" Tom

asked him casually, and Bill shook his head.

"There are waiting lists a mile long for churches in the city, and the suburbs aren't much better. And we can't get too far out of town. I can't do that to Jenny. She has too much work." Tom nodded, well aware that she was some kind of hotshot in the field of fashion, although he had no exact idea of what her job was. He knew she ran her own business, but it always sounded frivolous to him. It was not a business that interested him.

"Do you two ever think about having kids, or is that not in the picture?" Tom asked Bill for the first time. He had no idea that they had been trying to get pregnant for the last two years, but Bill didn't tell him that. Jenny was discouraged about it, but her job was stressful, and she was running around all the time. Bill was sure it would happen at the right time. Maybe when they had a vacation, which they hadn't had for a year.

"We talk about it," Bill said quietly, not anxious to share his worries with his brother. Anything he ever confided to

them, they used against him later. And
that was too sensitive an issue for him
to want to discuss with anyone but
Jenny. He would have felt as if he were
betraying her, if he shared their concerns with Tom. "There's no hurry," he
said vaguely.

"You two aren't getting any younger,"
Tom said bluntly. "But I guess her career means more to her than a baby,"
he added unkindly. His family didn't even
know her, but they never cut her any
slack. They were all too willing to believe that she was a bad person because
she had been born on what they considered the wrong side of the tracks.

"I'm sure she'll be a wonderful mother,"
Bill said fairly. "And I need to find a
church before we start having kids. First
things first." He looked calm about it.

Tom hesitated only for a moment before he dove in. "What about coming
back to the firm? You have a ready-
made job just sitting there, waiting for
you. You don't have to knock yourself
out finding a church. You can do volunteer work on weekends." They still considered his dedication to the ministry an

eccentric hobby, not a vocation. Bill had long since given up trying to convince them how much it meant to him. "Dad's not getting any younger. He's going to retire one of these days, and I think it would be a great comfort to him if he knew you were back in the fold. I know how much the pro bono work meant to you. Maybe we could make some arrangement. You could be a full partner, and take a lesser share of the profits, if you don't want to take on paying clients." It had been an issue for them before.

"It's not about money," Bill explained to him quietly. "I feel strongly that we each have our destiny to follow. This is mine. It took me a long time to figure it out. I know I'm on the right path, with the right woman. My marrying Jenny wasn't an accident. It was meant to be. Just like your being married to Julie." Tom didn't comment, he just nodded, but Bill noticed a troubled look in his brother's eyes.

"How can you be so sure?" Tom asked him, suddenly serious. Bill seemed so certain about what he was doing, and

Tom was never quite sure if he had a crazy streak or was saner than all of them. He seemed totally at peace.

"It'll sound stupid to you, I'm sure, but I pray a lot. I try to listen. And I always know in my gut if what I'm doing is right. Or very wrong. I was miserable when I was working at the law firm. I knew it wasn't right for me. I hated going to work every day, I felt like I was crawling out of my skin. And as soon as I started seminary, I knew I was on the right path. I knew it with my first theology class. It was like a magnet. Everything clicked. It was like that when I met Jenny. From the minute I met her, I was sure. I knew we were *meant* to be together." He said it with such certainty that Tom stared at him for a long moment, trying to understand. "Didn't you feel that way about Julie? You two were so in love," Bill asked his older brother earnestly.

"I'm not sure I ever felt that we were 'meant' to be together," Tom said honestly. "She was just the prettiest deb of the season, and that I'd been out with until then, and we had a lot of fun. We were both young. Twenty years later, it's all different. You need more than just a pretty deb. And people change when they grow up. Neither of us knew who we were then." Tom had married young, five years younger than Bill had been when he married Jenny, and not as wise.

Bill wasn't sure what his brother meant by what he'd said and he didn't want to pry. Tom didn't look happy. Both he and Peter had been married for a long time, to women Bill wouldn't have wanted to be married to, but it had seemed to work for them. Julie and Georgina were like everyone else they'd known growing up, but their marriages had lasted, Bill had always thought they were content, and they had decent kids. Jenny was very different, she was deeper, stronger, her own person, and he loved the life they shared. And everything between them was honest.

"Whatever works," Bill said reasonably. "Jenny and I are happy. I hope you are too. No one in the family ever gave Jenny a break, and God knows she deserved one. She's a terrific person. But we've done fine anyway."

Tom didn't comment. Occasionally he

felt guilty about it, but not enough so to make an effort to get to know Jenny. And Peter made no effort at all. He was still outraged by Bill's choice of wife, and so were their parents. It was as though they considered it a personal affront to them. Tom was more reasonable about it, and simply ignored Jenny when he saw her, and only addressed Bill. But at least he wasn't overtly rude to her, like Peter and their parents.

"Do I have any chance of talking you into coming back to the law firm?" he asked, giving it one last shot, and realizing once again that the chance was slim to none. His younger brother shook his head.

"It may take a while, but I want to find a church. I got an offer from one in Kentucky, but I refused it. Something will turn up. Jenny keeps telling me to be patient."

"Let us know if you change your mind," Tom said, as he picked up the check. He had invited Bill. But he knew Bill wasn't going to alter his course now. He was eager to find a church so he could enter the active ministry, not practice law.

"I'm as likely to go back to being a lawyer as you are to enter the church," Bill said, laughing, as they walked out of the restaurant. "Thanks for lunch." He smiled at his brother and hailed a cab. Tom walked back to the office, thinking about what Bill had said. He seemed so sure about everything. Tom envied him that. And Peter asked him about how Bill was when he got back to the office.

"He's fine. He seems happy in his life, and sure of what he's doing. Maybe happier than we are. Who knows? Maybe he really does have a vocation. I can tell you one thing—he's never coming back to the firm."

"He's always been a little nuts," Peter said, sounding dismissive and very smug.

"I don't think he is," Tom said honestly, more respectful of Bill than Peter ever had been. "He's doing what he wants to do, and believes in, and he's married to a woman he's crazy about. What's so nuts about that?"

"You can't just walk away from history and tradition, give up a career with the most respected law firm in New York, and marry some girl from nowhere. What's that all about? Teenage rebellion? He needs to grow up," Peter said with a sour look.

"I think he has grown up. He doesn't want the same things we do. He never did. He never went out with the kind of women we did, and I think he hated every minute he worked for the firm. He wants to go out and help people. Maybe that's not so wrong." Tom was trying to be fair.

But Peter was having none of it. He thought Bill's marching to a different drummer was juvenile, and their father thought so too. Their mother was more upset about Jenny than the law firm. Not one of them approved of him, or the choices he had made.

"That's fine if you want to join the Peace Corps at twenty. He's thirty-four years old, and he wants to be a Boy Scout." Tom was shocked at what Peter said. After what he'd heard at lunch, it sounded disrespectful. Bill was joining the church, after all, not the Boy Scouts.

"I'm not sure most ministers consider themselves Boy Scouts. There's room for both camps in the world," Tom reminded him. "What we do, and what he does. Bill wants to repair the broken of spirit. We just handle their taxes." Bill's choice seemed nobler to him.

"Try telling Dad that. It nearly broke his heart when Bill left the firm. And Mom's, when he married Jenny. How much sense does that make? I never questioned following in Dad's footsteps, and neither did you. What makes Bill so special?"

"Maybe we should have. Maybe he's got more guts than either of us," Tom said, looking thoughtful. The peaceful look in Bill's eyes at lunch had impressed him, and he was envious of it.

"Oh, for God's sake," Peter said, shaking his head. "Not you too. We have a great life, partnership in the best law firm in New York, permanent job security until the end of our days. What more do you want?" It was a big question, and Tom didn't answer him, but he was still thinking about it when he went back to his own office. Peter was the most similar to their father, dictatorial, authoritarian, traditional, and he expected his sons to be the same and follow in his footsteps. Peter had done it without wavering for a moment. And Tom as well, until now, but somehow he wondered if there wasn't more to life than living by tradition. And Bill had balked and refused to do any of it, and as far as Tom could see, Bill was happier than either of them, and more at peace. He admired him for that. Tom was beginning to ask himself questions, and lately he had none of the answers. His life was the sum of its parts, and some of it seemed sadly lacking. Bill seemed to have it all. A vocation he was certain of, and Jenny, who made him happy, and seemed like a nice girl—more than that, she was a good person, and so was Bill.

When Bill got back from lunch, he went through the mail and found several answers from churches he had sent letters to. Three had turned him down, and another one said they had put him on a waiting list. And he read the last letter several times. He had gotten it as a result of the letters sent out by the placement service for ministers. It wasn't a church he had solicited or even one he could consider. He read the letter one last time, folded it, and put it back in the envelope. And then he slipped it into a drawer in his desk and sat down to work on his thesis.

He had enjoyed seeing Tom, more than he usually did. He had expected him to try and convince him to come back to the law firm, but he had backed off faster than usual, so it hadn't turned into an argument. And he had no idea why, but as he thought of his older brother, he felt sorry for him. He had bought the party line, both his brothers had. But something about Tom seemed defeated now. He had sold his soul to be what their father expected, and so had Peter. Bill was so glad he hadn't stayed. Their lives seemed so empty to him.

*   *   *

Bill told Jenny about his lunch with Tom when she got home that night, tired after a long day.

"Did he ask you to come back to the firm?" she asked, relaxing on the couch, as he handed her a glass of wine. She loved coming home to him and telling him about her day. And he was happy to see her after hours of studying and working on his thesis. It was going well.

"Of course." Bill smiled at her. "After five years, I'm surprised they still care. I should be flattered." But he wasn't. They just wanted to bring him to heel, and force him to be like them.

"It's threatening for them that you flew the coop. It puts their lives in question," she said wisely. "They'll never give up trying to make you come back. Or about me. Our being different is scary for them. And even more so if we're happy." He didn't tell her that Tom had brought up the issue of their having children. He knew it was a subject that upset her. Every month they hoped that she had gotten pregnant, and each time it was a disappointment. They had agreed to see a fertility doctor if nothing happened in the next few months. A baby was the only thing missing from their life now. But Bill thought that was meant to be too, and it would happen when they least expected. It was way too soon for them to panic, but after two years of trying, unsuccessfully, they were both getting worried, even though they didn't admit it to each other. Maybe when he got a church, he sometimes thought.

And as he mused about it, he remembered the letter he had put in his desk drawer that afternoon. He didn't mention that to Jenny either. He never kept secrets from her. But he knew there was no point telling her about it—it would just upset her. A church would come, he was convinced, and a baby. They just had to be patient. Destiny would bring them what they needed, yet again. Bill was certain of it.

They made love when they went to bed that night, and Jenny fell asleep in his arms afterward, hoping as she always did that she had gotten pregnant. Other than that, as far as she was concerned, and she knew Bill would agree with her, they had it all.

Chapter 3

Other than the day of their marriage, Bill's graduation from Union Theological Seminary was one of the most important days of their life together.

The graduation ceremony took place in the Seminary Quadrangle, and Jenny cried during most of it, as she looked at Bill in his cap and gown. He had earned a joint degree from Columbia and the seminary, and now had a master's of divinity. And it meant infinitely more to him than his graduation from Harvard Law School, although that had been much harder. And now he was officially a minister, but he still had no job and no church. So far everyone had either put him on a waiting list or turned him down.

He had successfully completed his evaluated field education experience at a church in the Bronx, and had taken additional classes to qualify as a hospital or prison chaplain. And he had taken extensive psychology classes to help him counsel, with a specialty in the field of abuse. Bill was particularly sympathetic to abused women, and had done countless hours of volunteer work at a church that assisted the homeless. And after classes every weekend for five years to prepare for the Episcopal ministry, he had been quietly ordained as a minister the week before his graduation. He had everything he needed, except a church.

Helene had gone to the actual graduation ceremony with Bill and Jenny. Jenny had invited his parents and brothers and their wives, and his nieces and nephews, to attend, but all had claimed they were too busy. But they had agreed to come to the luncheon Jenny had arranged for him after the ceremony, except for his nieces and nephews, all of whom were still in school for another week. Jenny had reserved a table at "21" for all nine of them, since it was the family's favorite restaurant, and she knew the Sweets would be comfortable there.

She hadn't seen any of the Sweets in several years, but since they had accepted her invitation, she assumed they would be civil to her. It was a monumentally important day for their brother and son. He was a full-fledged minister of the Episcopal Church, having the right to marry people and perform all the rites and sacraments of the church. And all he wanted now was a place to practice what he'd learned. And in the meantime, while he waited for a church to hire him, he had signed on to act as relief chaplain at two hospitals and the downtown women's jail. At least it would keep him active, and he was looking forward to starting his chaplaincy duties in two weeks. Jenny was relieved that he'd have something to do. The search for a position in a church had taken longer than they thought it would. He had been looking for almost six months.

They went straight to the restaurant after the graduation ceremony, and his parents were already there. His father had a Bloody Mary in his hand, and his mother was looking grim, sipping a gin and tonic. She nodded at Jenny, and looked at Bill as though he were severely ill. She treated his new career path, and marriage to Jenny, like a manifestation of mental illness, from which she hoped he would recover soon. She said nothing at all to Jenny's mother, and Jenny shook hands with her parents-in-law with a pleasant smile, which they didn't return. They were off to a bad start, and Bill was instantly tense. Bill, Jenny, and Helene had just sat down at the table when his brothers arrived with their wives and filled the table, which was something of a relief. No one mentioned the graduation ceremony or congratulated Bill, which shocked Jenny. It was as though they thought it was more tactful not to mention it at all, like a terrible blunder he had committed that they were hoping to overlook, like his marriage to Jenny. After how hard he had worked to become a minister, Jenny thought it rude as well as cruel to ignore it. Tom finally said something halfway through lunch.

"How does it feel to be a man of the church?" Tom said to his younger brother with a slow smile.

"A little bit unreal until I find a church. Maybe I'll feel more like a minister when I start working as a chaplain at the downtown women's jail next week," he said honestly, as his mother frowned.

"How awful," she said in a strangled tone. "Can't you do something else while you wait?"

"I'm also going to work as a chaplain in two hospitals," he reassured her, and his father just shook his head.

"There's plenty of work for you to do at the law firm. You don't have to hang around hospitals and jails, looking for work," he reminded Bill. "You're still an attorney. You can come back to work anytime." And it was clear that he thought Bill should.

"Thank you, Dad," Bill said politely. Jenny was furious that no one had spoken to her mother so far, but Helene didn't seem to mind. She remembered how they had treated her at the wedding, and she expected no better from them today. She had only come to the lunch out of respect for Bill. Bill's mother looked through her as though she didn't exist, and she made an effort to speak to Jenny but looked pained each time she did. Bill's brothers' wives spoke mostly to each other. Only Tom was pleasant with Bill and tried to lighten the mood, with very little success.

Jenny had ordered a cake, which said "Congratulations, Bill," and they served it with champagne, for dessert. And by the end of the meal, Bill's father had had too much to drink, Peter was visibly bored, and their mother appeared ill. It was over in less than two hours. Bill and Jenny were exhausted when they left the restaurant with Helene, as Bill carried what was left of the cake. It had been a painful lunch, and Jenny was sorry she had invited them at all. They were incapable of being nice to him and celebrating his accomplishment. Bill commented on the way home that he had been to funerals that had been more fun.

"They act like I've just been sentenced to prison," Bill said to Jenny in the cab on the way home. Tom was the only one who had made an effort, and Jenny had noticed that he watched her closely at every opportunity, as though trying to figure out who she was, and why his brother loved her. And they had all mentioned several times during lunch the fact that she and Bill hadn't had children and asked if it was because of her work. Clearly, they thought she was to blame, as they did for his abandoning his law career and joining the church. She fielded all their questions lightly, saying that they had wanted to wait to start a family until Bill graduated, but Bill noticed that she looked crestfallen every time the subject came up. Their failure to have a child so far was the only real sadness in their life. She had discussed it with her mother recently, who sympathized and said that she and Jenny's father had never been able to have a second child, although they had tried and lost several after Jenny was born. They had wondered if it had something to do with Jack's work, since Jenny had been conceived easily when he was in the army and not working in the mines. But they never knew for sure.

They dropped Helene off at the train station on the way home, so she could go back to Philadelphia, and she congratulated her son-in-law again and told him how proud of him she was. And then Jenny and Bill went home and collapsed on the couch with a look of relief. Azaya called Jenny almost the moment they sat down. One of her clients was panicking over a fabric that had gotten lost on the way from France, another wanted to know if she could go to Milan with him the following week, and she'd had at least a dozen calls with questions that needed immediate responses. Twenty minutes later she was back on the couch with Bill, where he sat staring into space, and then he turned to look at her with saddened eyes. It had been an extremely difficult two hours, for an event that should have been meaningful and fun.

"For all their pretensions about good

breeding and impeccable pedigrees, I think my family are the rudest people I've ever met. I'm sorry, Jenny, I won't subject you to them again. And your poor mother." Bill was the only person at the table who had spoken to her at all. The others had acted like she didn't exist.

"They're still angry you married me," Jenny said matter-of-factly. It didn't surprise her anymore.

"I would have died of boredom if I'd married Julie or Georgina. Even my brothers look bored to death with them." Jenny had noticed several times that both women had an edge to their voices whenever they spoke to their husbands. She had the distinct feeling that all was not well in their worlds, particularly Tom's. Julie had snapped at him and made nasty comments in his direction several times. Bill and Jenny, on the other hand, had held hands through most of the lunch. They both needed the support, especially in light of the hostility directed at them almost non-stop. Jenny had barely eaten, it was so stressful, and Bill had had a Bloody

Mary and several glasses of wine, which he never did at lunch. But it had been the only way to get through it. He realized now more than ever that Jenny was his family. His parents and brothers no longer were. Their relationship had deteriorated so badly, over their objections to his marriage and his new career path, that there was just no bond between them now. When he was with them, it felt like six against one. They were no longer his allies and showed no compassion for him or Jenny. He was sorry she had made the effort to invite them to lunch.

Jenny went to make some business calls then, and Bill opened the mail. He frowned as he opened the last letter, read it a second time, and then sighed as he folded it, put it back in the envelope, and went to slip it into his desk with the other one from the same source. He didn't mention either letter to Jenny when she came back to the living room an hour later. She said that Azaya was coming over in a few minutes with some fabric samples she had to look over for a client, and with mail. She could see that Bill was troubled and assumed that it was from their unpleasant time spent with his family.

Azaya arrived half an hour later, and Bill said he was going for a walk. It gave Jenny time to work, and as soon as he left the apartment, Azaya turned to her with concern.

"How was it? Were they all right?" She knew that Jenny's relationship with Bill's family was strained, and how nervous she had been about the lunch.

"It was awful," Jenny said honestly, putting off their work for a few minutes. "They're so nasty to him, they ignored my mother completely, and they hate me. It's so hard on him. They're so unbelievably rude. And so mean to him because of me. You'd think that after all this time they'd give it up. I guess they never will." She was sad about it but put it out of her mind while they did their work. She chose the fabrics to suggest to the client, signed several letters, and looked over some files, and an hour later Azaya left. She was perfectly capable of handling their clients while Jenny took a day off, which was rare for her. Bill got home half an hour later and found her in the kitchen. He was seriously depressed.

"I'm sorry I invited them," she apologized, and he pulled her into his arms. But he was upset about something else.

"I honestly don't care. I don't want to see them again, not for a while anyway. We have better things to do. They're petty people with small lives, trapped in a little box. They can't stand the fact that I walked out of that box, with you. And I'm so glad I did." He smiled at her.

He had made a decision on his walk. He had never kept secrets from her, but he had for the past three months. It wouldn't change anything to tell her, but she had a right to know the truth. He gently took his arms from around her, opened the drawer in his desk, and removed the two letters. "I've been wanting to tell you about these. I didn't have the guts, and I didn't want to worry you. I got a letter in March offering me a church in Wyoming as full pastor, and I turned it down. I wouldn't do that to you, Jenny. I know how important it is for you to be in New York. So you don't need to be afraid. We're not going anywhere.

But I'd like you to look at their original letter. I just got another one today. They haven't found a minister yet, and they're begging me to come. It's everything I want, except it's twenty-one hundred miles from where we want to be. Other than that, it's perfect. At least somebody wanted me, even if I turned it down. They got my résumé from that service I signed up for. I told the agency I wanted to stay in New York, but I guess they sent some of them around the country. This church in Wyoming responded immediately." He looked flattered as he handed both letters to her. Jenny read them, appearing nervous, and she gazed at him with frightened eyes after she read them both.

"Are you considering this church?" She was visibly panicked. They both knew it would mean giving up her career. She couldn't move to Wyoming and consult in New York, given her demanding clients, and her work was very hands-on. The only two churches that had wanted him so far had been in Kentucky and Wyoming.

"I told you, I turned them down. We're

not moving to Wyoming. But they're nice letters, and they sound like good people. I just wanted you to see it. I haven't dared show you the first letter until now." And the second letter sounded even more desperate than the first one. They had offered him more money and reminded him that the pastorship came with a house. "I felt wrong not telling you about it, Jen. At least it was an option." He didn't want her to think he was a total loser, and had no offers at all, or wasn't trying. He truly was trying to find a church and a job.

"I'd have to give up work if you took it," she said, and he could see that she was close to tears as he put an arm around her to reassure her.

"I won't do that to you, Jenny."

"But you need a church. What if you can't find one?" There were tears in her eyes.

"I will. It may take a while to locate one around here. I can do the chaplaincy work till then. It's something to do."

"But that's not what you want," she said miserably. It had never occurred to her while he was studying that he wouldn't find a church. They had had no idea how scarce available churches were, or how far away. She didn't want to hold him back, but she wasn't ready to give up her career and move to a place like Wyoming, and she knew she never would be. Bill knew it too.

"It has to bless us both. Not just me," he said calmly. "It sounds great, though. All we have to do is find something like it around here."

"What if we don't?" Her eyes were huge in her face.

"We will," he said, trying to exhibit an optimism he no longer felt. He had written hundreds of letters with copies of his résumé in the past six months, and this was by far the best offer he'd had. But it was one he couldn't take. He didn't look angry about it, just sad and disappointed, which made her heart ache for him.

He put the letters away then, and they had a quiet dinner that night. It had been an important day for him, and a hard one at the lunch. And now Jenny felt as though the offer of the pastorship in

Wyoming was hanging over their heads. And she knew it was important to him, or he wouldn't have shown her the letters. She was quiet that night, as she thought about it, and lay in bed next to him wide awake, in the dark.

"I can hear you worrying," he said gently as he put an arm around her. "Don't. I'm not going to drag you to Wyoming. I wouldn't ask that of you." She wanted to say "Thank God," but she only nodded as tears slid down her cheeks.

"I'm scared you won't find anything else," she admitted. She felt as though her whole work life was on the line, and it meant so much to her. Not as much as he did, but she had been building her career for the past fourteen years, since she started Parsons at eighteen. It would be a lot to give up, if it ever came to that. She couldn't even imagine it.

"We just have to be patient." Like the baby, which hadn't happened either, and she was worried about that too. She wondered if he'd be willing to adopt. Until then, they had assumed they'd have their own. But she was beginning to doubt it, since it hadn't happened in two years. She hoped it wouldn't take him as long to find a church, but it might.

"I'm sorry, Bill," she said sadly, thinking as much about the baby as the job.

"I knew when I married you how important your career is to you. You didn't hide it from me. It's not a surprise. I love what you do. I'm proud of you, Jenny. I don't want something that works for me, at your expense. That wouldn't be right." She nodded and snuggled up closer to him. And then very gently, he began making love to her, and their sadness and fears turned to passion. They forgot everything in each other's arms, and afterward they lay breathless, having been swept away by a tidal wave of love and emotion. She had seen stars while they made love.

He lay holding her, smiling at her, and he didn't want to say it, but if all it took was love to make a baby, he was sure they had made one that night. And she was thinking exactly the same thing as she kissed him and fell asleep.

Chapter 4

Bill started doing his chaplaincy work at the hospitals and the jail two weeks later. It was challenging and interesting, and he even visited patients in a locked psychiatric ward. All his training in psychology served him well. He spent time talking to all the patients on his list, and although he was only filling in, people began asking for him, and the chaplaincy service increased his days from three to five. And he even enjoyed the work he did at the jail. The women inmates were there for a variety of crimes, including murder, and they found him

easy to talk to. He came home exhila-
rated and with a lot to tell Jenny every
night. Neither of them mentioned the
church in Wyoming again.

Bill was busy all through June and
July, and so was Jenny. On the first of
August, the fall Fashion Week was still
seven weeks away, but things were
heating up, and some of her younger
designer clients needed a lot of help.
Bill noticed that she was coming home
exhausted every night, from running
around in the heat. They had been invited away for several weekends, but
she had to work. And he used the time
to send out more letters with his résumé.
So far nothing had turned up. They were
both relieved when they were invited to
the Hamptons by one of her more important clients. It would be good to get
out of the city.

They talked on the way out, crawling
through the weekend traffic leaving New
York on Friday, and then Jenny fell
asleep in the front seat. She had had a
long week. They wanted to go to Maine
in August, or Martha's Vineyard, but
Jenny wasn't sure she could get away.

This was the start of a busy time for her, which would become frantic all through September. With one collection following another, it was hard for her to leave her clients at any time of the year. And Bill was anxious to spend some vacation time with her. He was thinking about it when she woke up an hour later, and they were only halfway there.

"Sorry I fell asleep." She smiled at him. But she felt better and less tired.

"You need it. You're exhausted. You've been running around like a maniac all week." She didn't usually get tired, she had boundless energy, but everyone was tired in the crushing heat, even Jenny. He could hardly wait to get to the beach and swim and relax and enjoy the weekend. And he liked their host. When Bill started to say something to her about it, he noticed that she was distracted. She took out her datebook and glanced through it, calculated something, and then looked at him in amazement.

"Oh my God . . . I just realized something . . . I've been so busy for the past few weeks, I didn't notice . . ." She was smiling at him mysteriously, and he had no idea what she was talking about, as they finally picked up speed.

"Didn't notice what? Please don't tell me you forgot ten more appointments and two new clients and you have to work this weekend," he teased her, but he wasn't far off the mark. She had been working seven days a week for months.

"I think I might be pregnant," she said softly, as though she were afraid to say it, and he glanced at her sharply, and then turned his eyes back to the road.

"Are you serious?" He was as excited as she was and a little shocked.

"I think it happened the night you graduated. I'm late. Really, really late. Like four weeks late. I forgot all about it." And as she said it, he felt a shiver run down his spine. Suddenly he was as sure as she was. He remembered their sudden passion, after the hideous lunch with his parents, and talking about the church he had turned down in Wyoming. He remembered thinking that she might have gotten pregnant that night, and then he had forgotten about it too. He reached over and touched her cheek gently with his hand, and she turned to look at him with eyes full of hope.

"I'll check it out on Monday," she said in barely more than a whisper, and then she put her arms around him and kissed him. But there was no other reason either of them could think of for her being late. That never happened to her. It was going to be a long weekend, waiting to find out on Monday, but suddenly they were both sure. It had finally happened, after two years. They tried not to get too excited, but by the time they got to the Hamptons, it was all they could talk about or think of. If she was really pregnant, their dream had come true.

They spent a wonderful weekend with her client, and enjoyed the people he had invited for dinner. He gave two beautiful dinner parties, and they had a room with an ocean view. Bill and Jenny took long walks on the beach and swam in the ocean, and on Sunday night they went back to the city, relaxed and tanned and in great spirits. She could hardly wait to call her doctor in the morning. Bill was up before she was and brought her a cup of tea. They didn't dare talk about a baby until they knew, but it was on their minds.

She stopped and had a blood test on the way to the office. They had to wait a day for the results. And she tried to concentrate on her work, which was nearly impossible. Even Azaya noticed something different about her, after the weekend. Nelson Wu was working with them too, helping them get ready for the shows. They were a good team.

"You're in a great mood. Did something happen?" Jenny avoided her eyes, afraid that something would show. She didn't want to say anything yet, and jinx it.

"We had a terrific time," she said blithely. She worked till nine o'clock that night, and Bill was home when she got there, relaxing and watching TV, after spending the day counseling inmates at the jail. He had dinner waiting for her, and they went to bed early. She called the doctor from home the minute their office opened the next day. And she almost screamed when the nurse told her she couldn't give her the results until the doctor came in. Nurses were not allowed to give test results over the phone.

They called her back at nine-thirty, and Jenny held her breath, waiting for the results, and then her doctor came on the line and told her the good news. She was pregnant. They had finally done it. Bill was in the shower when she walked into the bathroom and stood smiling at him with tears rolling down her cheeks. He stuck his head out of the shower, saw the look on her face, and gave a whoop of glee. He stepped out, took her in his arms, and kissed her, and she was soaking wet as soon as he did, but neither of them cared. It had been worth the wait. Bill stood there holding her and kissing her, and telling her how much he loved her. As much as she loved him. And the baby they had wanted so badly and waited so long for was on the way. Their life was complete.

Chapter 5

Jenny was seven weeks pregnant the first time she saw the doctor at the beginning of August, and Bill went to the appointment with her. The baby was due in early March, and everything seemed to be in order, although the doctor said she was a little on the thin side. He wanted her to gain a few pounds, and Bill told him that she worked too hard, and came home late every night. Jenny pointed out that Fashion Week was coming up and she couldn't let her clients down. They were moving into high gear and pulling her in a million directions with their needs and demands, collections to complete and runway shows to plan.

"I'm not going to stop working just because I'm pregnant," she said quietly. She was hoping to work right till the end, and the doctor didn't see why she shouldn't, as long as she was reasonable about it.

"*Reasonable* isn't in your vocabulary," Bill scolded her. "Not as far as work is concerned. Your work isn't compatible with that word," nor her style. She gave everything she did two thousand percent, and it showed in the results. That was why her clients loved her the way they did, and needed her so much. They all claimed they couldn't do what they did without her. She knew that wasn't true, they had the talent, but she fine-tuned it for them and put it in sharper focus. And it was always nice hearing their praise. Mrs. Vreeland had said it about her too, that she had the best eye of anyone she knew, particularly for someone so young. She had an instinctive sense of what was right for each designer's collection and was able to home in on each one's unique style, without borrowing from anyone else.

"Will you please try to slow down a little?" Bill begged her when they left the appointment. She'd been given a prescription for prenatal vitamins and iron pills, which the doctor had warned her might upset her stomach, but she felt fine so far. She had none of the symptoms of pregnancy yet, which was why she hadn't suspected it sooner, and she'd been too busy to notice the missed period. She hoped she'd continue to feel well, she didn't want to get behind on her work, although she promised Bill that she would rely on Azaya more than she had, if her clients were amenable to it. And she would ask Nelson to come in more often too.

"I don't care what they want," Bill growled at her. "This baby is too important to us." And just as he had known would happen, it had come at the right time, for both of them. They were ready, he had graduated, all he needed now was a church, and in the meantime he was keeping busy with his chaplaincy work at the hospitals and women's jail.

He had a gift for talking to people, with understanding and compassion, and making them feel that someone cared. He was holding church services at the jail now and was surprised at how many women came. He wanted to start a group for abused women, which in most instances was related to their crimes. He was nonjudgmental about how they'd gotten there and already knew many of the inmates by name. He had just gotten a request to start working at the men's jail as well and was looking forward to it.

After the doctor's appointment, Bill went to one of the hospitals where he was doing relief work for a minister who had been sick for several months, and Jenny went to meet a new client, a young Swedish girl who had enormous talent and was going to show her first collection during Fashion Week in the fall. Jenny was helping her put the show together to get the greatest impact on the runway. It was exciting to work with her right at the beginning of her career. She could really make a difference for her, and gave her great advice. They spent most of the day together, and she stopped in to see David Fieldston briefly after that. He had added two new looks to the line he was showing in September and wanted to know what Jenny thought about them. She told him they were incredible, although she suggested modifying the silhouette of one of them to give it a cleaner line. They pinned the sample he was working on, and it looked better immediately. She left his office at six o'clock and went back to her own.

"You've been a whirlwind today," Azaya commented as she handed Jenny a stack of work and messages the minute she sat down at her desk. It was a typical day in the life of Jenny Arden, and she tried to remember that she was supposed to slow down. But when, and how?

She hadn't had time to eat since a slice of toast for breakfast, and she had a slight headache when she left her office at eight o'clock, trying valiantly to finish before nine, for a change. And she took a stack of work with her in two shopping bags, which were heavy as she got into a cab. She looked exhausted as she came through the door of the apartment, and Bill glanced up from the letters he was opening. They all said the same thing they had for the past seven months. They would love to have him but there were no positions open at their churches, and they would let him know if anything changed. He looked discouraged and lay back against the couch, with the letters still in his hand. She was relieved he hadn't mentioned Wyoming again, especially now. She didn't want to give up her career and have a baby in the wilderness somewhere. She was glad Bill hadn't pressed the point. Staying close to New York, even if it meant taking longer to find a job as minister, was a sacrifice he was willing to make for her.

"I wanted to take you out to dinner tonight to celebrate," Bill said, sounding disappointed, but he could see how tired she was. They settled for a salad in their kitchen instead. He opened a bottle of champagne and poured them each a glass. The doctor said she could drink in moderation, but she only sipped the sparkling wine. She still had the headache she'd had when she left work. They talked about their days over dinner, and Bill couldn't help thinking how different his life was from what it would have been if he had continued to practice law at the family firm. He liked this so much better. And after dinner, Jenny went to work at her desk with the two shopping bags full that she'd brought home. She didn't finish until one A.M. Bill had fallen asleep on the couch.

She woke him gently, and he followed her into the bedroom, pulled off his clothes, went to brush his teeth, and slid into bed next to her. He gave her a sleepy look and pulled her into his arms, feeling her long lean body against him. He could hardly wait until he could feel their baby in her belly between them. It still seemed unreal to both of them. It was hard to believe that in only seven months there would be a little person living with them. Jenny had already realized they would have to move to a bigger apartment. They had two bedrooms now, but she used one of them as a home office, and she couldn't give it up.

There were going to be so many

changes in their life, but it felt totally right to both of them. She wanted to tell her mother but hadn't had time all day to call her. She was going to wait as long as possible to tell her clients. She didn't want to make them nervous, or have them think that she would no longer be available. She fully intended to manage having both a family and her work, and knowing her, Bill was sure that she could do that, with efficiency, creativity, and grace. It was all going to work out just fine.

They decided to go to Maine instead of Martha's Vineyard for a week's vacation mid-August. They stayed at a tiny bed and breakfast, drove around the area, and rented a sailboat for two days. It was one of Bill's passions—he had sailed since he was a boy. Jenny had never sailed until she married Bill, it wasn't part of her experience, growing up with her mother and grandmother, but she had come to enjoy it a lot. He made her wear a lifejacket as she wasn't a strong swimmer. But she never got seasick, and she trusted him completely. They talked about the baby as they walked through small quaint towns and explored old cemeteries with touching inscriptions on the headstones. They stopped to look at two of them, a mother and infant who had been buried side by side, and near them the young widower, who had died only months later. It told a story of loss and love that brought a lump to Jenny's throat and tears to Bill's eyes.

"I always think that when people really love each other, they find each other again, in another life," Bill said quietly. It touched her to hear him say it, and she thought he meant that people who loved each other would meet in heaven, like this young couple with their baby. She noticed that it had been a little girl, who died three days after she was born, and the mother the day before, probably due to some mishap at the birth. And the woman's husband and baby's father had followed shortly after. The young couple had been only eighteen years old and lived two hundred years before. Jenny liked what Bill had said, that they had all found each other in heaven, in a better life. It followed her belief system as well.

"I'm sure they wound up in heaven together," Jenny said softly, holding Bill's hand. She was haunted by the couple, and the story that the dates on the gravestones told. They had been so young.

But Bill's idea on the subject was subtly different from hers. "I think if you really, really love each other, you get another chance. I don't think even death can keep you apart," he said in a firm voice, keeping her hand in his, as she turned to look at him in surprise. He had never said anything like it to her before. It went beyond their traditional views to something more.

"You mean like you come back and find each other again in this life?" she asked him, looking startled, and he nodded.

"I don't know why, but I've always believed that. I think true love lives on until the end of time, and you find each other again. If anything happened to us, I'm sure we'd find each other. It wouldn't

just end there. We were meant to be together, in this life or another. I knew it
the first time we met. What we have is
too strong to just die with us. I don't
think God would let that happen. We
would find our way to each other again,
even if we didn't know it. Our story won't
be over for a long, long time." What he
said frightened her a little—she didn't
believe in the supernatural or reincarna-
tion. She believed in the life they had,
dying one day, and their spirits going to
heaven. Coming back, to be together
again, whether they knew it or not, or
recognized each other, was too big a
stretch for her, but Bill seemed very sure
of it, as they walked away from the three
graves. But if what he said was true,
then had the young couple met again in
another life? The theory was a little too
"out there" for her.

"Well, let's just stay alive in this life,
so we don't have to go looking for each
other. I might not recognize you next
time," she teased him. "I'd rather we just
stay together now."

"So would I," he said peacefully as
they left the graveyard and gently closed

the gate behind them. There were so many like it in New England, always so picturesque and so sad, no matter how long the people in them had been gone. He spoke quietly, as they walked back to the car. "I believe that our destiny is forever, not just for a short time, or even just this lifetime." She nodded, listening to what he said, wishing it were true, but not sure it was. He seemed so certain, and his belief in what he said seemed so strong.

"I'm just grateful we have each other now," she said gently. It was enough for her. She didn't expect to have more than this life with him, and being with him was all she wanted. And with the baby growing inside her, their life seemed fuller than ever. They were both silent as they drove away and stopped at the next town for lunch. What he had said had left her pensive. They would never know if it was true, but it was something to think about.

"I told my brother about my theory once," Bill said to Jenny at lunch. As he thought about it, he smiled. "He thought I was nuts. But they think that about me anyway. I never fit into the parameters of what they want from me—they always act disappointed." It was true of his parents and his brothers, the only one who appreciated him just as he was, was Jenny. She was all he needed now, and their baby, when it was born. He had his own family at last. And Jenny felt the same way about him. He was everything she'd ever wanted and dreamed of in a man. Bill had never let her down, and she knew he never would. And as he liked to say to her, he loved her "until the end of time." You couldn't ask for more than that.

They drove around Maine and Vermont and spent a day in New Hampshire, visiting a college friend of Bill's who was teaching at Dartmouth. He was fascinated by Bill's decision to go into the ministry, and they spent a lovely day with him, his wife, and their three children, and after eight relaxing days in New England, Bill and Jenny drove back to New York. And then as it did every year, in the weeks before Fashion Week, all hell broke loose, and despite her promise to be careful, she was working eighteen-hour days, trying to satisfy all her clients, who would be showing their spring lines on the runways.

Venues got canceled, fabrics failed to appear, samples didn't arrive, fittings went awry, models showed up stoned or missed their flights from other countries, production samples looked different from the original specifications, and Jenny was expected to help solve all of it, and she did a heroic job for every one of her clients, most of whom were hysterical by the Labor Day weekend. And by the time Fashion Week actually arrived, with runway shows scheduled back to back, the press watching them all closely, and everyone's nerves rubbed raw, Jenny had lost five more pounds even though she was pregnant, and looked exhausted. She promised herself and Bill that she'd take a few days off to relax when it was over.

Her three most important clients showed their spring lines in the first two days, and two of them were smash hits and got rave reviews from the press. The third client, a new one for Jenny that season, had made too many changes at the last minute, and the press called the collection weak and indecisive, and Jenny thought they were right. She hadn't been able to convince the client to stick with his original inspiration, which had been stronger and had had an exotic Asian theme she liked. Some of her favorite young designers had shown their wares that season, although none of them were her clients. She tended to work with bigger designers, or brand-new ones who had money to spend to establish themselves faster. Some of the young ones she liked had come up through the ranks and were greatly respected. And they brought in their wake a group of young artists and followers who added color to the show.

It was a scene every time Fashion Week happened. She had seven clients doing runway shows that season, two of them on the last day, and she was running like a maniac, and so were Nelson and Azaya. Everything had gone smoothly so far, and Bill came to every show and was impressed with the quality of their work, and Jenny's, to showcase it for them and maximize their talent. He thought that particular season was the best she had ever done. She was three months pregnant on the day of the last runway shows. No one could tell, and she hadn't announced it, not even to Azaya. She was thinner than ever and had had no symptoms of the pregnancy, just occasional exhaustion because she'd been working so hard for the last two months. She had told her mother about the baby, and like Bill, Helene urged Jenny not to work too hard, and take it easy, which she promised to do, right after Fashion Week was over.

She stopped in at two parties that night, on the way home, one at a glamorous apartment on Fifth Avenue, at the home of a major designer, and the other in a loft in the East Village, given by the young Swedish designer, whose runway show had gotten rave reviews from the critics, thanks to Jenny. And when she got home, she nearly crawled into the apartment, she was so tired. Bill had gone home hours before and had skipped the parties. He was doing a six A.M. service at the men's jail these days, and he didn't have Jenny's endless en-

ergy and drive, even when she was
pregnant. He was already in bed when
she got home. And after unwinding for
a little while, she got into bed with him
and cuddled up beside him. The week
had been a resounding success. She
always felt so lucky. For a little girl from
Philadelphia, and Pittston before that,
which was barely on the map, and where
her life had begun in poverty, she had
become the toast of the fashion industry in New York, a key player, and at the
eye of the hurricane that was fashion.
Where she was now had been hard
earned, and she loved every minute of it.

She went to sleep that night, thinking
of the last two shows she'd done that
day, and anxious to see the press on
them in the morning. Bill didn't stir when
she got into bed—until he heard her
moan just after four in the morning. He
thought she was having a nightmare,
and still half asleep himself, he rubbed
her back and started drifting back to
sleep, when she moaned again, louder
this time. It was a long slow, growl of
pain, and then he heard her say his

name in the dark, and she sounded breathless.

"Bill . . . I can't move . . . I'm . . . it's so bad . . . make it stop." He heard her crying and came awake immediately. He propped himself up on one elbow, and then turned on the light. She was curled into a ball, with her entire body tensed. She had her back to him, and he gently tried to turn her over so he could see her, but the moment he tried to do that, she let out a scream.

"What's happening . . . Jenny . . . talk to me." Her face was sheet white, and her lips were gray. He pulled the covers away instinctively, so he could see her body, and there was blood everywhere in the bed. She was smeared with it, as she clutched her stomach. It looked like someone had been murdered, and Jenny looked like she was dying. He fought his own panic and tried to speak to her calmly. "It's okay, sweetheart. You're okay. Everything is going to be fine." He wasn't even sure she knew what was happening, or that she was bleeding. She was in so much pain, she was almost incoherent, and her body was rigid as she braced herself against an avalanche of contractions. He turned away from her, picked up the phone, dialed 911, and asked for an ambulance. He said his wife was hemorrhaging and told them she was three months pregnant. He knew as he looked at her that there was no way the baby could have survived it, and all he wanted now was to save Jenny. He wanted to tell the operator it was a matter of life or death, but he didn't want to scare Jenny if she heard him. She looked like she was dozing or slipping into unconsciousness, and he shook her and told her to talk to him while they waited for the ambulance.

Her eyelids looked too heavy for her to keep open, and her face was getting grayer by the minute. Their bed was filled with blood, and he was covered with it now too, as he ran to grab a towel, wiped it off his legs and hands, and put on his clothes, while still trying to rouse her. The ambulance arrived eight minutes later, and the paramedics rushed into action. They put her in a pressurized inflatable bodysuit to try and slow the bleeding, ran an IV into her arm, and had her on a gurney and out the door in less than two minutes. Bill pounded down the stairs behind them and jumped into the ambulance next to her before they could stop him. They had the siren on, and Jenny was no longer conscious as they drove through the city careening around corners with all lights flashing. They took her to Lenox Hill Hospital and rushed her into the emergency room, where they asked Bill for her blood type, cross-matched her immediately, and gave her a transfusion on the way to the operating room. A doctor shoved a clipboard at him and told him where to sign the surgical release form, and gave him a serious look as Bill handed it back to him, all within seconds.

"Is she going to be okay?" Bill asked, choking on a sob, and the doctor hesitated just long enough to terrify him.

"It's not looking good," he said honestly, not wanting to lie to him. "She's lost a lot of blood. She would have bled out in another five minutes. We're pretty close here. We'll do what we can to save her. She already lost the baby." Bill nodded. He would mourn their baby later—right now all he wanted was to save his wife.

"Do everything you can!" Bill shouted at the doctor as he rushed off to join the team working on her. Bill sat alone in the waiting room for three hours until a nervous new father came in, waiting for his wife to deliver. He complained that he wanted to be in the delivery room with her, but a nurse told him with a disapproving look that it was not allowed. The young man tried to strike up a conversation with Bill, who was beyond talking to anyone, and five minutes later a nurse came to move Bill to a small private room, where he could wait alone for news of Jenny. The nurses had already been told that they were fighting for Jenny's life and her condition was poor. They offered Bill a cup of tea or coffee, which he declined. He just sat there, waiting and praying in silence.

Half an hour later, two doctors in surgical pajamas, wearing caps and masks, came to talk to him, with grim expressions.

"Is she—" Bill looked like he was about to pass out as he met their eyes.

"She's alive," they told him quickly. "Your wife had an ectopic pregnancy. It's rare, but it happens. The fetus was developing in her fallopian tube, instead of her uterus. Sooner or later that creates a life-threatening situation for the mother. The baby must have been growing very slowly, she should have had some pain and cramping as a warning. She's conscious now—we asked her, and she said she didn't. Simply put, under pressure from the growing fetus, the tube explodes and creates the kind of hemorrhaging you saw tonight. The baby isn't viable in that situation and probably never was. And nothing she did caused this. It's an anomaly that occurs. It sounds like she's a very active person, so maybe she missed the early signs. Many women die when an ectopic explodes, the way it did tonight. She's very lucky. She lost the tube and the ovary on one side, but there's no reason why she can't get pregnant again and have a normal pregnancy with one tube and one ovary, after she recovers. She'll have to be carefully watched to be sure it doesn't happen again, but this kind of lightning usually doesn't strike twice. It's very unfortunate, I'm sorry about your baby," the doctor speaking to him said somberly, but at least Jenny had lived through it. He admitted that it had been touch and go for a while, and the surgery had been delicate to save one side of her reproductive organs, so they didn't leave her sterile.

"How is she?" was all Bill could think of. Her ectopic pregnancy had been more dangerous because it had gone on longer, and she almost died.

"She's still groggy from the anesthetic and weak from the blood loss. We gave her three transfusions in the OR, but she'll be shaky for a while. I'd give it a few months of rest before she gets pregnant again, but there's no reason why she can't conceive and deliver a healthy baby in the future. It's just a trick of nature that happens sometimes, and unless she had severe abdominal pain, there was no way for her doctor to suspect it, and nothing she could have done except terminate the pregnancy before she wound up in a situation like the one tonight. She's going to be fine," the doctor reassured him again, "although of course she's upset about the baby." She had cried when they told her, and she wanted to see Bill, but she was still in the recovery room, so they could observe her, and he couldn't go to her until they took her to a room. They didn't want the hemorrhaging to start again. At this point she wouldn't survive it, and Bill got that message loud and clear as he listened to the two doctors. He was only slightly cheered to hear that she could still have another baby. He was too worried about Jenny to care about that right now, and sad about the one they'd lost. The second doctor informed him that it had been a boy, which made it even worse. They had a real person to mourn now, a son they would never know.

While he waited for them to bring Jenny from the recovery room, he hounded the nurses for bulletins about her. He begged them to let him go to her, and showed them his ID as a hospital chaplain at another hospital, but they still insisted that he couldn't go to the recovery room to see her, unless he had been called to administer last rites, which fortunately he wasn't.

It was afternoon before Jenny was wheeled into a private room on the maternity floor and they let him see her. He had called Helene by then and told her what happened, and let Azaya know that she wasn't coming into the office, and he called the chaplaincy service and told them that his wife was in the hospital and he wouldn't be in for several days. Helene was devastated for them when she heard about it and worried about her daughter. She said she knew of two women who had died of ectopic pregnancies when she was younger. It had been in Pittston, and they had bled to death before anyone knew what had happened, or why. She was infinitely grateful that Bill had gotten her to help in time. He shuddered thinking what might have been if he hadn't woken up and heard her moaning, or if she had bled out so fast, she never woke up and died beside him. It had been a very, very close call.

He bent to kiss her the moment he saw her, and she started to cry, from the relief of seeing him, the terror of what she'd been through, and sadness over their lost baby.

"I know, sweetheart, I know . . . ," he crooned to her, sitting on a chair next to her, stroking her hair, and holding tightly to her hand. "We'll have other babies. All that matters is that you're okay. I don't ever, ever want to lose you. You have to get well now. And then we'll have another baby."

"I want the one we just lost," she said, sobbing. "It was a boy."

"I know. I promise, we'll have others." She nodded, clinging to him, and he put his arms around her, and she lay there and cried. And Bill was crying too, as much for the wife he loved so much as for their lost infant son.

"I kept thinking of that family we saw in the graveyard in Maine this summer. . . . I don't want us to die. . . . I want us to live forever. I don't want to leave you, ever," she said sadly, and he smiled.

"You won't. And you'll never get rid of

me," he promised. "I'm in forever. So you'll just have to get well and put up with me." She smiled and closed her eyes, still weak from the acute blood loss, and she was having severe cramping, and pain on one side from the tube and ovary they'd removed. They gave her something for the pain a little while later, and another transfusion that night. Her blood count was still too low, and she was deathly pale. Bill sat in the chair next to her all night, and in the morning she looked better, although her eyes were sad. She told him then that she had had no warning signs, no pain from the baby growing in her tube instead of her womb. She had thought everything was fine, and so did her doctor. She had an appointment to see her that week for her three-month visit, which was irrelevant now.

Her own doctor came to see her that morning, distressed for her about what had happened. The doctor reiterated everything the surgeons had told them and assured them both that in the best case, she would conceive again and carry the next baby to term, even with one ovary and one tube. But it had taken her two years to get pregnant, and Bill was worried that it might take even longer next time, particularly with the insane work life she led. And her doctor said that it might make things a little easier if she reduced her workload. Jenny nodded and said nothing. She was too weak to argue, and Bill knew that this wasn't the time to discuss it.

Jenny stayed in the hospital for five days, until her blood count improved slightly. They were still concerned about another hemorrhage and urged her to take things easy for the next two weeks, but she didn't feel up to running around anyway. As soon as she got back to the apartment, she had Azaya bring her some work, and her assistant was shocked at the condition she found Jenny in. She was rail thin and so pale she was almost gray. And Jenny had no choice but to tell her what had happened.

"I'm so sorry, Jenny," her assistant said, feeling terrible for her. "I had no idea you were pregnant."

"I didn't want to tell anyone till later," Jenny said sadly.

But in spite of how weak she still felt and how upset about the baby, she started working from home right away, and talking to her clients on the phone. She was relieved that it had happened right after Fashion Week and not before. And she told none of her clients that she'd been sick, just that she was working from home, and none of them suspected that anything was wrong.

She was opening their mail one morning after Azaya dropped off more work for her, and fabric samples her clients wanted her to look over. The designers had already started their research for the next season. Most of them started the day after their shows. And as she went through the stack of letters, she saw another one addressed to Bill, from the church in Wyoming. Feeling guilty, she opened it.

They were begging him again to come. They still hadn't hired a minister and were hoping he would reconsider and take the job. Jenny felt her heart sink as she read it. It was a very nice letter, and

Bill hadn't found a church yet, and was getting seriously discouraged that he ever would. He had even talked about going back to the law firm. He said he couldn't stay out of work forever, and it was beginning to look like that could happen. There were just no churches that needed a minister anywhere within a reasonable radius of New York, so Jenny could continue to work.

She put the letter on his desk, and it haunted her all day. Part of her wanted to throw it away so he wouldn't be tempted to accept their offer, and part of her felt that she was being unfair to him, forcing him to stay in New York. But she couldn't give up a career that had taken her fourteen years to build and that she loved. What would she do if she gave up fashion? And in Moose, Wyoming? The prospect of living in a place like that gave her chills. The church wasn't even in Moose, it was fifteen miles out of town. The nearest big town was Jackson Hole, which was a nice place, but Wyoming just wasn't on her map. Only New York was. She tried to forget about the letter and concentrate

on her work, until she saw him reading
it with a serious expression late that afternoon when he came home. He had
already scolded her for doing too much
work, but she was looking better every
day.

He had brought home a roast chicken,
Jenny had made some vegetables, and
she was trying to force herself to eat.
She still had no appetite and was fright-
eningly thin. And she knew that if she
wanted to get pregnant again in a few
months, she'd have to gain weight and
maybe even work less. Her doctor had
stressed that to her, and Jenny knew it
too. She had heard it all before, for the
past two years. And having lost half of
her reproductive anatomy, it might be
even harder for her to get pregnant now.
No one could say for sure.

"I saw that the church in Wyoming
wrote to you again. I'm sorry I opened
it," she said in a soft voice about the
letter, slightly embarrassed. "I just wondered what they had to say. They still
want you." She looked worried.

"Yes, they do," he said simply. "That's
beside the point. I heard from that church

in Brooklyn that I wrote to last week."
He looked discouraged as he said it.
"They turned me down. They hired a
new young minister last year. They said
he waited seven years for the job."

"I'm sorry," Jenny said, looking deeply
sympathetic. She knew how hard he
had tried to find a pastorship for the last
nine months. All the positions within
hundreds of miles of New York, and in
commuting distance certainly, seemed
to be filled, and people weren't giving
up their jobs.

"Don't worry about it. The right thing
will come at the right time." That was
what he always said, but he was sounding less convinced. And he'd been down
since they lost the baby too. Their
dreams were slow in coming. And for
now, no baby, no job—they were both
disappointed and trying hard not to give
up hope on either front.

Bill changed the subject then and told
her about the people he had seen that
day at the jail. He had met with a serial
killer who was awaiting trial, and was a
surprisingly intelligent man, who had
studied theology himself. They had had

a very interesting exchange, which made the man's situation seem even more eerie. How could someone that intelligent be a serial killer, who had killed seven women before he was caught? It was fascinating, tragic, and very strange. But at least Bill wasn't bored.

And the following week Jenny went back to work. With a vengeance. She saw all her clients and was trying to make up for lost time. And Bill looked worried when he saw how exhausted she was when she got home.

"Don't you think you're pushing a little too much?" he said gently. She was still anemic and underweight after what had happened.

"I've been stuck at home for nearly two weeks. I can't let my clients down." Bill nodded and said nothing. And Jenny went to see her doctor at the end of the week, who was unhappy that she had lost more weight. There was no denying that she was very, very thin, and very pale. The massive hemorrhage had taken a toll.

"You may want to rethink your lifestyle at some point," her doctor told her.

"You're working awfully hard. It's difficult to get pregnant and maintain a pregnancy with those kinds of demands on your body and time. People do it, but it's not easy. And before you get pregnant again, this may be a good time to slow down." She had gone to the appointment alone, and she didn't say anything to Bill when he got home. But as soon as she opened the door, she saw him hunched over a stack of letters on his desk, with the same beaten expression he had worn for months. He felt defeated by his inability to find a church, and all she wanted to do as she looked at him was take him in her arms and comfort him. She walked quietly across the room and sat down across from his desk. It was one of those defining moments in life when you throw everything you believe out the window and caution to the winds.

"Tell them yes," she said in a single breath, feeling like she had just boarded a roller coaster for the wildest ride of her life. She hadn't planned it. What she had just done was totally spur of the moment.

"Tell who yes?" He looked up in surprise, wondering if she meant his father and brothers. He had had lunch with Tom that week and had a serious discussion with him about going back to the firm. He didn't know what else to do. He didn't want to be out of work for years. "My father?"

"Of course not." She looked incensed at the idea. She would let him do anything but that. They would eat him alive. "The people in Wyoming. I think we've got to do it. You're not going to find anything here, and they've been begging you for months." There was even a small cozy house for them near the church. Bill stared at her as though she had lost her mind, and for a minute she felt like she had. The words had come out of her mouth before she had time to measure them or even think about it. But she knew in her gut it was right.

"Are you serious? But what about you?" Suddenly he looked panicked, wondering if she was leaving him. "Would you come with me?"

"Are you crazy? Of course. What would I do here without you?"

"Work in fashion, maybe," he teased her with a slow smile.

She sighed as she looked at him. "I love my job, and the work I do. But you're my whole life." She had realized it more than ever when she almost died. His brother Tom had been horrified when Bill told him about it. They had never accepted Jenny as a suitable spouse for him, but no one wanted her to die. Tom felt sorry for them both, and was glad that she'd survived. He knew how much Bill loved her and how devastated he would have been if she hadn't.

"You can't just move to Wyoming, Jenny. That's not fair to you. I won't let you do that. You've invested fourteen years in your career. You can't just throw that away."

"Maybe I could take a year off, while you see how it goes, and we decide if we like it there." They both knew she'd probably lose some clients and some momentum in her business. Most of her clients wanted more attention than she could give them from a distance. But others would come back to her if she returned. "It's worth a try. What have we got to lose? And it might be a better place to be pregnant and have a baby than running my ass off here. Maybe we just have to do this, and take our chances on Moose, Wyoming." Her eyes filled with tears as she said it, but she was smiling. It was a huge sacrifice for her to make, but she loved him and she felt as though she owed it to him. He had tried valiantly to do the right thing for her. Now she felt like it was her turn. And she wanted to do this for him.

"I want you to think about this," he said sternly, "before I say anything to them. You can claim insanity for what you just said to me, and I won't hold you to it. Maybe you just had a bad day." She laughed and put her arms around his neck.

"I have a great husband. That's more important than any bad day. I want you to be happy, and have a shot at the life you want. And who knows, maybe we'll love it." She couldn't imagine it, but she was willing to try. For him. It was the greatest gesture of love she had ever made in her life, and he was deeply cognizant of it. But he didn't want to ruin her life and career in the process.

"Just think about it, Jen. We don't have to rush into this. Take your time. And it's okay if you change your mind and decide you want to stay."

She kissed him again, and Jenny told her mother about it the next day. Helene sounded instantly worried. It sounded all too familiar to her.

"That's how I felt when I agreed to go to Pittston with your father. I thought I was doing the right thing for him. And when we got there, it was so much worse than I'd imagined. If he had lived, we would have had a horrible, horrible life. We did for the three years we were there until he died. I felt like I was buried alive." And she couldn't imagine her daughter in Moose, Wyoming. She had been part of a sophisticated scene in New York, in the fashion industry, for fourteen years, including her three years at Parsons. What could she possibly do in Moose, other than cry?

"Bill says we can do it for a year, and if I hate it, we'll come back." Jenny tried to sound confident, but she was scared too. And her mother was echoing her own fears, and fanning the flames of panic. But Jenny had made up her mind.

"In your business, you can't just come and go like that. People will find other consultants quickly. It could hurt your business badly if you left."

Jenny sounded serious when she answered. "Maybe it could hurt my marriage if we stay. Bill really needs a break. He's been thinking about going back to the law firm, if he doesn't find a church by the end of the year. He would hate that. I don't want that to happen to him. And this church sounds like exactly what he wanted. It's just in the wrong place. But who knows, maybe it's the right one." Her mother couldn't believe how brave she was being, and how kind to her husband. It was a huge sacrifice for her to make. And Bill knew it too. Jenny talked to Azaya about it in the ensuing days, and Azaya said she would try to do her best to keep Jenny's business alive, though in a somewhat reduced way. And Azaya was sure that Nelson would help too. There was no way that Jenny could provide the full services she had while she was in New York. But she could consult with them on the phone and they could send her fabric samples and drawings to look at. It would keep her hand in, and for some it might be enough. And she could come back for Fashion Week in February, and again in September, if they hadn't moved back by then.

Azaya agreed to service their clients to the best of her abilities, for a year anyway, and she and Jenny could talk by phone every day. It wouldn't be enough to make some clients happy, but it would work for others. And it was only for a year. After that Jenny could come back and take over the reins again, or maybe they'd stay in Wyoming. For the moment, Jenny was open to anything.

Azaya was stunned, just as Helene had been. Jenny was planning to go with her whole heart and an open mind. It had been a week since she and Bill had first discussed it, and she brought it up with him that night.

"So when are we moving to Wyoming?" she said casually, as she cleared away their dinner plates. Bill had brought home Chinese takeout. He looked at her in surprise.

"Are you kidding me?"

"Nope. I'm serious. If it's okay with you, I'd rather not sublet the apartment, just so we know it's here, as a kind of security blanket in case something goes wrong. Azaya says she'll babysit my clients, the ones who don't dump me flat. And I'd probably need about a month to get them ready." It was the first week in October. "I think I could do it in early November. What about you? I think we've got to give it a try," she said, and her voice sounded stronger, when she talked about it, than it had the week before.

"Are you just doing this for me?" he asked, with a look of astonishment. He had fully expected her to change her mind, and wouldn't have been angry at her if she had.

"I'm doing it for us," she said simply. "And who knows, maybe we'll have better luck having a baby there. It's worth a shot. And most of all, I want you to have a church. You deserve one, and if that's the one you want, I'm game." She was smiling at him, and he hugged her so hard, he nearly knocked the wind out of her.

"Remember, if you hate it, we'll come back in a year. Less, if you want." He thought it was a good idea to keep the apartment. For the moment he thought it wiser to keep a foothold in New York. "I will never, ever forget what you're doing for me, Jenny," Bill said gratefully. They talked about it all night. And he called the head of the church board in Moose, Wyoming, the next day. They asked Bill to come out in a week, and he said yes. And Jenny would follow him in a month, after she tied up all the loose ends in New York. She and Bill agreed to buy simple furniture locally for the house that came with the ministry. She wanted to leave all their things in the New York apartment and not disrupt their home there, which Bill thought wise too. And it would be nice to start fresh with simple furnishings. Their lives were about to change radically. For better or worse, they were on their way to Moose, Wyoming.

*   *   *

His brother Tom nearly fell out of his seat when Bill called to tell him before he left.

"Are you serious? I thought we almost had you convinced to come back to the firm. Dad will be crushed." Tom sounded disappointed.

"You nearly did. My wife talked me into going to Moose."

Tom laughed at the idea. "You're either a lunatic or a saint, I'm not sure which. That is one hell of a change for both of you. What's Jenny going to do about her business?" He knew how important it was to her, and she couldn't take it with her.

"She's leaving her assistant to run it for a year. And she'll do what she can by phone and mail. And she'll come back a couple of times. She expects to slow down, though. She's been an incredibly good sport about it. She's the saint. I'm the lunatic."

"I think I have to agree. When are you leaving?"

"In two days."

"Stay in touch," Tom reminded his little brother. He had to admire him for his perseverance and guts. And one thing was for sure, he had a wife who loved him more than anything in the world. Tom had no illusions that his own wife would have done the same for him. It was a huge sacrifice to make, as Bill was well aware.

"Come and visit us in Moose," Bill said, sounding happy and excited about what they were about to do. This was what he had been waiting for, through all his years of seminary, and the four months since.

Tom laughed. He was still laughing when he hung up the phone, as Peter walked into his office.

"Who was that?" Peter asked in his usual querulous tone.

"Our baby brother Bill," Tom said, still smiling.

"Is he coming back in?" Peter asked, bored.

"No, he isn't," Tom answered him. "He is going to Moose, Wyoming, to be a minister. I have to hand it to him." And to Jenny. And for a fraction of a minute, he envied them for what they shared, even if he thought they were crazy for moving to Moose.

"Moose, Wyoming?" Peter said to Tom, stunned. "You're not kidding?"

"No, I'm not," Tom said with an amused glance in his brother's direction. "I almost wish I were going with him," he confessed. It suddenly sounded like a lot more fun than his own life in New York.

Chapter 6

Bill flew to Salt Lake City, and from there he took a small plane to Jackson Hole. It was snowing when they landed. Winter had already set in, and a tall man with gray hair, in cowboy boots and a Stetson, was waiting for him in the small airport. He was the head of the church board, who had been corresponding with Bill since June, hoping to convince him to take their offer. He had a serious face, with deep weathered lines and electric blue eyes. And he smiled as soon as he saw Bill, in jeans, hiking boots, and a parka, and somehow he still looked like New York, compared to Clay Roberts, who looked like he should have been riding a horse, and most of the time he was. He owned a ranch in the same county as the church. He was a widower and had lost his wife ten years before. He had a big black truck with the insignia of his ranch on the door, and he had come to drive Bill to fifteen miles outside Moose, to Sts. Peter and Paul Church, which was about to become Bill's new home.

Clay explained to him about the district and the ranches, some for cattle, others for horses. He mentioned a few of the ranchers by name, although he said they hardly ever came to church. And he explained that the area around the church was populated by several hundred people, most of whom knew each other. There was a school, a main street with two restaurants, a general store, a post office, a drug store, a laundromat, and two motels for people passing through town. He said there was a very respectable library, a movie theater twenty miles away, and a supermarket a little closer. And they were less than an hour from Jackson Hole, where the rich and famous were starting to gather and it was slowly becoming a tourist town. And in the summer there was a rodeo. He asked Bill if he liked to ride.

"Not lately. But I enjoyed it a lot as a kid." He and his brothers had ridden at camp every summer and had gone to a dude ranch in Montana several times with their parents. He was a competent rider, which Clay said would be useful, since in the spring when the snows melted, and even in the winter, there were areas you could only reach by horseback, if he needed to visit members of the congregation who were sick or elderly or shut in for some reason. He said that the church had been built with a capacity of two hundred, which had been optimistic, but considering the size of the community, there had been a fairly decent turnout on Sundays, of somewhere around a hundred people. And there was a Catholic church in the next town, Our Lady of the Mountains.

As they drove toward Moose, avoiding Jackson Hole on the highway, Bill could see the Grand Tetons in the distance. They were breathtaking, and looked as though they had been painted shades of violet and dark blue, with pale blue sky above them, and a pink light in the sky at sunset. The view was dazzling, and the mountains looked powerful and mysterious. Bill thought he had never seen anything as beautiful, and Clay was easy to talk to as they drove along.

When they reached Moose, Clay drove him past all the places he had mentioned, the restaurants, the post office, the general store, and then drove another fifteen miles out of town, to where the church was. And as they approached it, Bill could see the steeple of the white wooden structure rising into the sky with a bell tower on top. The building looked freshly painted and in good order, and there were neat hedges, flowerbeds, and a picket fence around it, and two huge trees providing shade. And just behind it was a small neat yellow house, with white shutters, its own picket fence, and red roses in the front garden. Clay explained that the women in the community took care of the garden. He said they had provided the basics, a bed, a chest, some lamps, a desk, a kitchen table, and some chairs. But Bill would have to provide the rest of the furniture. He said that they would find what they needed at a shopping mall fifty miles away. Bill said he wanted to pick up some things so that Jenny would not arrive to an empty house.

They got out of the truck in front of the church, and Bill walked inside with a feeling of awe. It was his first ministry, and he wanted to shout. There were beautiful stained-glass windows, some statuary, simple pews, and a dignified altar. It was a plain building, but lovely in an unpretentious way. And the rectory was right behind the church, with a small waiting room, and an office for the pastor. And right out the back door was the little yellow house that was about to become their home. He walked through it with Clay. There were three bedrooms upstairs, in case the pastor had children, a big living room downstairs, a cozy country kitchen with a dining area, and a playroom in the basement. It was all they needed. And Jenny could use one of the bedrooms as her office. Bill could see that the house was freshly painted. The bedroom was pale blue, and everything else was white, except the kitchen, which was yellow. It was bright and cheerful. There was a washing machine and a dishwasher and two bathrooms. It was more than adequate, and had a warm, cozy feeling to it. Bill turned to look at Clay with a happy smile.

"It's perfect," he said, feeling like a kid with his first bicycle.

"I'm glad you like it. Call me if you need anything. I left one of our trucks from the ranch out back so you can get around, but you'll need to buy your own, and I put one of our horses in the stall. He's a good, solid ride named Navajo. He's sure-footed, which is useful around here." Bill nodded. They had thought of everything to make him feel at home. Clay jotted down his phone number and handed it to him, and as Bill looked around the kitchen, he realized that there was food everywhere, in casserole dishes, baskets, and bowls, with cellophane around it, with big red bows. The refrigerator was full. Bill looked at Clay in surprise, and he laughed. "Your congregation will take good care of you. At least you won't starve. They wanted you to feel welcome." He felt *very* welcome, and he shook hands with Clay and thanked him again. And after he left, Bill looked around again and did a little jig all by himself. And then he walked back into the church, knelt down at the altar, and said a prayer of deep thanks. Sts. Peter and Paul had been worth waiting for, and he could hardly wait for Jenny to see it.

He called her that night and described everything to her, and hearing him so elated told her that their decision had been the right one. She had spent the day explaining to her clients that she was taking a year off to support her husband in his ministry. Everyone was shocked and couldn't believe she was moving.

It made the front page of *Women's Wear Daily* a few days later, and all her clients were in a panic. Two of them told her that they couldn't manage with reduced creative input and asked her to help them find new consultants, which she agreed to do. And five of them agreed to try and work with Azaya, and Jenny herself long distance, if she would agree to fly in to help them occasionally if a crisis came up. She promised to be there for Fashion Week, and a week before that to set up their shows. She was impressed that they were willing to stay with her, despite her unexpected relocation to Wyoming, and it made the move considerably less traumatic for her. She didn't have to give up everything and everyone, and she and Azaya had endless meetings to brief her on what she didn't know. She went to all of Jenny's meetings with her before she left, so the clients would start getting used to dealing with her when they needed face-to-face meetings in New York.

And on her last weekend in New York, Jenny's mother came up from Philadelphia to spend a few days with her. Helene was sad to see her leave, but Jenny was so excited about it that Helene was hopeful for her that it was the right thing to do. She tried not to compare it to her own dark memories of moving to a coal mining town thirty years before. And from everything Bill was telling her, Jenny said the area was beautiful, and their new home looked like a dollhouse. He had taken photographs of it, and she showed them to her mother. And it did in fact look like a very nice place. And between preparing his first sermon, and driving around the area to meet the members of his congregation, he had managed to go to the shopping mall Clay had told him about, and he had bought a truck, so he could return Clay's, and some basic furniture for their new home. None of it was stylish, but it was functional and modern, and he was sure that Jenny would somehow add her own touches and turn the house into a home when she got there.

She could hardly wait to do that, and after seeing the photographs, she had shipped a few small decorative items, and some photographs and watercolors for their walls. The house had a light, airy feeling, and her mother said that if she sent the measurements, she'd make curtains for them. It was the kind of thing her grandmother would have done, and it touched Jenny when her mother offered to do that. Jenny promised to send the measurements as soon as she arrived.

Bill had bought them a couch by then, in a soft beige velvet, and two comfortable armchairs. There were hardwood floors, and he had gotten a simple hooked rug in neutral tones. It was like starting out and getting married all over again. And Jenny felt that way too. Going to Wyoming with him was like renewing their vows, for better or worse, richer or poorer, until death did them part.

And during the weeks while he waited for her, Bill delivered what he thought were three very strong sermons, and he read them to Jenny over the phone before he gave them. The first one was about what home meant to him, and how grateful he was to be there, and how home was a place in their hearts, more than a physical structure. The message was simple but heartfelt, and a number of people commented on it when they shook his hand and introduced themselves after the service. He had already met several of them, from dropping by their homes as he made his rounds.

His second sermon was on resurrection, being reborn and starting fresh, after something bad happens, and having the courage to start again. That moved a number of people too, and Jenny thought it was excellent when he read it to her. And the third one was on forgiveness, and how vital that was in all relationships, particularly in marriage, and even in friendships, business relationships, or family relations. Several people thanked him for the sermon on the way out after church.

He had also managed to visit the elderly and the sick, and a young widow managing with three teenage boys. And he found that his brief time as chaplain before leaving New York had served him well. He discovered that there were a number of children in the community, and a very pleasant woman ran the Sunday school, which was full every week. Bill wasn't sure, but he had the feeling that the numbers in church increased slightly every week, as people came to hear his sermons. And everyone said they were looking forward to meeting Jenny and anxious for her to arrive. So was he. He was lonely at night without her and had so much to tell her every day, while she was busy wrapping things up in New York. He had explained to several of the women who had asked that she worked in fashion, and was a consultant to several designers, although he found it difficult to explain to people who were so far removed from the fashion industry and knew nothing about her job. It was hard enough for him to understand the intricacies of it, even though he had lived with it every day for nearly six years.

And he was surprised when his brother Tom called him a week after he arrived. "So are you ready to come back yet?" he asked as soon as Bill answered the phone, and they both laughed.

"No, it's great here. The Grand Tetons are gorgeous, the church is just what I wanted, and the house is very cute. And my congregation is full of nice people. They keep bringing me enough food to feed an army."

"Good lord, you sound like a country minister. Wait till Jenny gets there. That should stir them up a little. She'll be teaching them about fashion trends in New York. I hope your house has enough closets."

"It doesn't. But I bought a few old armoires at a yard sale." For the time being, he had turned the second bedroom into a dressing room for her, and the third bedroom into her office. If they had a baby, she'd have to give up one or the other, but for a nursery he was sure she wouldn't mind. "I bought a truck, and I have to visit some of the congregation on horseback. It's beautiful country, Tom." Tom had never heard his younger brother so relaxed and so peaceful. Clearly, he had done the right thing. Tom just hoped Jenny thought so too when she arrived. It was an enormous leap of faith for her. It had endeared her to him, as nothing else ever had.

"I'll have to come out and see for myself when I have time," he promised, and he hung up a few minutes later. He didn't bother telling his brother or father. He knew they wouldn't understand. He had

had a hard enough time understanding Bill himself over the years, but he was beginning to get glimpses of the kind of man he was, and how different he was from them. He wasn't a misfit, as Tom had suspected for so long. He was a much, much better man than any of them. It had taken him all thirty-five years of Bill's life to figure that out.

Bill rode Clay Roberts's horse, Navajo, for his home visits over rough terrain, and Clay had told him to keep the horse for as long as he wanted. He was reliable and solid, and Bill enjoyed the rides. There was a small horse stall behind the house, and he was coming back from feeding Navajo one morning, before going out on some visits, when he saw a young boy standing outside the house, afraid to go in. He was wearing jeans and a cowboy hat, and well-worn cowboy boots. He had come on foot, and he had the gangly look of a fourteen-year-old, as he looked nervously at Bill. And there was a Lab puppy sitting patiently at his feet, gnawing on the toes of his boots as the boy shooed him away.

"Hi there," Bill said with a broad smile, as the boy looked at him with wide eyes. "What's your name?"

"Tim Whitman," the boy said cautiously. "People call me Timmie. My aunt wanted me to bring you a cake, but I brought you something else," the boy said. He had wheat-colored hair, green eyes, and freckles.

"Do you live nearby?" Bill asked pleasantly. It was early for a visit, and the boy had surprised him. The Lab was the same wheat color as his hair, and he could tell the boy was shy.

"Just over that hill," he waved vaguely.

"It was nice of you to come by for a visit. Would you like something to eat?"

Timmie shook his head. "I just had breakfast. Thank you, Reverend."

"You can call me Bill." He didn't want to be formal with a boy that age, and wanted to put him at ease.

"I liked your sermon last Sunday," the boy said with a serious expression, as the puppy scampered around his feet. "The one about forgiveness. Sometimes it's hard to forgive people who do bad things."

"Yeah, I know. And sometimes it takes a long time, but it's nice if you can do it. It kind of lightens the load," Bill said, leaning against the fence, and then he bent down to play with the puppy. "How old is your puppy?"

"He's three months old. My dog had three of them. One died. I'm keeping the other one. My aunt says three dogs is too many . . . so I thought maybe . . . I wondered if . . . you know, I wondered if you'd like to have Gus," he said, pointing at the puppy, who was running circles around Bill by then, barking and wagging his tail.

"You mean to keep him?" Bill looked shocked. He hadn't had a dog since high school. It had been too much trouble to keep one in New York, because he and Jenny were too busy.

"Yeah, if you like dogs and all. He's a good dog. I've been training him a little myself. His mother is really smart. I bred him to our neighbor's dog, who's a Lab too, so he's purebred, not a mutt or anything." Bill looked at the boy with gentle eyes filled with gratitude for the generous gesture. "My aunt said you might not want a dog."

"I'd love him," Bill said, picking the dog up. He was all gangly legs and his tongue was hanging out from running. "Are you sure you don't want him?"

"No, I'm fine with the two I've got." The boy smiled at him then, and Bill could see sadness in his eyes.

"You live with your aunt?"

Timmie nodded. "Yeah, my mom's sister. My parents were killed in a car accident last year, going to Cheyenne." Bill wondered if that was what Timmie had meant about forgiveness. If so, he had a lot to forgive, if he had lost his parents at thirteen. "It was hit and run," Timmie explained. "No one knows who did it. Probably just someone driving through the state. My little sister was with them, but she's okay. She was in the hospital for a long time. She hurt her legs. But she's walking fine again." And then he rolled his eyes, appropriately to his age. "She's kind of a pest. She's seven. But I'm glad she's okay now."

"Me too," Bill said warmly. "Can I give you a ride back to your place?" He thought it might be a good opportunity to meet his aunt and sister, and to know where Timmie lived. Timmie hesitated and then nodded.

"Sure."

Bill put the new puppy in the house and closed it in the kitchen, still amazed by the kindness of his gift. He couldn't wait to tell Jenny. And he came back out with the keys to the truck, and waved to Timmie to get in.

"I'm sure I could use some help around here sometimes, giving me a hand to fix things or get ready for church. If you ever want to come over and hang out, or do some chores, feel free to drop by anytime. And I'm sure Gus would love to see you."

"Okay." Timmie smiled brightly, and Bill had the distinct impression that Timmie was hungry for male companionship, particularly if he'd lost his father the year before. There had been no mention of an uncle, just an aunt.

He followed Timmie's directions, to a slightly battered-looking ranch house with a barn behind it. Bill could smell horses and hear them in the distance.

There were several in a corral, and there was a little girl in pigtails playing out front. When they got out, and she smiled at them, Bill saw she had no front teeth. She was wearing overalls, a pink T-shirt, and sneakers, and her hair was the same color as her brother's. And a few minutes later a small thin woman came out of the house in jeans and an apron looking to see who was there. She looked nervous when she saw Timmie with a strange man, and Bill was quick to introduce himself and explain who he was, and to thank her as well for the gift of the Lab puppy. She relaxed as soon as he said it.

"I told him you might not want a dog. You can give him back if you want," she said, smiling. "By the way, my name is Annie Jones. Timmie is my nephew." She looked about thirty years old, young to be bringing up two kids, one of them Timmie's age.

"I know. He told me."

"We're not big churchgoers, but we came to see you last week. Your sermon was pretty good," she said, and then told her niece to get down off the fence. Her name was Amy. She got into mischief while they were chatting, and then she ran up and tackled her brother, who pushed her away with a groan. Bill couldn't help laughing at her antics. She found a small pail by the water trough and put it on her head like a hat.

"Thank you." Bill was pleased at the compliment about his sermon. "That young lady must keep you busy," he said as Annie laughed.

"Yeah, she does, but it's nice to see her running around again. She was in a body cast all last year, after . . ." Her voice trailed off, and Bill nodded.

"Timmie told me. My wife will be here in a week or so. Come by and visit us sometime at the house." He had a feeling they would have a lot of visitors once Jenny was there. The locals were friendly people, and curious about them. "And thank you again for the puppy," he said, and then he left them, and got back in his truck and drove home. When he got there, Gus was happily gnawing one of the kitchen cabinets and had eaten a small rug Bill had put in front of the sink,

and he had unsuccessfully tried to over-
turn the garbage.

"So that's how it's going to be, is it?"
he said, patting the dog and straighten-
ing up the kitchen. He hoped Jenny
would like the puppy. He thought it was
an awesome gift. And as he looked at
the chaos in the kitchen, he decided to
surprise Jenny with it and not tell her till
she came out and saw him. He didn't
want her to make him give the puppy
back, which made him feel like a kid,
and he laughed as Gus barked and
wagged his tail.

Five days later Jenny boarded a plane,
after leaving Azaya a ream of instruc-
tions, and calling her clients to say
goodbye the day before. She had given
them her phone number in Wyoming,
and their address. Their address for
Federal Express was "Fifteen miles
north of Moose, Wyoming." Her clients
laughed when she told them.

She closed the apartment, and their
cleaning lady said she would come once
a week to check everything, dust, and

make sure that there were no problems. The post office was forwarding their mail. Everything was done.

She followed the same route Bill had, with a flight to Salt Lake City, and a second one to Jackson Hole, and instead of Clay Roberts, Bill was waiting for her at the airport, wearing a cowboy hat and a heavy coat. And he had a hat for her, which he put on her head after he hugged her. He was thrilled to see her after nearly a month. She noticed that he looked relaxed and happy, and he said he had a surprise for her at the house. He pointed out things along the way and seemed totally at home, and she laughed watching him drive his new truck.

"What are you laughing at?" he asked her. There was still an aura of New York about her, in black slacks, alligator loafers, and a fancy black down coat.

"You look like a cowboy." She chuckled. "You went native pretty quickly."

"I like it here," he said honestly. "It feels like home."

She was impressed when she saw the church, and pleasantly surprised by the house. He had added some more furniture and it was cozy and warm when they walked in. And as soon as they did, the puppy leaped at them, put his paws on Jenny's legs, barked, and wagged his tail in greeting as she stared at him in surprise.

"What's that?"

"That's Gus. He was a gift from one of our neighbors. Can we keep him?" he asked, sounding like a little kid, as she put her arms around Bill and kissed him.

"Looks like he got here first," she said, smiling. "Will he let you keep me?"

"He'd better," Bill said tenderly. "Welcome home, Jenny," he said softly, and then took her upstairs to see their bedroom, her office, and her dressing room. And a minute later they were in their new bed, making love, and feeling as though they'd always been there. And Jenny knew, as she looked at him, that this was exactly where they were meant to be.

Chapter 7

Jenny spent her first day in Wyoming unpacking and settling in. Bill had created the perfect dressing room for her, although she had brought and sent ahead far too many things. Warm sweaters, ski clothes, down coats and parkas from Eddie Bauer, fur jackets, and an absurd number of high-heeled shoes. Having seen the place, she realized now that she would never wear them here. She was wearing slim black slacks and a simple black cashmere sweater and ballerina flats, her favorite work outfit, while she unpacked. Her shining straight dark hair brushed her shoulders and had been freshly trimmed before she left New York. She wore hardly any makeup but had had her nails done, and she was wearing a big gold cuff, designed by David Fieldston for his last runway show, and he had given it to her. She stood in their kitchen, watching Bill play with the puppy before he went out, and he smiled as he gazed at her. She looked straight out of New York, still. Even the cowboy hat would have made no difference. She was chic to the core, and even in flats, black pants, and a black sweater, she looked like what she was, someone who had lived and worked in fashion for all of her working life. Bill loved everything about her, including her casual, sexy chic appearance. She was so sleek and elegant, in a totally natural, unaffected way.

"What are you looking at?" She noticed him staring at her as he stood up.

"You. I missed you so much."

"Me too," she said, and gave him a hug. She wanted to hang the pictures she had sent out, for their half-empty living room. Bill had done well with his purchases before she got there, but she wanted to get a few more things. She called her mother with the measurements for the windows and told her the kind of curtains they needed. She wanted to keep everything simple, bright, and clean. They both favored light colors, and she thought it would keep the house looking cheerful in the dark of winter. The few things she set around made the house look stylish and cozy. She had a great eye and a light touch and was as talented with decorating as she was with fashion. And she made Bill promise to take her to the mall later that day. He had three people to see first and went outside to saddle Navajo. Jenny followed him and fed the gentle horse an apple. She wanted to ride him when Bill didn't need him for work.

Jenny waved goodbye at Bill from the kitchen door as he rode away, then went back inside to organize the kitchen a little differently, and she was hanging one of the photographs in the living room when she heard a knock on the front door. She set the photograph down, and the hammer she'd been using, and went to open the door. She found herself looking at a woman who appeared to be ten years older than she was, wearing a heavy plaid jacket, jeans, and battered cowboy boots. She was slightly overweight and had dyed blond hair. She was wearing turquoise eyeshadow at ten o'clock in the morning, and she was holding a pan of brownies and a perfectly iced chocolate cake that said "Welcome" on it, as Jenny gazed at her in surprise.

"Hi, won't you come in." Jenny wanted to be welcoming to all of Bill's congregation, and he said they had been dropping by, mostly with gifts of food, for weeks. He hadn't had to cook since he'd been there. Jenny led the woman into the kitchen, and she set her offerings down on the kitchen table. The brownies smelled delicious, and the cake looked like something in a cookbook or a magazine. "Would you like a cup of coffee, or tea?" she offered, as the woman glanced around and then smiled at Jenny, noticing how slim and stylish she was.

"You sure don't look like Wyoming,"

the woman said, grinning from ear to ear. "We need to get you some cowboy boots. You won't get far in those shoes around here."

"I usually wear them to work," Jenny said, embarrassed. She thought she was a mess by New York standards, as she realized how "done up" she looked here. The woman took off her plaid jacket and seemed like she was getting ready to stay.

"What kind of work do you do? Are you a dancer?" She had met Bill the previous three Sundays and enjoyed his sermons, but she didn't know much about Jenny yet. Others had asked Bill about his wife, but she had only heard garbled things about Jenny. Some said she was a dancer, others thought she was an actress. Someone said she was a model. She looked like one to her.

"I'm a stylist, in fashion. I advise dress designers about what they do, and organize fashion shows for them," Jenny explained, and then introduced herself to her guest. "Actually, I guess I'm a minister's wife now. That's new for me."

"I'm Gretchen Marcus," the woman

said, as Jenny poured her a mug of coffee and handed it to her, and then put some of her brownies on a plate. "You must not eat a lot of cake," Gretchen said, laughing. "We have hard winters, and sit around and eat too much when it's cold outside. And I have five kids. I've never lost the weight."

"How old are they?" Jenny asked with interest, wondering how many of these visits she would get. Gretchen seemed friendly and warm. And the brownies were so good that Jenny had a second one.

"My youngest is five," Gretchen answered. "My oldest turned fourteen in June. He just started high school, and he's driving me insane." Both women laughed, and Jenny would have been shocked to know that she and Gretchen were exactly the same age. But the dyed blond hair and turquoise eyeshadow aged her, as well as the excess weight. She had worn makeup just to impress Jenny, since she was from New York. But Jenny looked surprisingly plain to her.

They sat in the kitchen and talked for

a while, about people in the community, whose names meant nothing to Jenny, about their children, and Moose itself. Gretchen's husband Eddy was a car mechanic and owned a garage in Moose that did all the local repairs. She managed to fill Jenny in on all the local dirt, faster than she could absorb it. The librarian who was having an affair with the owner of the coffee shop. The woman from Laramie who had come through town and stolen someone's husband. Clay Roberts, who was the local catch, and everyone thought was secretly in love with a married woman in Cheyenne, although no one had ever seen her, but they'd heard about her. She told Jenny about the women whose husbands were drunks, and the women who drank too much. And two teachers at the high school who everyone thought were gay but didn't know for sure.

"Wow, it sounds like a busy place," Jenny said, more than slightly overwhelmed. It struck her how many husbands Gretchen said were alcoholics, although she spoke in glowing terms of Eddy, who sounded like a saint, and who Gretchen said helped her with the kids when he wasn't working. "Is there an AA group here?"

Gretchen shook her head. "There's one in Jackson Hole. No one ever bothered to start one here."

"Maybe someone should," Jenny said, helping herself to another brownie, and Gretchen looked pleased. She had been looking forward to meeting Jenny, and she liked her a lot. She seemed honest and open and funny, and she wasn't stuck up because she came from New York. And Gretchen said something to that effect.

"I'm actually from Philadelphia. I went to design school in New York, to study fashion, and I just stayed. I was born in a little mining town in Pennsylvania called Pittston. My father died when I was five, in a mine accident, and my mother moved away."

"Your father was a miner?" Gretchen looked impressed. She had thought Jenny would be some fancy debutante from New York, but instead she was a simple, unpretentious person. It was Bill who had the fancy background, which

Jenny didn't say, and Gretchen didn't know.

"Yes, he was. And my mom is French. She and my grandmother made beautiful clothes for society ladies in Philadelphia, which is how I got interested in fashion. I wanted to be a designer, but I didn't have the talent. I'm actually much better as a stylist."

"I wish I were as thin as you are," Gretchen said wistfully, "and I like the way you dress. You should wear a little makeup, though." She thought Jenny looked too pale, but was beautiful and had a natural elegance. And she had noticed the big gold cuff. She would have loved to have a bracelet like it.

"I've been thin all my life, and I work too hard," Jenny confessed. "I'm always stressed. There's a lot of tension in the fashion industry. It's going to be nice being here." She almost said "for the next year," but she and Bill didn't want people to think that they were temporary, so the fact that they were trying it out for a year was something they planned to keep to themselves.

Gretchen stood up regretfully after

they'd talked for about an hour. "I'd better get back. I left my two youngest with my neighbor, and they've probably destroyed her house by now. I'll come back and visit soon. Come over and see me sometime. Everyone knows where I live. Just ask," she said, and gave Jenny a warm hug.

"You'll have to give me a refresher course about who's sleeping with whom," Jenny said, laughing, as she walked her to the kitchen door. "And thank you for the brownies and the cake. My husband will be thrilled." Gretchen thought he seemed like a nice man too. She liked them both. They seemed like honest, wholesome, warm people, and she was impressed that they had come out from New York.

Gretchen waved as she got into an old pickup that she said her husband had rebuilt. With five kids to feed, there weren't a lot of luxuries in their life, although she said that Eddy did well at the garage.

It had been a pleasant visit, and much to Jenny's amazement, there were two more after that—an older woman who said she was a retired schoolteacher, and a young woman in her twenties with a baby in a stroller and a toddler on her hip. The schoolteacher had brought a lemon cake, and the young mother had just come to say hi. And Jenny noticed a nasty bruise along the side of her face. She said she had taken a fall off a horse. And Jenny guessed she couldn't be more than twenty-five, and she said she had four kids. She didn't stay long, and she seemed shy and nervous, but it was obvious that she had been anxious to meet Jenny. The young mother's name was Debbie, and Jenny thought there was something very touching about her. She seemed so vulnerable that Jenny almost wanted to hug her. Instead they just chatted for a while, while Jenny played with the toddler to distract her, and Debbie nursed the baby. Afterward she put the baby in the stroller, and a few minutes later, they left.

Jenny was thinking about Debbie when she hung the photograph in the living room, and Bill came home for lunch. It was already past noon, and the morning had flown by.

"That's nice," Bill said admiring her work. "What have you been doing all morning?" he asked with interest.

"Entertaining," Jenny said, looking pleased. She wanted to meet the locals and members of Bill's congregation. Everyone she had met so far was so kind and welcoming. "People keep dropping by and bringing us things to eat. I met a woman called Gretchen Marcus. They have five kids, and her husband Eddy owns the garage in Moose. A retired schoolteacher named Ellen brought us a lemon cake. Gretchen brought brownies and a chocolate cake. And a little girl named Debbie Blackman came by with two of her kids. She had a nasty bruise from falling off a horse. Gretchen makes it sound like half the town is alcoholic," Jenny said, sharing all her new information with him, and he seemed surprised. "And the other half are sleeping with someone else's husband," she announced.

"Wow, you have been busy! No one told me all that. What makes you think they're all drunks?"

"Gretchen was telling me who drinks

too much and who's having an affair. I couldn't keep track. It sounds like there's a lot of action around Moose." Jenny smiled at her husband. It had been interesting meeting the three women, especially Gretchen, who seemed anxious to make friends, unlike Debbie, who was too young and seemed frightened, and the retired schoolteacher, who was adorable but ancient. "You should start an AA group at the church," Jenny said, brightening. "Gretchen says the closest one is in Jackson Hole, which is a long way to go in the winter. Maybe we could start an Al-Anon group too."

"You sound like a minister's wife already," Bill said, kissing her. "I can't keep up with you. If you want to start an AA group, go ahead. Whatever makes you happy. It can't hurt." And then Jenny's face grew serious.

"I think Debbie, the woman with the two kids, is sad and scared. She said she bruised her face falling off a horse, but she looked nervous when she talked about it," Jenny said, looking concerned.

"Take it easy, baby," Bill told her gently. "We just got here, and it's fine to try to help people and provide services, but we don't want to intrude on their lives, or interfere where we shouldn't. I don't know these people yet, and they don't know us. We have to go slow at first." But slow had never been Jenny's style. She called Azaya a short time later and asked her to get some material from AA, about how to start an AA group, and an Al-Anon group, the twelve-step group for people who were involved with alcoholics, and send it to her in Moose. Azaya was impressed with what Jenny wanted to do in Moose, and she brought her up to date on her clients, and said that all was well in New York. She said everything was under control, and Nelson had come in several times to help her.

Jenny made Bill a sandwich after that, and he returned some calls. A member of the congregation wanted him to visit her sick father. A young couple wanted premarital counseling. An elderly man had just called to talk and sounded lonely. He didn't ask Bill to visit, but Bill offered to come and see him sometime that week anyway. People were reaching out, which was gratifying to him, and Jenny was happy for him. His new congregants were responding to him and liked his style.

She reminded him that she wanted to get to the mall that afternoon. There were some things she needed for the house, some hardware supplies, more furniture, and more hangers. And she was anxious to check out the local stores.

"This isn't Paris or New York," he reminded her, but she liked practical things too. And she loved hardware stores. When they got to the mall, she had a ball, checking out all the stores, and they ran into Clay Roberts at a bookstore, where Jenny bought a book about abused women and domestic violence, and another one about AA. Bill introduced Jenny to him, and her eyes lit up immediately. After he was gone, she spoke conspiratorially to her husband.

"He's having an affair with a married woman in Cheyenne," Jenny said, and Bill burst out laughing.

"Are you serious? You got here yesterday. How do you know something like that? And how do you know it's even true?"

"My new best friend Gretchen told me. And it sounds like she knows the scoop on everyone," Jenny told him with a mischievous smile.

"Just watch out she doesn't say things like that about you."

"Of course not," Jenny said as they got back in the truck, and they stopped at a car dealership on the way out of town. She wanted to look around. She needed a car of her own, but she had no idea what she wanted, until she saw a bright yellow 1959 Chevy pickup truck sitting on the dealer's floor. It was in perfect condition, the salesman said the engine had been rebuilt, and the upholstery looked almost new. "It's exactly what I wanted," Jenny said with delight. It was funny and crazy and a little bit eccentric. And the dealer had already put snow tires on it for the winter.

"You should get something new," Bill told her. "I don't want you driving around in some twenty-year-old relic. Driving conditions are bad here in winter."

"It has snow tires," she pointed out to him. "It's only sixteen years old, not twenty. And I love the color." Bill rolled his eyes at the way women bought cars, and Jenny wrote a check from her own money. The old Chevy truck was ridiculously cheap, and she thought it was adorable. And buying a truck like that seemed so "Jenny" to him, it had humor and style and was something different. To most people it would have just been an old truck. But with Jenny driving, the yellow pickup suddenly seemed humorous and chic. He could see why she loved it. She followed him home and parked right behind him when they got to the house. He knew that she'd be famous in the area as soon as she started driving her new yellow truck. Jenny was a minister's wife who was not going to go unnoticed, but that was why he loved her. And they talked animatedly over dinner that night. She had lots of bright ideas about how to help him. And as they sampled all the cakes they'd been given, Jenny came up with another idea.

"Why don't we have a potluck lunch after church on Sunday?"

"At the house?" Bill looked shocked at the idea. The house was much too small to accommodate the entire congregation. Not to mention, who would clean up after they left? There were no fancy New York caterers in Moose, Wyoming.

"No, at the church. There's a nice big hall in the basement. I looked. Gretchen said they used to have church socials there. It would be a nice way to meet everyone. I'll tell everyone to bring one dish. They don't have to come if they don't want to. But at least we can extend the invitation." Bill was watching her with obvious pleasure. She had stepped right into her new role with ease. She was organizing potluck lunches, starting AA groups, and making friends among the local women. And she had bought a few things that afternoon to spruce up the house a little, which, along with the things she had sent from New York, made it look really pretty and suddenly like home. Jenny had a magical touch wherever she went.

And he could see that Moose was about to get a dose of her magic. He loved it. And all he could think as he listened to her was "Watch out, Moose, Wyoming! Here comes Jenny!"

Chapter 8

Jenny managed to call the entire congregation the next day to tell them about
the potluck lunch she was organizing
after the Sunday service. She told them
that she and Bill were looking forward
to meeting everyone. Many of them
sounded startled to hear from her. And
she sounded so at ease. No one had
done anything like it before, and certainly not so soon after they'd arrived,
but Jenny never let the grass grow under her feet. And Bill could see that she
would find a way to be as busy in Wyoming as she had been in New York, and

all to help him. Only a few people were less than friendly, and most of the people on her list thought it was a good idea. She had used the church roster, and by three o'clock she had called them all and told everyone to bring one dish. She was even thinking about doing something like it once a month, or a potluck dinner.

Several of the women she contacted had asked her if she had children and were disappointed she didn't. But she also thought it would be a good idea to do things at the church for young people, especially teenagers, to keep them out of trouble. She had a million bright ideas. And Gretchen had been thrilled when she called her, when Jenny got to her name on the list. She told her she thought it was a fine idea, and promised to drop by again later that week and help her run it. She said she would have Eddy organize a clean-up crew, since they knew who the most efficient people were, and she volunteered two of her kids, her twelve- and fourteen-year-old sons. "There's no point having five kids if you can't put them to work," she said gamely, and told Jenny again what a good idea she thought it was. She loved how involved Jenny wanted to be. Their last minister had died a year before. He'd been in his late seventies and had been a widower for fifteen years. They had all agreed that they needed a younger minister, and their church needed a woman's touch as well.

Clay Roberts called Bill the next day and told him how pleased he was with what Jenny was doing, and he said he'd come to lunch on Sunday. Bill reported it to Jenny, and then he said wryly, "I didn't tell him to bring the married woman from Cheyenne that he's allegedly having an affair with."

"Damn," Jenny said, looking disappointed, "you should have. I'd like to meet her."

"I bet you would." He rolled his eyes and then put his arms around her. "You're busy enough without checking out the love life of the president of the church board." He chuckled as he said it.

And the next day the material Azaya had sent her, on AA and Al-Anon groups, arrived by Federal Express with the address Jenny had given her, "Fifteen miles north of Moose, Wyoming." Much to Jenny's amazement, it had actually worked. And she'd also gotten an envelope of fabrics to look at for her clients. The AA material Azaya had sent her was very interesting. It told her how to start a twelve-step group, the format, the rules, and various suggestions. The purpose of the AA group was to give up drinking, and Al-Anon was to support those involved with alcoholics. The groups seemed surprisingly simple to set up. All they needed was a secretary of the meeting, and she could be it. There was a set format to follow. And in time she could hand over the AA group to a recovering alcoholic, but until they had one who was willing to run it, Jenny was planning to do it herself, and the Al-Anon group as well. And with Bill's permission, she posted a notice announcing both meetings in the entrance to the church, just inside the main doors, where people would see them. She offered one on Tuesday night and the other on Thursday. And because she had no children, she had more time to spend, organizing things that would help Bill with his congregation.

She called Gretchen and told her about both meetings.

"Good for you!" Gretchen praised her. "Probably no one will show up at first. But if you keep sitting there for long enough, some Tuesday or Thursday people will start coming. That's how it works. I know, my father was an alcoholic, and my mom and I used to go to Al-Anon meetings. My father never made it to AA. He died of cirrhosis at forty-five. I can run some of the Al-Anon meetings for you if you want, if Eddy can stay with the kids and doesn't have to work late. He's always great about helping me out." Jenny could already tell they had a solid relationship, and he sounded like a good man, from what Gretchen said.

"I'd love that," Jenny said, grateful for the help from her new friend, and the wealth of information she provided. "What do you know about Debbie Blackman, by the way? She dropped by here the same day you did. She had a big bruise on her face. I was kind of worried about it. She seems so shy and scared."

"Her husband Tony is a drunk. I wouldn't be surprised if he did it. He was kind of a juvenile delinquent, went to jail for drunk driving a few times, used to get into bar fights. She's a lot younger than I am, so I don't know her that well."

"She seems like a sweet girl. She looked nervous. I think she said she has four kids."

"I see her around town, but I don't really talk to her. She's about twenty-five years old. She's just a kid. She was a waitress at the coffee shop until she got married. Her husband could probably use your AA group. And Al-Anon wouldn't do her any harm. It really helped me and my mom."

"Maybe we should put together a group for abused women," Jenny said, sounding pensive. "Is there a lot of that around here?"

"Some. It relates to the drinking. If you get the guys into AA, they won't abuse their women. Or get the women into Al-Anon. And there are plenty of women who drink too much too. People get bored when they're snowed in all winter. They screw like rabbits and get drunk on weekends. There aren't a lot of cultural activities around here," she informed her. "No ballet, no symphony, no opera, no theater. Just sex, booze, and TV." They both laughed at what she said, although the abuse issue was serious, and Jenny couldn't help wondering how common it might be.

She was touched when Debbie showed up again on Friday morning, this time with only the baby. It was a warm day, she was wearing a T-shirt and a down vest, and Jenny noticed that she had a fresh bruise on her arm. This time she didn't explain it and Jenny pretended not to notice. She was pleased that Debbie felt comfortable enough to drop by again. She seemed intrigued by Jenny, and a little infatuated with her. She looked as though she felt safe sitting in her kitchen, talking about nothing in particular as she nursed her baby. He was four months old. Debbie said she didn't want to get pregnant again. She had all she could handle with four kids. And she didn't say a word about her husband, except that they had gone to high school together, and got married when she got pregnant right after graduation. She was twenty-four years old, and her oldest son was six. She also had a four-year-old, a two-year-old, and the baby.

"You don't want kids?" she asked Jenny with interest, but she looked as though she was afraid to offend her.

"Yes, I do," Jenny said quietly. "I had a hard time getting pregnant, and I had an ectopic pregnancy two months ago. It was kind of a big deal. We thought we'd wait a few months till we try again." She didn't say that it was one of the reasons they had decided to come to Wyoming. For a better, quieter life, so she might have a baby more easily.

"That's too bad. I'm sorry," Debbie said sympathetically, holding her sleeping baby, who had fallen asleep at her breast. She looked like a child herself, and the bruise on her arm looked nasty. Jenny thought she could discern a handprint in the shape of the bruise but she wasn't sure, and she was afraid to ask her and frighten her from coming to visit again. She wanted to establish a bond with her and see if she could help her. The bruise on her face was fading, and Jenny could tell she'had put makeup on it to conceal it. But the bruise on her arm was fresh and clear. Jenny was surprised she had worn short sleeves. Maybe no one paid attention to her bruises or cared.

They talked for a while again, and then Debbie got up to leave. Jenny reminded her of the potluck lunch after church on Sunday and Debbie looked embarrassed.

"My husband doesn't like me to go to church. He thinks it's stupid. I only go when he's out with his friends. But Tony sleeps late on Sundays."

"Does he help you with the kids?" Debbie didn't answer at first and then shook her head.

"No, Tony works late. He's a bartender at the bar in town." Jenny thought to herself that it was a great job for a drunk, or an alcoholic. "He doesn't come home till about two-thirty in the morning, so he sleeps late. He hates it when the kids wake him up, so I take them out in the

morning. He expects me to be home in
the afternoon, to make him dinner before he goes to work. Sometimes it gets
pretty crazy with the kids." Given the
ages of her children, that was easy to
believe, especially if he didn't help her.
"My mom gives me a hand sometimes,
but my sister here in town has three
kids, and she's two years younger than
I am, so between the two of us, we keep
her busy. I have a sister in Cheyenne
too." Debbie smiled shyly, and put the
baby in a car seat and carried him out
to the car, with Jenny walking beside
her. Debbie said she was driving her
husband's car while he was asleep. But
when he was awake, she had no means
of transportation for the kids. And she
laughed when she saw Jenny's new
truck.

"Where did you get that?"

"At the mall two days ago," Jenny
beamed. "I love it. I know it's kind of
crazy, but it's fun. If you need a lift sometime, call me, although there's probably
only room for one car seat." So she
could only give her a ride with one child,
but maybe even that would help her, if

she had someone to babysit the others, maybe her mother. "Try to come Sunday," Jenny encouraged her. "Bring your husband, or your mom and the kids. And your sister. Everyone is supposed to bring one dish, but I'm sure there will be enough to go around. It will be fun." At least she hoped so. Debbie looked like she needed some fun in her life. She appeared tired and disheveled, she was wearing chipped nail polish, and her hair was greasy. She had no time for herself, and her eyes told Jenny that something was wrong, even if Debbie didn't say it. She didn't tell her about the abuse group she was contemplating. She didn't want to let her know that she had guessed. And she could be wrong.

Debbie waved as she drove off, and Jenny looked pensive as she walked back inside, and a few minutes later Bill came home for lunch.

"Everyone's talking about your potluck lunch on Sunday," he said, pleased. They were off to a great start in the community, thanks to Jenny. And he had been working hard to meet everyone for weeks. Together they were an efficient team. But that was Jenny. Days after she'd gotten there, it seemed like she'd been there for months. He had seen the notices for the AA and Al-Anon groups at the church, and he approved. She was reaching out, or trying to, wherever it was needed.

She told him about Debbie over lunch, and he looked sympathetic but warned her again to be careful. "Let her come to you, Jen. If her husband thinks you're on to him, he could hurt her."

"I think he already has," Jenny said firmly. She didn't believe Debbie's first story about falling off a horse.

"Then he could hurt her worse. You're doing the right thing, letting her come here. Domestic abuse is a very dangerous thing." She nodded, and believed what he was saying. He had counseled abused women during some of his internships while he was training, and he knew the risks to those women. Two of the women he had counseled had been killed. It had given him a healthy respect for how dangerous some of their men could be.

She spent Saturday cleaning the

church hall and setting up long tables for people to put the food on. There were other tables where they could sit to eat. And she put out tall stacks of paper plates and cups, and disposable utensils. They had everything they needed, right down to the paper napkins. By Saturday evening, everything was ready for the next day.

And on Sunday, she was excited to hear his sermon. He had chosen the topic of gratitude, and how being grateful for small things, instead of lamenting big ones, could turn your life around. And he had cited several examples in his own life. And as they had been with his first three sermons before she got there, people were impressed by the simplicity and strength of his message. And they liked the fact that he was a very humble man, who had a strong affinity for people. He was intelligent, compassionate, and warm, with deep convictions about his beliefs. He was someone who lived his faith as well as preached it.

And as soon as the service was over, people went downstairs. They had left their food offerings there before the service. The church had been packed that day, with people looking forward to the lunch. The church hall with the long tables had been turned into a feast. Gretchen came to find Jenny halfway through it. "Well, Mrs. Sweet," Gretchen said to her with a look of open admiration, "your potluck lunch is a huge success. And all the women in town are in love with your husband. He's a very handsome guy."

"Yes, he is." Jenny looked at him from across the room. "And he's all mine."

"They're falling in love with you too," Gretchen reassured her. "This was a great idea. I don't know why we never did it before."

"Sometimes it takes fresh eyes to see the obvious. I think we should do this the first Sunday of every month."

"I second the motion," Gretchen said, keeping an eye on all five of her kids, who were running around with countless others. "I see people here today who haven't come to church in years. They like Bill, and if you feed people on top of it, you'll have a real winner. Maybe we should do bingo nights too," Gretchen said thoughtfully.

"And an abused women's group," Jenny said quietly, and Gretchen nodded. Although they might not have been otherwise, and their paths would never have crossed, Jenny felt like she had a new friend. The two women got on well, although their lives had been very different to that point, and Gretchen was teaching Jenny a lot about their new home, how to fit in there, who people were, and how it all worked. There was so much Jenny wanted to do. And Gretchen loved it. She had already infused new life into Moose, which was just what it needed.

The lunch was almost over, when Debbie appeared with all four of her kids. She said Tony had gone out with his friends, and they had walked over. It was a long way for the kids, and Jenny heaped food on plates for all five of them, and sat down to chat with her while they ate. She had served the kids hot dogs and a burger, and gave Debbie a good assortment of delicious foods on her plate. The fare was simple, but there appeared to be plenty of good cooks in Moose. Jenny had enjoyed the lunch herself. And Bill had made a point of greeting everyone who had come and stopping to talk to them. And he had met a number of new people he hadn't seen in the past month. Several of the people he'd visited came as well, including Timmie, who'd given them the dog, and his sister and aunt.

"I feel like Jack Kennedy when he was married to Jackie," Bill said, smiling at her. "I have no illusions. I think they all came here to meet you. I'm the guy who came to Moose, Wyoming, with Jenny Sweet. But whatever gets them through these doors works for me. After that, it's up to God. You can be my shill any day."

"Happy to oblige," she said, as Debbie went off to chat with some of the friends she hadn't seen since high school. She was laughing and talking and having a good time, and so was everyone else.

Jenny and Bill stood in the doorway and thanked everyone for coming, as they left. Jenny was pleased to see that Debbie looked relaxed and happy. She said she'd had a really great time, and it was obvious that she meant it. Although she'd said they weren't frequent church-goers, she seemed totally at home.

It was after four o'clock, and they all spent an hour cleaning up. Bill and Jenny, Gretchen and Eddy and two of their kids, and three women and two high school boys made up the cleaning crew. They got the place back in order in no time.

That night Bill thanked Jenny again for everything she'd done.

"You are turning out to be the perfect pastor's wife," he told her, and she beamed.

The AA and Al-Anon groups were harder to get started than the potluck lunch had been. No one wanted to be identi-fied as an alcoholic, or living with one, so it took time for people to show up for the groups. There was no one present at the meeting the first week, and Bill mentioned the two groups gently from the pulpit the following Sunday. And that time two women showed up for Al-Anon, and Gretchen came too, to share her experiences about her father. She did it to help Jenny get it going. Jenny was holding the groups in the rectory, which was small and cozy and had enough chairs if more people came.

And it took two more weeks for one woman to show up at AA, and no men. But it was a start, and Jenny conducted the meeting just for her. The woman who came said she had been drinking heavily since her husband died two years before, and her married children thought she should join AA, as she had embarrassed them several times recently, drinking to excess at family events. She had passed out cold at the dinner table at the last one, and she wanted to get some support before she did it again at Thanksgiving. Jenny told her that it was smart of her to come, and the woman looked pleased. She had identified herself only as Mary, according to the rules of AA. Last names were never used, since anonymity was the cornerstone of the program. The purpose of anonymity in the groups was that people could feel safe there. Jenny knew to remind them each time, at the end of a meeting, that they were not to disclose whom they had seen there, nor what was said.

At the end of that week, Bill and Jenny shared a quiet Thanksgiving in their kitchen. They'd had several invitations but didn't want to offend one person by accepting the dinner invitation of another, so they decided that it was wisest to stay alone, and they really enjoyed it. Jenny had cooked a small chicken for them with all the traditional trimmings. And they got up from the table afterward, feeling like they were going to explode after a delicious meal. They called her mother in Philadelphia, and she was planning to spend the evening with friends. She missed Jenny, but was pleased that everything was going so well. And she told her mother everything she had done in the past weeks. It was only when she told her about it that she realized herself how much she had accomplished. She and Bill were both very busy in Moose. He was counseling and visiting people, preparing his sermons, and trying to spend time with everyone

on repeat visits. And he was surprised
by how many of his congregants he had
to visit on his borrowed horse. A lot of
them lived well off the main roads and
said they were snowed in for months at
a time in winter. Bill had found an old
horse-drawn sled in a small barn behind
the church, and he was planning to try
and use it that winter if Navajo was willing. Bill hoped he would be. The sled
was so picturesque.

And after Thanksgiving, the time flew
by until Christmas. Jenny organized a
Christmas potluck lunch again, and a
bake sale, to raise some money for the
church. And after Thanksgiving, atten-
dance at both her AA and Al-Anon
groups had picked up. People who had
behaved badly over Thanksgiving, due
to alcohol, had turned up for the AA
group, and those who had been impacted by it went to Al-Anon. The congregation was talking about both meetings, and after a strong reminder each
time, about preserving the anonymity of
those who had attended, people were
being remarkably good about not di-
vulging who they saw. By Christmas

both twelve-step groups were notice-
ably larger and well attended. She had
moved the meetings to their living room,
so they'd have room for more partici-
pants. They had outgrown the rectory in
less than two months. Bill could hardly
believe it. And Jenny's goal for the new
year was to start the women's abuse
group, but just before Christmas, she
got an unexpected request from two
teenage girls. They talked to her after
Sunday school, before they left church,
and they said they loved the way she
did her makeup, and the way she
dressed, and they wanted to know if she
would do classes to teach them how to
look more like her. And they said they
had other friends who wanted to join
them too. Jenny was their new hero.
She was shocked and flattered, and
since the theme was more frivolous in
nature, she asked Bill what he thought
she should do. And much to her surprise, he loved the idea.

"But it's not religious based," she reminded him with a look of concern, but
Bill wasn't worried.

"Who cares? You're a minister's wife—

you can teach them how to do their makeup, and you can be talking about values and drugs and sex and all the issues that are important to them at the same time. What a great way to reach out to local kids and get them to church!" He was fully in favor of the project, and she contacted the two girls who had approached her, and said she would meet them at her home after the new year. She suggested Friday afternoons after school. That way it wouldn't interfere with their weekend social life, or their homework, and parents were less likely to object, which made perfect sense, and the girls liked it too. They were fourteen and fifteen, and their friends were roughly the same age, although one of them knew an eighth grader who wanted to come too, which sounded fine to Jenny. Bill had made a good point about the value of the group.

Before she started the group, she had Azaya send her several books about how to apply makeup, since Jenny wore very little, and had never applied it to anyone else, although she had seen lots of models being made up for shoots, both in her recent work and in her years at *Vogue*. Azaya promised to have Nelson send her a bunch of cosmetics samples, and she was impressed but not surprised at how enterprising Jenny was. And much to Jenny's relief, Azaya said that none of her clients were complaining, although Jenny called them once a week to touch base, and more often if there was a problem. So far dealing with them from a distance had gone well, with Azaya and Nelson meeting their needs, and there was no reason to think that would change.

Bill held a special service at the church with Christmas carols the day before Christmas Eve, and they had a midnight service on Christmas Eve, which was heavily attended, and on Christmas Day Bill and Jenny visited many people in the congregation, particularly the sick and elderly. It was a very rewarding day. And that night, they wished each other a merry Christmas and exchanged presents. They had agreed to buy all their gifts for each other at the mall that year.

Bill bought her a new warm jacket, a cowboy hat, and a beautiful pair of black lizard cowboy boots with a matching belt, and a set of fuzzy dice for her yellow truck. And she had gotten him cowboy boots very similar to the ones he gave her, and two warm sweaters to wear when he visited people in the congregation, a camera he had wanted, riding gloves, and a black Stetson just like Clay's, which he had admired, and which looked great on Bill. They bought a new collar for Gus, who was growing by leaps and bounds. Timmie had come to visit him several times, and he had gone riding with Bill a few times, and they were becoming good friends. Timmie seemed to revel in the company of a man, and admitted to him how much he missed his father.

They were enjoying their new life in Wyoming, and they called Tom, and Jenny's mother, on Christmas Day. Their old life seemed light-years away, and it was hard to believe that Bill had been there for only three months, and Jenny for two. And when she went back to New York in late January before the shows, it felt like another planet. But she was relieved to see that her clients were doing well. They were happy to see her, and grateful that she had come back to help them with their shows. She had consulted with them frequently about their selections and was fully prepared when she got to New York. She had even helped them choose the models for their runway shows from the distance, with Azaya's help. And the clients were all pleased to be working with Azaya too. She had been well trained by Jenny and had good ideas of her own.

Jenny was happy to get back from New York and everyone in Moose said how much they'd missed her while she was away, particularly Gretchen. Jenny brought some clothes back for her, which fit her perfectly, and a bracelet she loved. Gretchen was thrilled with her new fashions from New York.

As soon as she returned to Moose, Jenny started her teenage group on Friday afternoons. It was more fun than she had expected. The girls were outspoken and funny and open about their concerns. They wanted to learn more

from her than how to put on makeup—
they wanted to learn about fashion and
style. And they wound up talking about
boys, and sex and drugs, birth control,
and how to deal with their parents. Some
of them talked about college and wanted
to leave Wyoming, while others were
terrified to leave the womb they had
grown up in. And every week a few more
girls joined them.

There were fifteen girls in her group
within a month, and in February there
were so many, she split them into two
groups, and she was impressed by how
great they looked and how much they
were learning from her. They looked
cleaner and sleeker, got better haircuts,
did their nails, wore less makeup, and
saw the merits of simpler clothes. She
bought them makeup herself and went
to the mall to shop with them. They
looked so pretty and fresh, even their
parents were impressed. And so was
Bill. Jenny had a wonderful way with
them, and they all loved her.

On Valentine's Day, after she returned
from New York, they surprised her and
gave her a party to tell her how much

they appreciated her. They made cup-
cakes with her initials on them, and had
T-shirts made with their pictures on
them inside a big heart. They called
themselves "Jenny's Girls," and it was a
status symbol in Moose to be one of
them.

Also in February, Jenny started her
abuse group, under the heading DVA,
Domestic Violence Anonymous, and like
the other groups, she held it at her
house. And just like AA, it took time to
get started, but word of mouth traveled
fast, and by the end of February, there
were six women in her living room on
Monday nights. They told their husbands
that they were going to an embroidery
class at the church. And they all referred
to it as the Embroidery Group. But the
women in town all knew what it was. It
was a secret code that allowed them to
attend and discuss it among themselves.
Jenny was disappointed to see that
Debbie never joined them. She had
talked to her about it, but Debbie said
her husband would kill her if he found
out, so she didn't push it. By then, Jenny
had seen her with blackened eyes and

bruises several times, and Debbie no longer pretended that she had walked into a door or fallen off a horse. They both knew how the bruises had occurred. Her husband Tony beat her up every time he got drunk, or anytime the kids annoyed him, made noise, or woke him up, which they did often, but Debbie never left him and was afraid of his reaction if she did. She had a sister in Moose, and another one in Cheyenne, but they couldn't take her in with four kids. And history was repeating itself. Her mother had been beaten by her alcoholic husband until he died. Debbie had grown up watching that and thought it was her lot in life to be abused whenever her husband felt like it. She had no money, no job, and nowhere to go, and four kids to take with her if she left. Her life was a dead end at twenty-four. It broke Jenny's heart seeing that, and she spoke to Bill about it often, but they were afraid to interfere and make it worse.

Right after Valentine's Day, Jenny discovered that she was pregnant. She and Bill were ecstatic, but cautious this time.

They were afraid to get too excited in case she lost it again. They told her mother and Gretchen and no one else. She continued running all her groups, and she felt fine. She was seeing a doctor in Jackson Hole, and he was satisfied with her progress and sure she wouldn't have another ectopic, but on a quiet Sunday afternoon in March, watching movies on the couch with Bill, she started getting cramps, and when she went to the bathroom, she saw that she was bleeding. She was eight weeks pregnant, and she came back from the bathroom in tears.

"What's wrong?" Bill looked at her in panic, remembering what had happened last time. But this was different. She called the doctor, and he told her to come in. He admitted her to the hospital to be on the safe side, and Bill stayed with her, holding her hand and talking to her through the night as the cramps got worse and turned into contractions. In the morning she lost it, and sobbed uncontrollably as Bill held her. They let him stay with her this time. Her life was never in danger, but she miscarried. They did

a D and C, and she went back to Moose
in a deep gloom. The doctor had told
her that some women were able to get
pregnant, but not to carry a baby to
term, and she might be one of them. It
was hard to predict. He told them that
they should consider adoption, which
neither of them wanted to do. They
weren't ready to take that route.

"It's not the end of the world, Jenny,"
Bill said gently. He was as heartbroken
as she was to have lost another baby,
but he was grateful that this time her
own life hadn't been at risk. But she had
had two miscarriages in six months, and
she was profoundly depressed. Gretchen
took over her abuse group that night
and came upstairs to see her afterward.
The women in the group were all sorry
to hear that she was sick, although they
didn't know why. Gretchen came and
sat on her bed, after the group.

"I'm sorry, Jenny. Life just isn't fair.
Half the women in this town got married
because they had to and don't want the
babies they have. And then someone
like you is desperate to have one and
can't." Gretchen was wearing one of the

pants outfits that Jenny had bought her in New York, and she told her friend how nice she looked. Jenny was singlehandedly changing the women of Moose, just by who she was. "Why don't you and Bill try adopting? You can always have your own baby, if you can. It might take the heat off. I've often heard about people getting pregnant after they adopt."

"I'd probably lose it," she said sadly.

"Lots of girls from around here wind up at St. Mary's in Alpine and give their babies up for adoption," Gretchen said quietly. "You should talk to them."

She and Bill had discussed it. Jenny wasn't sure how she felt about adoption, but she didn't want to spend the rest of her life without children. After Gretchen left, Jenny told Bill about St. Mary's home for unwed girls. Gretchen had said that some of the girls who went there to have babies were as young as twelve or thirteen, which seemed tragic to Jenny. It reminded her that she wanted to talk about birth control again with her group for teenage girls. Several of them

were now on the Pill. She didn't want
any of them to wind up at St. Mary's.

She and Bill decided that night that it
was too soon for them to make a decision. They hadn't fully given up yet on
having their own children, and Jenny
wanted to try again. But this time she
knew she hadn't overdone anything, she
wasn't stressed or overworked. She had
had the miscarriage for no reason at all.
But at least it had been less traumatic
than the ectopic pregnancy, and she
knew she could get pregnant again, with
only one ovary and one tube. But she
hadn't been able to carry it to term.

Gretchen took over all her groups that
week, and Jenny stayed in bed, not for
any medical reason, but just because
she was depressed. She got up on Friday finally, to meet with her teenage
girls. She didn't want to let them down.
She had some new makeup for them,
lots of magazines, and a book she
wanted to share with them. They discussed a variety of topics, and she
brought up the subject of birth control
again. She reminded them to be honest
with themselves about what they were

doing and not trust to blind luck or phases of the moon for protection. And if they were having sex, they needed to get birth control. All the girls seemed to agree with what she was saying.

A girl she didn't know as well stayed to talk to her after the group. Her name was Lucy and she was fourteen years old. She was a freshman in high school, and she had mentioned in the group several times that she didn't get along with her mother, and that her father hit her mother when he was drinking. Jenny would have liked to get her mother into Al-Anon or the abuse group, but she had never met her, so she couldn't suggest it. She wondered if Lucy wanted to talk to her about the violence at home or her father's drinking, and she handed her a Coke after the others left.

"How's everything going?" Jenny asked her with a warm smile. It had been a lively group that night, with lots of discussion about turning down drugs and not getting into a car with a boy who had been drinking. They had gone way past makeup and hairdos since the group started, although they talked

about appearance too. Being with them
had boosted Jenny's spirits a little, and
she felt better than she had all week. It
was her first step back into the world.
"How are things at home?" Jenny asked
her, and Lucy shrugged. She was a
pretty girl, with dark hair like Jenny's,
and dark eyes. She had an exotic look
and a full figure, and she appeared older
than she was, which Jenny knew could
be hard on girls her age, when older
boys pursued them and then manipu-
lated them into doing things they couldn't
handle. She encouraged the girls to
avoid situations they weren't comfortable with, or that didn't seem safe, which
wasn't always easy to do.

"Things are okay at home, I guess.
My dad hasn't been as bad lately. My
mom says we just can't get him mad."
Jenny knew that Lucy had an older
brother who was eighteen. He had run
away from home, was living in Laramie,
and was working for a rodeo. Lucy
hadn't seen him in two years. Her father
had been angry ever since, at the son
who had escaped, and he took it out on
everyone else, particularly his wife,

whom he blamed for driving the boy away, when he had really run away because of him, a fact the father was unable to face.

"Jenny," Lucy began hesitantly, "I think I have a problem. Kind of like we were talking about tonight." Jenny ran down the list of topics in her head and guessed that it might be birth control, or a boy pressuring her into things she didn't want to do, and how hard it was to say no, especially if the boy got mad, or was cute. The problems of young girls were universal. They were problems Jenny had faced herself in her youth, not that long ago.

"A problem about boys?" Jenny asked her gently.

Lucy nodded. "Kind of. There was a boy I really liked. I went to the Halloween dance at school with him. He's a senior, and he didn't know I was a freshman. I lied to him and said I was sixteen." And with her lush figure, it was easy to believe. She wasn't the first girl to have lied about her age in order to attract an older boy. And no one would have guessed how young she was. "My dad wouldn't let me go to the dance, so I lied to him too. My mom knew, though. I always tell her the truth." Jenny nodded, waiting for the rest.

"It's always important that someone knows where you are. In case anything happens."

"Something did happen," Lucy said miserably, with tears bulging in her eyes. "He had a bottle of bourbon with him, in his pocket. I drank some of it, and it made me feel sick. And then I drank some more, and I don't know what happened. I think I did it with him, but I can't remember. He took me home, and I went right to bed, and the next day I wasn't sure if I dreamed it or it was true, and I didn't want to ask him. He never called me again or asked me out, so I figured maybe I didn't do it and he was mad . . . but I think I did. . . . I just don't know." She started crying then. "And I just kept believing I didn't do it. I wouldn't do something like that. . . ."

"You can find out, just so you know," Jenny said, trying to reassure her. "A doctor can tell you if you're still a virgin or not," Jenny said, and with that Lucy pulled up her shirt, and Jenny could see the bulge that was there, like a small round ball on her belly. They both knew the answer to her question then, and Jenny tried not to look shocked, so as not to scare her, or appear judgmental.

"I never got my period again after Halloween," Lucy said softly. "I just figured maybe it stopped, because I hadn't had it for that long, and sometimes that happens, but now it's growing, and I know I must have done it. I can't even tell him, because he moved to another school. And he never talked to me again after that night. Jenny, my dad is going to kill me if I tell them. And he'll kill my mom." She dissolved in a river of tears next to Jenny, who put her arms around her, as she did a rapid calculation. It was March. And Lucy was five months pregnant. Here she had lost her own baby, when she wanted it desperately, four days before, and this child who didn't even remember having sex was having a baby she didn't want, that would ruin her life. Life truly was cruel. But in spite of that, Jenny did all she could to console her and waited for Lucy to calm down, trying to think what she could do to help.

"Do you want me to talk to your parents with you?" Jenny offered. Lucy hesitated and then nodded. "Don't let my dad hurt my mom," she begged her. "He'll take it out on her if he gets mad at me."

"We won't let that happen," Jenny said, hoping that would be true. "When do you want me to talk to them?"

"Will you come over tomorrow? My dad goes out on Saturdays. He goes to the bar in town and drinks with his friends. My mom and I will be home alone."

"What time?"

"Like twelve o'clock? He'll be gone by then. My mom just does laundry all day."

"I'll be there," Jenny said, and gave Lucy another hug, and she left a few minutes later. Jenny went upstairs to find Bill and told him what had happened. Bill had been waiting for her upstairs, so as not to intrude on her and the girls.

"Poor kid," he said, thinking about her. He had seen her in the group, although her parents didn't come to church, but Jenny's groups were open to anyone, whether churchgoers or not, and he approved of that. "What do you suppose they'll do to her?"

"I have no idea. Her father has been violent to her mother when he gets drunk. And he's not going to be happy about this with a fourteen-year-old kid. I'm going over to talk to her mother with her tomorrow when he's out. I guess she'll have to have the baby—she's five months pregnant. It's a crime for a kid that age to go through that. She's a child herself." The evening and Jenny telling him about it sobered them both, and Jenny got up early the next day. She was in her yellow truck and on her way to Lucy's house shortly before noon, and Lucy was waiting outside for her.

They went inside together and found her mother folding laundry in the kitchen, humming to herself. She looked shocked when she saw Jenny in her kitchen. She knew who she was, and that Lucy went to her group.

"Is something wrong?" She looked at Lucy immediately. "Did you do something bad in the group?" Her voice was filled with fear and accusation, as Lucy shook her head and her eyes filled with tears.

"No, she didn't." Jenny answered for her, which confused Lucy's mother even more. She looked like a nervous woman, and she had been quick to accuse her daughter, which was what Lucy had said often in group. Her mother was always blaming her for something.

"I'm pregnant," Lucy said, burst into tears, and threw her arms around her mother's neck, who began to sob too. Jenny got them both to sit down at the kitchen table with her, and they went through the whole story. Lucy's mother was distraught and kept asking her how she could have done it. But she had. Nature, a bottle of bourbon, and a persuasive boy had convinced her, and now there was a baby growing inside her that nobody wanted.

Her mother told Lucy that her father would kill them both, which had been Lucy's fear too when she said it to Jenny. And Jenny offered to be there when they told him, but Lucy's mother, Maggie, looked frightened and defeated and said it would only make things worse. She thanked Jenny for her help but said they would have to take care of it now. Lucy would have to go to St. Mary's, before anyone knew what had happened, and give the baby up for adoption. The whole thing was so depressing, and Lucy just sat at the kitchen table and sobbed. She was still crying when Jenny left an hour later, and she was distressed when she went home. She talked to Bill about it, and there was nothing they could do.

She called Lucy that night but there was no answer, and Lucy showed up at Jenny's house at eight o'clock the next morning. She had run all the way there. She said they were taking her to St. Mary's that morning, just as her mother had said. Her father said he didn't want to see her again until after she had the baby and gave it up. Her mother was driving her. She said her mother had cried all night, but she hadn't let her dad hit her. He had hit her mother instead, several times. She thanked Jenny then, threw her arms around her neck and hugged her, and ran back to her house across town. Jenny promised to visit her at St. Mary's, and she knew the other girls would suspect what had happened when she disappeared for several months. The baby was due in July, and Lucy would be back shortly after, never quite the same, after going through childbirth and giving up the baby. She would spend the rest of her life wondering where it was.

Jenny was haunted by it all day, and she went to see Lucy's mother the next morning and found her crying in her kitchen with a black eye. She looked at Jenny in despair. She seemed like a woman who had no hope and no way out, like so many victims of abuse, and Jenny's heart went out to her. Jenny told her about the abuse group, on Monday nights, and Al-Anon, and urged her to come. Maggie said she might but looked frightened and uncertain. And much to Jenny's amazement, she showed up that night, looking terrified, but she came. Jenny went to see Lucy at St. Mary's the next day. She looked heartbroken and subdued. The nuns were very nice to her, and they told Jenny that Lucy had been examined by a doctor and had confirmed that the baby was due in July. It would be put up for adoption, and they assured her they would find a good home for it, and Lucy would go home as soon as she delivered.

When she saw Lucy again, she clung to Jenny and sobbed and begged her not to leave her there, but Jenny had no other choice. She sat with Lucy until she calmed down, and then Lucy turned to her with a strange, haunted look.

"Will you take my baby, Jenny? I know you want one. I don't want it to go to anyone but you. I know you'd be good to it, and it would never have to know it was mine. But I would know, and you and Bill would give it a good home." She was sobbing again, and Jenny was shocked at what she had said, although it seemed strangely providential. This was the kind of situation Gretchen had talked about, a young girl who got in trouble and was going to give up her baby. She had told her to come to St. Mary's for an adoption. She and Bill had decided to try again, but this might be a blessing for everyone. She didn't know what to say.

"I'll talk to Bill about it," she promised, and Lucy was calmer when she left. There were twenty other girls there from neighboring counties all in the same situation, waiting to give birth, relinquish their babies, and go home. Some of them looked even younger than Lucy. It was heartbreaking. And all the way back to Moose, Jenny thought of what Lucy had said. She went to find Bill as soon as she got back. He was at his desk, working on his sermon. He knew where she had gone, to Alpine to visit Lucy, and he could see the deep concern in Jenny's eyes.

"She wants us to take the baby," Jenny said in a strangled tone, as she sat down across from Bill. "I don't know if her parents would agree to it, but it's a thought. We could still have our own," she added sadly, wondering if that was true. "The baby is due in July."

"Is that what you want?" Bill asked her softly, sounding surprised. Adopting Lucy's baby hadn't occurred to either of them. They were just worried about Lucy and her mother. This was not what they'd expected or wanted. They weren't ready to adopt yet, but it was a baby, and it needed a home, Lucy was a sweet girl, and she wanted to give it to them. "Let's think about it," he said quietly. "We can talk to her parents in a few days." Jenny agreed. She didn't want to rush into anything. And this was so sudden.

They spent the weekend thinking about it and discussing it some more. They both liked the idea. It seemed like a ready-made situation for them, and it would be a blessing for Lucy and her parents as well. Bill called Lucy's parents and made an appointment with them for Sunday, after church, allegedly to talk about Lucy. And they offered to adopt Lucy's baby. Her mother looked relieved, and her father said that he wanted an agreement from them that they wouldn't disclose whose baby it was, ever. They could say they had adopted it in New York. And if Jenny and Bill were willing to do that, Lucy's parents would let them have the baby. It was a simple arrangement, and both

sides agreed to let St. Mary's know.
Jenny said she wanted to be at the birth
with Lucy and her mother, to see the
baby born. Her father didn't care. He
looked like he'd been drinking before
they got there, and as soon as they con-
cluded their business, he stormed out
of the house and slammed the door.
Jenny hugged Lucy's mother, who was
crying, and they left.

And Maggie showed up at the abuse
group again. This time she had a determined look in her eyes. She said she
wasn't going to let her husband push
her around anymore. And she wouldn't
let him lay a hand on Lucy when she
came home. When Jenny called Lucy to
check on her, she said that she and her
mother were getting along better. Jenny
suspected that the abuse group was
having a positive effect on Maggie.

Jenny went to see Lucy later that
week and told her that she and Bill would
adopt her baby and were thrilled to do
so. And Lucy looked enormously relieved. All she wanted was to know that
her baby would be in good hands, and
she was sure that Jenny and Bill were

the best parents she could have chosen. All they had to do now was wait for the baby to come. It was only four months away.

"I can't believe this is happening," Jenny said to Bill that night. "We're going to have a baby in four months." He smiled at her and took her in his arms. They had four months to get ready for the most important day of their lives. The day they brought their baby home. Jenny didn't mind at all that she wasn't giving birth to it. She would be there when it was born. Bill would have liked to be too, but he didn't want to intrude on Lucy, so he would have to wait until the baby left the delivery room in Jenny's arms. It had all worked out in the end. They had lost two babies of their own, and now this fourteen-year-old girl was giving them their dream. It was the greatest gift she could have given them. Jenny told her that every time she saw her, and thanked her for the gift. She and Bill talked about it all the time now when they were alone. It was all Jenny could think about, and she finally admitted to Gretchen that they were adopting a baby, but they didn't know who the parents were. And Gretchen was so happy for them. Jenny had told her mother as well, who was cautiously happy for them and hoped it would work out well. She was afraid the birth mother might change her mind and Jenny would be disappointed. Jenny assured her that wouldn't be the case.

Jenny moved her office to a corner of the living room, and they started getting the nursery ready in May. And Maggie had continued coming to the abuse group for the past two months. Her stories were the same as all the others, of being beaten and slapped around by her husband, as she had been for years. But something had changed. She was no longer willing to accept the treatment from him that she had taken before.

And as they waited for their baby to come, Bill never missed an opportunity to tell Jenny that he loved her until the end of time.

Chapter 9

Jenny was painting the nursery one morning in June, when she heard the doorbell ring. Bill had gone off to see Clay Roberts about some repairs they needed to make to the church, and Clay wanted to discuss them with him, as the head of the church board. She went downstairs and opened the door, and found herself looking at Debbie, with three of her children all around her, and the baby in her arms. She looked frightened, she had a huge black eye, and her arm was in a sling.

"Jenny, can you help me?" she said

without preamble, and Jenny stepped aside immediately so they could come in. The children were all wearing pajamas, Debbie looked hastily dressed, and she had nothing with her except a shopping bag full of diapers for the baby and some snacks for the kids.

"What happened?" Jenny asked her, looking worried. She went to the fridge to get juice for the kids and poured Debbie a cup of coffee.

"He said he was going to kill me," she said in a hoarse whisper, as they walked a few steps away, so the children couldn't hear them. "He thinks I've been cheating on him, and I haven't. He's crazy. One of his friends came over and tried to help me fix Mikey's crib. He must have said something to him when they went out drinking together, and Tony came home, threw me down the stairs, and gave me a black eye. I want to go to my older sister in Cheyenne. She said I can stay there until I find a job. I didn't tell anyone where we were going. I just left when he went out. He's crazy. I think he really would kill me. He started using uppers, and he drinks all the time now.

I can't stay there anymore, he's going to do something terrible to me or the children. I can't take the chance." She was willing to run away to save her children, but for herself she had stayed there and taken the abuse for years. Jenny was just glad that she had finally gotten up the guts to get out. She was young, and she could start over and have a good life.

"How are you going to get to Cheyenne?" Jenny asked her, and Debbie looked blank. There was a bus, but she had no money, and if Tony saw her at the bus station, he would force her to go back. "I'll take you," Jenny said without hesitating, realizing Debbie had no plan. She just threw the diapers into a bag, grabbed her children, and ran, before he returned to the house. It would take him a while to figure out that she had escaped. She had left no note, and for a short time he would think they had just gone out. It gave her several hours' jump start on him before he started looking for her. Time was of the essence. And Jenny knew that it was a seven- or eight-hour drive to Cheyenne. "Okay, let's go," she told Debbie. They would take Bill's truck. It had a backseat and a front seat, with six seat belts all told, enough to get them there safely, even though they had no car seats, but Debbie could sit in back and hold the baby, and there were seat belts for all the other kids. And whatever they did, it was safer for all of them than staying at their house.

She left Bill a note on the kitchen table for him to find when he got home. "Sorry I hijacked your truck. You can use mine. Gone for a while. Will call you when I can. Don't worry, I'm fine. Mission of mercy. I'll explain. I love you, J." She was afraid to write anything more in case Tony showed up at her house, broke in, and found the note. She shepherded Debbie and the children out to Bill's truck and settled everyone in. She had grabbed her purse and still had paint on her hands. She hadn't stopped to change or clean up. She just wanted to get Debbie and her kids out of town as fast as possible. Debbie was finally doing the right thing. And Jenny didn't want her to lose courage or momentum now. She had been hoping for months that Debbie would leave. And whatever it took, Tony had finally crossed the line.

Jenny drove for two hours until the kids all started to complain that they were hungry. She stopped at a Burger King and bought everyone lunch, and after that they fell asleep. And it was a long silent drive for the next several hours. Even Debbie fell asleep in the back, slumped over, with the baby in her arms, and the seat belt around both of them. Jenny turned on the radio, to keep her awake, and for distraction. It was nearly four o'clock when they all woke up again, and they had been on the road for six hours. It was another two hours before they reached Cheyenne at six o'clock. The kids were hungry again, but Debbie didn't want to stop and was anxious to get to her sister's. She gave Jenny directions to her sister's house.

She was a carbon copy of Debbie, in a slightly older version, and there were children running all over her house, the moment she opened the door. The place was tiny, the living room was full of toys, and her husband was watching TV. He had just come home from work and had a beer in his hand, and her sister hugged Debbie as soon as she saw her. She knew what Debbie was doing there, and Jenny was dismayed, as she followed them in, to see how small the house was. It would be tough for two families to live there, even for a short time. But Debbie's sister had always promised to help her find a job in Cheyenne if she left Tony, and she finally had. Her sister looked relieved, and thanked Jenny for getting them there.

One thing was certain, Debbie could never go back to Moose. Particularly with Tony so angry now, the risk of being anywhere near him was just too great. Tony's perception would be that she had stolen their children from him, and it would anger him even more. But it had been the right thing for her to do. She had had no other choice.

Jenny gave her all the money she had in her purse when she left. She didn't want to linger, as she had an eight-hour drive ahead of her through the night. She had given Debbie less than two hundred dollars and it wouldn't take her

far, but it was better than nothing. Afterward Jenny thought she should have
tried to cash a check, and given her
more, but she didn't think of it until she
was on the road again. She stopped at
a gas station to put gas in the truck for
the trip home and called Bill. He answered on the first ring and had been
frantic, wondering where she was. She'd
called earlier from a gas station on the
way to Cheyenne, but no one had answered.

"Where are you? I've been sick with
worry. I came back and you were gone."

"I'm sorry, baby. Debbie showed up
with her kids, with a black eye and her
arm in a sling, and she finally decided to
bail. She asked me to get her to her sister in Cheyenne. I just dropped her off.
I'm heading home now."

"I'm supposed to be the angel of
mercy around here, not you. I don't want
him coming after you if he figures out
you helped her escape. I want you to be
very careful and keep the doors locked
from now on. What time will you be
back?"

"I'm leaving Cheyenne now. I'll be

home in seven or eight hours." He hated the idea of her driving for so many hours with no one with her. But there was nothing they could do, and she was a good driver.

"I hope she stays there," Bill said, sounding worried about Debbie.

"She will. She's never coming back. She's too afraid of Tony to even think about it."

"Don't be so sure. Abuse victims have a way of returning to their abusers. It's an addiction that's hard to break." He had learned that from working with abused women. Too many of them went back to their abusers and paid a high price for it in the end.

"I don't think she's addicted to him. She just had nowhere to go, and her sister's place is too small. She has to find a job soon."

"Just come home now, Jenny. And drive carefully. If you're tired, pull over and sleep." If she drove straight through, she'd be home around three in the morning, even later if traffic was bad leaving Cheyenne.

"I will. I promise," she told him, and

she was wide awake. She had been on edge all day, trying to deliver Debbie and her children to Cheyenne safely. She put the radio on when she got back in the truck, and had bought coffee at the gas station. All she wanted now was to get home to Bill. She had completed her mission and hopefully delivered Debbie to a better life.

She drove through the night and got home at two-thirty—she had made good time. And Bill woke instantly, the moment she slipped into bed. She had taken off her clothes and dropped them on the floor, and was wearing her underwear and a T-shirt, when he put his arms around her.

"Thank God you're home," he said, sounding sleepy in the dark. "I was worried about you all night." He had finally gone to bed around two.

"I'm fine," she said, cuddling close to him, and nestling her face in his neck. She was asleep in two minutes and woke up late the next morning. Bill was downstairs making coffee when she got up.

"What a day that was," she said as

she sat down at the kitchen table, looking exhausted, and he handed her a
mug of coffee. She had driven sixteen
hours the day before, and she felt dazed
and was still stunned by Debbie's escape to Cheyenne with her children.
Jenny wondered how she was doing—
Debbie had promised to stay in touch.

After breakfast, Jenny went back to
painting the nursery, and they finished it
together that weekend. They had bought
nursery furniture in a shop at the mall,
and Jenny put appliqués of little teddy
bears on it when they were finished. It
looked adorable, and she was pleased.
The baby was only five weeks away
now, and Lucy was uncomfortable and
frightened of what lay ahead. She wasn't
emotionally prepared for what she'd
have to go through in the delivery, but
her mother and Jenny were determined
to get her through it, and the doctor at
St. Mary's was sympathetic and experienced at delivering girls her age. He had
promised to make both labor and delivery as easy as possible for her.

And then it would be over, she could
put it behind her and go back to her life

as a sophomore in high school in the fall. They were letting her take her exams at St. Mary's, and she had to do homework every day. The nuns told her that with time, it would seem like it had never happened, and she would forget. Jenny knew that was an even bigger lie than the ones the boy had told her to get her to have sex when she didn't want to. How would she ever forget giving birth at fourteen to a baby she was being forced to give away? Jenny couldn't imagine anything worse, and she still felt guilty at times that her greatest joy would cause Lucy so much pain, not just physically but emotionally, when she gave the baby up. But Lucy was in no way prepared to have a child, and her father had not relented, although her relationship with her mother had improved markedly in the last three months. Maggie was stronger and calmer after her months in the abuse group, and she was determined to help her daughter, and protect her when she got home. At least they all knew the baby would have a loving home. Of that there was no doubt.

It was all Jenny could think of now, and she was in town at the general store, buying diapers and nursery supplies two weeks later, when Debbie walked in with her kids. Jenny's jaw nearly dropped when she saw her, and she walked over to her with a look of panic. She had heard nothing from her since she left her at her sister's in Cheyenne, but Jenny had assumed she was safe.

"What are you doing here?" she asked in a whisper. "Why aren't you in Cheyenne?" She was terrified for her, seeing her back in town. She wondered if Tony knew she was there.

"I couldn't find a job," Debbie answered nervously, glancing over her shoulder. "Tony showed up and brought me back." Her eyes were deep pools of despair.

"How did he know you were there?"

She hesitated for a fraction of a second. "I called him. I had no money to feed the kids. My sister couldn't help me out, and there was no work for me there. I couldn't afford to pay a sitter."

"You should have called me. I would have helped." Jenny felt guilty again for not leaving her more when she left Cheyenne, and then she remembered what Bill had told her, that abuse victims often went back to their abusers and came to a bad end. She didn't want that to happen to her. She had walked right back into the lion's mouth.

Debbie looked at her imploringly then. "Don't come by the house. Don't call me. He really will kill me then. I'll call you if I can." And as she said it, Tony walked in, looking surly, and grabbed Debbie's arm. He walked right past Jenny as though he hadn't seen her, and didn't care. He told his wife to hurry up, and walked out again. Jenny watched in horror as she gathered up her children and left.

Jenny told Bill about it when she got home, and Gretchen when she saw her that night. She had come to admire the nursery, and shook her head when Jenny told her about seeing Debbie at the store.

"Poor kid. He's such a bad guy. Tony always was. She'd have been better off starving in Cheyenne with her sister, than back with him."

"I'm afraid of what he'll do to her now."

"There's nothing you can do about it, Jenny. She has to free herself, however long it takes. No one can do it for her. She probably feels trapped, with no money and all those kids." Jenny nodded, and they ran the abuse group together that night. Gretchen had never been an abuse victim, but she was good with the groups. And Lucy's mother Maggie was there as usual that night. She hadn't missed a meeting since she started and seemed to have gained confidence in the three months since Lucy was at St. Mary's. Maggie seemed like a different woman, and she was attending Al-Anon meetings too.

Jenny was having breakfast with Bill the next morning, when Gretchen called her in a shocked voice. At first Jenny didn't even recognize who it was.

"Oh my God, you were right" was all she said at first, and Jenny could hear that she was crying, and then realized who it was.

"About what?"

"He killed her last night. Tony killed Debbie. He came home drunk and threw her down the stairs. She died of a brain hemorrhage this morning. I just saw her mother."

"What about the kids?" Jenny said, sounding panicked.

"They're okay. They're with her mother. Apparently, he called the cops himself and said she fell, but they found evidence that he'd beaten her badly before he threw her. He's in jail, being held for murder. You saw this coming," Gretchen said in a choked voice.

"And I didn't stop it," Jenny said, devastated by what Gretchen had just told her. A few minutes later she hung up and told Bill. He had already figured it out from her end of the conversation, and he wasn't surprised. She had signed her death warrant when she came back. He had seen it happen before.

"I should have been more forceful with her," Jenny said, looking at Bill mournfully. "I didn't want to upset her. She was always so afraid to piss him off."

"It wouldn't have made any difference," Bill said, as he put an arm around her. "You couldn't make her leave him or stay away."

"I thought when she went to Cheyenne, she'd never come back." She had lasted two weeks and called him. And now her children had no mother, and she was dead at twenty-four.

Jenny was depressed about it all day, and to distract herself, she went to see Lucy. She was miserable in a summer heat wave and cried every time she talked about giving birth. She didn't want to go through it, but there was no turning back now. She clung to Jenny like a small child, which in many ways she was. And she was about to grow up. Fast.

Jenny stopped in to see Gretchen on the way home, and they talked about Debbie again. She told her what Bill had said.

"He's right. I don't think any of us could have stopped him, or gotten her away. She was too tangled up in his web, and too used to the abuse." But that seemed like such an easy excuse to Jenny. Gretchen asked about their birth mother then, to change the subject. All she knew was that they were adopting a baby in New York in July. She had no idea that the baby was Lucy's, whom she knew, which was their agreement with Lucy's parents.

"It's all going along fine," Jenny said, smiling. "It won't be long now. They're going to call us when the baby is born, and we'll go pick it up and bring it home."

"I'm surprised you don't want to be at the birth," Gretchen commented. It seemed like what Jenny would want to do, knowing her as she did now, and Bill just as much so. They were very warm, loving people who would want to be there the minute their child was born.

"The mother doesn't want us there. She's very young," Jenny said smoothly, and as she did, Gretchen gave her a long look.

"How young?"

"Fourteen," Jenny said, and was sorry as soon as she said it. She didn't want to blow the deal by violating their agreement. Lucy's father was capable of anything and didn't care about his daughter's baby. Gretchen didn't comment, or ask any further questions. Something told her she shouldn't, and Jenny was relieved.

And for the next several days all anyone talked about was Debbie, and Tony being arrested for murder. They took him to Jackson Hole for arraignment, and kept him in jail there. Jenny and Bill went to her funeral with Gretchen and Eddy, and everyone who knew her or had grown up with her, or had ever gone to school with her, was there. Her children weren't there at least, but her mother and sisters were crying in the front pew. It was the most depressing funeral Jenny had ever been to, and she and Bill were quiet when they went home afterward. It was such a waste.

Things had just begun to calm down a week before Lucy's due date. Jenny was trying to visit her every day. But there were flash floods in the mountains just as she was about to leave the house one morning to see her, and she was surprised to see Bill saddling up Clay's horse.

"Where are you going?"

"Out to see Harvey Adams. He's got pneumonia, and I promised I'd visit." Bill smiled at her. He was loving his work, and they both agreed that their destiny had led them here. It felt like it was a million miles from New York, and it was hard to imagine living there anymore. In nine months, this had become home.

"Why don't you wait till the weather clears?"

"I told Doc Smith I'd take a look at him, and see if he needs to go up there today too. His kids want him to move closer to town, but he's a stubborn old coot."

"So are you," she said as she kissed Bill. He was so dedicated to his congregation and loved the people here. He had said he would go out to visit Harvey, and he never broke a promise.

"I'll be fine," he assured her. Clay's horse was solid and sure-footed and used to the terrain. She didn't worry about Bill riding up the paths into the mountains, except in bad weather. But he had even done it in the snows that winter. And between showers, it was a beautiful day. "I'll be back in a few hours. What are you doing today?"

"I was going to see Lucy, but I think

I'll stick around. I have to call some of my clients, and Azaya and I need to go over some things. I haven't talked to her in a week." Jenny was finding it harder and harder to focus on her clients in New York. Her life was here now, with Bill, his congregation, and their baby in a few weeks. She didn't want to let her clients down, but it just wasn't the same, now that she was in Wyoming. And Nelson's business was taking off, and he had less time to help Azaya. Jenny was thinking of telling her clients that she was closing her business when she went back for Fashion Week in September, and then winding up her business in New York by the end of the year. It was time. Her life had changed too much. She had moved on. She had never thought that would happen, but it had.

Bill smiled at her before he walked out the door, and then he turned back and walked over to kiss her again. "Don't forget how much I love you," he said to her, wishing he could stay home and make love to her. She was more beautiful than ever, and he was more in love with her every day.

"Until the end of time, right?" She smiled at him, teasing him a little. He was so loving to her, and she knew how lucky she was to share her life with him. "And if the weather looks too lousy, come back. You can go see Harvey tomorrow." He nodded, and a few minutes later she saw him ride away on Navajo, and she went to call Azaya and spread a stack of fabric samples and photos out on her desk. Suddenly whether they used a print or a stripe, an organza or a gazar, just didn't seem to matter. Her heart wasn't in it anymore.

As Bill rode up the foothills toward where Harvey Adams lived, the weather cleared, and the sun came out in a bright blue sky. And the sure-footed horse led him up the familiar path. He was thinking about Jenny as he rode, about how happy he was with her, and how right it had been to come here. He was thinking about their baby too, and how different their life would be now. Lucy's baby would give even deeper meaning to everything they felt for each other.

He rode easily in the saddle, looking at the wildflowers on the hills around him, and down at the valley, as a flash flood came over the mountains. He never saw it coming, and it swept him and the horse to the edge of a ravine. He grabbed a low-hanging branch as the horse went over the edge and fell into a deep crevasse below them. The water kept coming in a torrent as Bill hung on, struggling to keep his grip. He was hanging over the edge of the cliff, as he felt his hands slipping. He never wore his gloves in the warm weather, and as he felt his grip going, he looked up at the sky, felt a wave of peace wash over him, and shouted at the sun as loud as he could, "I love you, Jenny!" He wanted her to hear him, and for those to be the last words he said. He felt himself falling with the water rushing below him. He wasn't afraid. All he felt was his deep love for her, more powerful than any ocean, as he fell to the floor of the ravine below.

Chapter 10

After Jenny spoke to Azaya, she went upstairs to the nursery, and put away some things she'd bought and hadn't had time to put in the drawers yet. Everything was ready. All they needed now was the baby. She could hardly wait. She was smiling to herself as she bustled around and was surprised when, three hours later, Bill wasn't home yet. Sometimes he spent hours with his congregants when he visited them, particularly Harvey Adams, who liked to tell stories, or any of the older ones who were lonely and sick. Bill had the proverbial patience of a saint. She knew there was no point worrying about him. Eventually, he'd wander home, apologizing for taking so long.

At five o'clock she took out some lettuce and tossed a salad for dinner. Bill was going to barbecue steak. And it was five-thirty when she heard a car drive up and looked out the kitchen window. It was the sheriff. It was the second time he'd been there that week, to question her about Tony Blackman and what she knew about his abusing Debbie. They were still investigating their history and the persistence of his abuse. It didn't surprise her to see the sheriff again, and he looked serious when she opened the door and invited him in.

"Hi, Clark," she said easily. "Bill isn't home yet. He should be here any minute. He went up to see Harvey Adams—he's been sick." The sheriff nodded and took off his hat when he walked in.

"Jenny, I have to talk to you," he said.

"I know. It's about Tony again." She hated going over it again, and hoped he would go to prison for a long time for what he'd done.

"It's Bill," he said quietly. He wanted to get this over with quickly and not draw out the agony. It was bad enough. "He got caught in a flash flood today, going up to Harvey's. He and his horse fell into the ravine." It was as simple as he could make it, as Jenny stared at him in disbelief.

"What are you saying?" Her mind refused to understand.

"He died, Jenny. He fell. We found him at the bottom of the ravine. They got swept away." For a moment he thought she was going to faint as she clutched his arm. The look on her face was one he knew he'd never forget. He just hoped someone felt that way about him when he died. She looked as though someone had just ripped her heart out through her eyes. "I'm sorry. I'm so sorry. He was a wonderful man." He helped her into a chair as she stared at him.

"That's not right," she said, wanting to argue with him and roll back the film. "It can't be. You made a mistake. Are you sure?" She was talking quickly and shaking her head. She couldn't believe what she was hearing.

"I'm sure. We brought him back." He didn't want to tell her that his broken, lacerated body was at the morgue. And the strangest part of it was how peaceful he had looked when they found him, almost as though he were asleep. He really was a holy man. Clark wondered if he'd been praying when he fell, to look like that. "I'm really sorry. Is there anyone you want me to call?" She couldn't think. She knew there were people she had to tell. And as soon as he left, she phoned Gretchen and told her in a shaken tone to come right away. She didn't say why. Gretchen thought maybe the birth mother had changed her mind. It never dawned on her for an instant that Bill had died. And the moment she saw Jenny's face, she knew. She had never seen anyone look like that, as though part of her had died at the same time.

"They're wrong. I know they are," Jenny kept saying as Gretchen sat with her and held her hand. "Bill wouldn't leave me like this." But he had. Life had intervened, despite their love and their plans. As Gretchen sat with her, she was terrified that she would come unglued. But she didn't. She just sat there for hours. And then she called Tom, to tell him, and he burst into tears. He asked when the funeral was, and she didn't know. She called her mother, who sobbed uncontrollably for her daughter's loss and grief. It reminded her of when her own husband had died when Jenny was a child.

Gretchen went with her to make the arrangements the next day. They set the date for three days later, at Sts. Peter and Paul. A minister from Jackson Hole was coming to do the service. Jenny called Tom and her mother to tell them, and Gretchen called Azaya, and she said she would let everyone else know. Gretchen never left her side for three days, and Jenny said she could feel him with her, that he would never leave her. He had promised he wouldn't.

Jenny called Maggie to tell her herself, and she said she still wanted the baby. Nothing had changed. The only difference was that she'd be alone. And Maggie sounded relieved that there had been no change of plan about the baby.

And she told Lucy that night, and she cried.

Her mother came from Philadelphia and stayed at her house with her, and Gretchen continued to come and go too. Jenny looked like a ghost and was still dazed by what had happened. Bill's family arrived the night before the funeral and stayed at a hotel in Jackson Hole. Tom came out to see her at the house, and they both cried. He hugged Jenny as though she were his own sister. He had come to love her at last for how good she'd been to Bill. He was going to give the eulogy at the funeral service, and Clay Roberts had agreed to say a few words. Jenny didn't really care. There was nothing they could say about him that she didn't already know. She couldn't imagine a life without him, and she spent hours that night, sitting in a chair outside, looking up at the sky, wondering where he was. He had always said to her that people who love each other find each other again. First they went up to the sky and became stars, and then they came back in other lives, and they knew each other when they met and went on. She had thought it was silly when he said it, but now she liked the idea, that they would share a life again. Hers had no meaning without him.

She had told Azaya not to come to the funeral. It was too complicated to get there, and dealing with Bill's family was hard enough. His parents looked devastated when she saw them the next day, and they said not a word to her. Both his brothers had come, but not their wives, and Tom and Gretchen stood on either side of her, and her mother right behind her, as Jenny stared at his coffin and looked shell-shocked, and they all felt helpless in the face of Jenny's overwhelming grief. His parents had wanted to take him back to New York for burial, and she had refused. She wanted him buried here. He had said that this was where they were meant to be, and she believed him. She knew it too.

Tom's eulogy was beautiful, about their childhood and the man Bill had become. Timmie and his aunt and sister were there. And all of the congregants he'd touched. Eddy cried like a baby, and afterward people drifted in and out of the house, talking to her, saying things she didn't care about or understand, and telling her how sorry they were for her loss. But how could they know? How could they possibly know how much he meant to her? She kept thinking about the day they met, in front of the Plaza in New York, and then when they saw each other again at the gas station in Massachusetts. It had been their destiny. But now none of it made sense with him gone. She felt like an empty shell without him.

Gretchen put her to bed that night after Tom said goodbye. Jenny's mother stayed at the house with her. Bill's family was leaving in the morning, and Jenny knew she'd never see them again and didn't care. But Tom had promised to visit her. And she convinced her mother to leave the day after. She wanted to be left alone with her grief, and Gretchen had promised to stay with her, so Helene reluctantly agreed to leave. All that mattered to Jenny was Bill. He was a part of her now, and always had been since the day they met. She didn't want anyone else around, not even her mother. And Gretchen was a discreet presence, like a guardian angel. She spoke little and was just there.

Jenny drove to see Lucy the next day. Lucy had been worried about Jenny—she hadn't seen her in four days. When Lucy saw Jenny's glazed eyes, she started to cry, and Jenny held her in her arms and told her that everything would be all right. It would all be better when the baby came. Her due date was two days away, and she was huge. Lucy cried all the time now, she was so afraid, and Jenny promised her that she'd be right there, with her mother, and it would be fine. When Jenny went back home, Timmie and his sister came to see her and brought her flowers. And Gretchen came back and brought her dinner, and she stayed late into the night with Jenny, sitting outside again, looking up at the stars. Jenny didn't say it, but Gretchen had the feeling she was looking for him, as though she would see him there, up in the heavens, waiting for her. They were like two people with one soul.

Gretchen had no idea how Jenny was going to live without him now. But she had to. She had no choice.

At Jenny's insistence, Gretchen went home to her own family that night. She knew that Eddy and her children needed her too, so she agreed.

"How is she?" Eddy asked when Gretchen came home, looking drained.

"I don't know. She looks like she died with him. I don't know what's going to happen to her now. She's so lost without him." Gretchen had talked to Azaya, who thought she should come back to New York and go back to work again, but Gretchen wasn't sure. They had made a life here, and she thought Jenny wanted to stay, although she'd have to give up the house when they found a new minister, but that would take time. And the baby was coming any day.

Jenny got the call from the hospital at four A.M., hours after Gretchen left. And she had promised Lucy she'd be there. She got up, and she could hear Bill in her head, telling her he was right there with her. He would never leave her. She felt peaceful as soon as she remembered the words. And it started to rain when she went out to the truck. She drove her own, instead of his. It was a half-hour drive to St. Mary's, and the nurse had said the baby was coming quickly, so she picked up speed. There were several sharp turns on the road, but the old Chevy truck held the road well. She was just nearing the last turn, when she turned and saw Bill sitting beside her, and smiling at her. He was right there with her in the truck.

"What are you doing here?" she asked him, as she smiled too.

"I told you I'd never leave you, silly." She remembered it perfectly. And she was still smiling at him, as her truck slid out of control on the last turn, in the rain, and she saw lights coming toward her. She turned to see what Bill would say, and he looked peaceful, as she reached a hand out to him, and the truck coming at her hit her head on, going at full speed, and the yellow truck disappeared under its wheels, as she and Bill quietly walked away.

Chapter 11

Maggie had gotten the call from St. Mary's at the same time Jenny did, that the baby was coming. She jumped into her clothes and grabbed her purse, as Frank woke up and looked at her.

"Where are you going? It's the middle of the night." He sounded as disagreeable as he always did when he drank too much.

"Lucy's having the baby," she said quietly.

"I don't want to hear about it. Give it to them and forget about it," he said, as though a life could be given up and forgotten as easily as that. She wondered if he felt the same way about her. She said nothing and walked out of the room. She went outside and got in her car in a light rain and wondered if she should have offered to pick Jenny up, but she hadn't thought of it. She was glad she still wanted the baby, in spite of losing Bill. It would give her something to live for now, Maggie thought as she drove, praying that Lucy would come through it all right. She was so young to endure so much. Her own delivery had been traumatic, and she'd been ten years older than Lucy was now. At fourteen, Lucy just wasn't ready for what was in store for her.

The rain slowed Maggie down, and an accident as she approached the hospital blocked the road. There were police standing by and an ambulance. A truck had overturned, and she explained to the officer, when he stopped her, that her daughter was having a baby and she had to get to the hospital, so they escorted her through, and she drove on. And as soon as she got there, they handed her surgical pajamas to change into and rushed her to the delivery room. It had all happened so quickly, and Lucy was ready to push. She was screaming piteously when her mother walked into the room, and Lucy grabbed her arm and clawed at her, as her mother tried to calm her down.

"Where's Jenny?" she shouted as they held her down so she didn't fall off the table, and finally they strapped her down which made her scream more. They were going to use forceps if she wouldn't push, which would only make it worse. But they couldn't reason with her, she was in too much pain. "I want her here too!" she screamed. "She said she'd be here!" Lucy said, terrified.

"She's coming," Maggie said with a calm she didn't feel. It was ghastly watching her child in so much pain, it made her feel sick. "They called her when they called me. It's raining and the road is blocked, so it may take her a while." But Lucy's baby wasn't willing to wait. It was ripping its way through Lucy's young body, and she felt like she was drowning as she screamed.

"Come on, Lucy, help us . . . we want

to help you . . . let's get the baby out. It will help us if you push," the doctor said gently, but she was in too much pain to listen or care. She felt like she was dying. And finally they used the forceps, which only made her scream more. There had been no time for an epidural, and it was too late now to give her anything for the pain.

"Can't you do something for her?" her mother begged, wishing that Jenny were there too. It might have helped. But she'd obviously been delayed on the way, or stopped by the roadblock.

"We can give her a C-section," the doctor said quietly, "but I'd rather not do that. It'll be an issue for her in subsequent births, I'd rather she deliver naturally the first time." But it was infinitely harder for her. Then finally, agonizingly, slowly, with the help of the forceps, as Lucy continued to scream, the baby's head emerged, with a look of surprise and a mass of dark hair like Lucy's and Jenny's. The baby looked like both of them. Then they delivered the rest of the body—it was a baby girl—and Lucy lay there sobbing as her

mother stroked her cheeks. They gave
Lucy something for the pain then as
they sewed her up and took the baby
away. Jenny was supposed to be there,
but she wasn't, and they carried the
baby to the nursery, to wait for her, while
Maggie stayed with Lucy until she drifted
off to sleep, still whimpering. It had been
a terrible night that her mother knew she
would never forget. And all for a baby
they were giving to someone else. It
made Maggie sad to think about it. Lucy
was still asleep when they rolled her out
of the delivery room and into a room
where Maggie sat in a chair, dozing all
night. In the morning, Jenny still hadn't
come.

Maggie called her house, and no one
answered. And when Gretchen arrived
to make breakfast for her, she saw that
she had left, and her truck was gone.
She didn't know who to call or where
she went, as she looked around. Jenny
hadn't left a note. She was about to
leave, when the phone rang and Gretchen
picked it up. It was Maggie calling again
to see where Jenny was. Gretchen
thought it odd that she was calling and

then wondered about the baby again and if it was Lucy's. "Her truck's not here," Gretchen said simply. Bill's was in the driveway, but the yellow Chevy was gone.

"I was expecting her last night," Maggie said without explaining, "and she never came." It had been a long ordeal, and she was exhausted. "There was an accident on the road," she told Gretchen, and then her voice trailed off into nothing, and there was silence on the line.

"Oh my God," Gretchen said. "I'll call Clark." He would know if something had happened to Jenny, and who was involved in any accident in the area. She called the sheriff's office, and he came on the line a few minutes later and confirmed Gretchen's worst fears.

"She lost control of her truck," he said, sounding devastated. "She got in a head-on collision with an eighteen-wheeler coming around the bend. She must have died instantly." He felt sick as he said it. She had died four days after Bill, and for an instant, Gretchen knew it was what she would have wanted. They were meant to be together, forever. Her

life would never have been the same
without him, even with the baby. She
hung up, feeling shaken, and called
Maggie back and told her. The two
women cried and then hung up. And
Gretchen called Azaya in New York and
told her. She promised to call Helene,
and Bill's family, to tell them. She couldn't
imagine telling Jenny's mother. Tragedy
had struck twice in one week.

Maggie sat for a long time, thinking
about it, while she waited for Lucy to
wake up, and it was almost noon when
she did. Lucy's voice was hoarse from
screaming, and she looked at her mother
with blank eyes. She hadn't even seen
her baby after it was born, and had
planned not to, since she was giving it
up. But now Jenny wasn't coming to
take it. Maggie told Lucy as gently as
she could what had happened to Jenny
the night before. Lucy lay there, sobbing
silently, with tears streaming down her
cheeks. She had loved Jenny, and now
her baby had no one to adopt her. She
looked at her mother with agony in her
eyes. But they were the eyes of a woman
now, not a child.

"Mama, can I keep her?" she begged, and without hesitating, her mother nodded, as Lucy sobbed in relief. It made everything that had happened to her the night before worthwhile. She could keep her baby. "What about Dad?" she asked with panic in her eyes. And with the same certainty she'd had a moment before, Maggie knew that it was time. She was ready.

"I'm going to leave your father, Lucy. We'll figure it out, the three of us, you, me, and the baby. What are you going to call her?" her mother asked her.

"Jenny," Lucy said with a sad smile, as her mother leaned over and kissed her.

Chapter 12

Gretchen made the arrangements for the funeral with Maggie's help, and Azaya's advice from New York. It was held at Sts. Peter and Paul. Her mother came back from Philadelphia and looked like a ghost herself, as Gretchen did her best to shepherd her around. Helene was incapable of making any decisions. She was too distraught. She looked very frail as she attended the funeral of her only child.

All the men and women who had attended her groups were at the funeral, and the teenagers in Jenny's Girls, everyone she had touched, reached out to, and helped in the eight months she'd been in Moose, which seemed like a lifetime to those who knew her. She had affected so many lives while she lived there, and before that. Two of the designers she had consulted for flew out to Wyoming, and the others sent enormous flowers. There was a memorial page in *Women's Wear Daily* that day, with the announcement of her death and a tribute to her enormous dedication, talent, and contributions to fashion. Tom was the only member of Bill's family who came out, and he looked shocked.

It was a brilliantly sunny day, and they laid her to rest in the cemetery where she had put Bill less than a week before. They lay together side by side, in the small cemetery surrounded by wildflowers. And afterward people milled around the house, looking lost, and they left quickly. It was just too sad being there with both of them gone now.

Helene offered to pack up the house, but Gretchen knew she wasn't equal to it and suggested she go home. It was just too sad and overwhelming for her in Moose. She flew back to Philadelphia that night, and Tom had promised to stay a few days after to pack up their things. He felt he owed it to Bill. He and Gretchen were going to do it together. Helene had been in no condition to help. Tom was planning to take Gus back to New York, as a way to feel closer to his brother. He wanted to keep the dog. Tom and Gretchen sat outside that night, talking about them, and Tom told her how funny his brother had been as a kid, and how different he had been from the rest of the family, even then.

"He was a much better person than we were," Tom said quietly. "It took me years to figure that out. I only got it last year. He was ten times the man my brother and I are, and my father. And he was so lucky he found Jenny. He adored her."

"And she adored him," Gretchen added.

"He had a crazy theory, that people who love each other like that stay together forever. They become stars in the heavens when they die, and then they come back and find each other again. I hope that's true for both of them. They deserve it." He was quiet for a while, and then he spoke to the woman who had become his friend through two funerals, of people they both loved so much, although he had hardly known Jenny. "I've made some important decisions lately," he confided to her. "I want what they had someday. I'm going to get divorced when I go back. I think my brother showed me that you really can find someone to love the way he did Jenny. I never understood it till recently, but he was right." She nodded. She felt that way about Eddy.

As they sat together, looking up at the night sky, they saw two falling stars shoot through the sky close together, and disappear.

"I hope that was them," Tom said softly, and Gretchen smiled, as tears rolled down her cheeks. She hoped so too. That they were in heaven now, two stars together, forever.

Robert and Lillibet

2013

Chapter 13

The day dawned warm and beautiful, with a cameo-blue sky, as carriage after carriage drew up to the plot of freshly prepared land. The men had organized and cut the lumber, and it was stacked and waiting. And the women had been cooking for several days. The younger children would play nearby, while the young girls helped their mothers with meals, and the able-bodied boys would help their fathers with the house raising, which was one of the happiest activities the entire community engaged in. And by nightfall, the family would have a new home. The following day the windows would be put in, the floorboards laid, and the plumbers among them would put in a simple indoor plumbing system, as well as an outhouse. The propane tanks would be put in, to light and heat the house and provide hot water, as there was no electricity.

The smell of fresh lumber was everywhere in the air, as the men began working. There was shouting and singing, and people calling to one another, and by mid-morning, the women had a hearty meal set out on long tables, and poured lemonade and cold tea from pitchers into tall glasses, to quench their mighty thirst.

Lillibet had loved house raisings since she was a child. All of her brothers would be helping that day, and she joined the other women in serving food onto plates. The men ate heartily and went rapidly back to work in order to finish by day's end.

The house was standing by dusk and finished on the second day. It had been a good weekend. They had returned back to work on it after the Sunday meeting. Vast amounts of wholesome foods were consumed that weekend, and Lillibet was tired but happy when she went back to their own home on Sunday afternoon. She had cooked six chickens to add to the lunch table, and ten the day before. She had made hard-boiled eggs and several salads with lettuce from their farm. The chickens were from their henhouse, and she still had to prepare dinner for her own family, her father and younger brothers, that night. Her four much older brothers from her father's first marriage were all married and would go home with their children and wives. Lillibet had her chores to do when she got home—the cows had to be milked as always, the chickens fed, and the goats fed and watered.

She chafed at her chores sometimes, but never during house raisings—there was always something so exciting about it. In this case, it had been for a family that had outgrown their old home with the birth of their sixth child, whose mother had gone to school with Lillibet, until they both graduated from the one-room schoolhouse in eighth grade. Their lives were not too dissimilar now, since Lillibet cared for her three younger brothers and father but had no husband or children of her own. She had no need of a new house, and the two young women had chatted amiably at the lunch table as her old school friend watched her new home materialize in a matter of two days. Her eyes had glowed as she held her baby in her arms.

When Lillibet went to bed that night, she was tired from her own contributions to the busy two days, but satisfied at having been part of it. Her brothers and father had been exhausted from hard labor and had gone to bed early. Lillibet lay in bed that night and thought about the life they all shared. She loved their community, and the way they helped one another. It gave her a sense of being part of something more important than just her own family. As she drifted off to sleep, she found herself thinking about her brother Markus and how warm he had been when she touched his cheek before he went to bed, and she wondered if he was falling ill. She'd have to check him more closely in the morning.

And the next day, shortly after she got up, she had her answer. All three of her brothers had come out in spots. She had acted as their mother for long enough to know that it was chicken pox, so she wasn't overly worried, but now all their chores would fall to her as well. That was not good news—she had enough to do without taking on their work too. But caring for them was all part of the duties that had fallen to her when her mother died, and she had acted as mother and female head of the household for the past seven years. After checking on her brothers and bringing them all breakfast, she went out to the barn to milk the cows. The boys were miserable with their chicken pox, which had burst forth during the night. She knew they had exposed others the day before, but there was nothing to do about it now.

Lillibet was a wisp-thin young girl with white blond hair poking out from under her black bonnet, and she pushed the last of the cows away as she finished milking. Usually her younger brothers helped her. They were eleven-year-old twins, Josiah and Markus. But since both were sick today, as was Wilhelm—Willy, her fourteen-year-old brother—all the chores would fall to her. Their sister Bernadette, who would have been nineteen now, had died before their mother, when she was ten. She had died of pneumonia during a flu epidemic. Now Lillibet was her father's only surviving daughter, and he relied on her to run their home.

Lillibet's father, Henryk Petersen, had married her mother when she was a mere girl of sixteen, after his first wife died, leaving him with four sons who were all older than his new bride. Rebekah, when Henryk married her, had been a studious, quiet young woman, who had turned out to be more strong-willed than he had expected, but a good woman who had borne him five children and was respectful of him, although she had her own ideas and always had her nose in books, more than he liked. She had shared her passion for literature with their children, but only Lillibet took after her, and read voraciously, under her mother's tutelage, and despite Henryk's objections. She gave Lillibet the classics to read as she was growing up: Jane Austen, Tolstoy, Shakespeare, Balzac, Proust, Henry James, Alexandre Dumas, all the greats of literature, which Lillibet devoured. Henryk preferred that they confine their studies to readings of the Bible, but Rebekah had been very brave in standing firm in her beliefs of what her children should read. The boys were more like their father, while Lillibet took after her. They worked hard on the farm, as did Lillibet in their home. She was a dreamer, but also a bright, hard-working girl.

Rebekah's own mother had favored education, and her father, like Henryk, had been an elder of the church, with traditional and extremely conservative ideas. And Henryk was much like him, and hadn't mellowed over the years. If anything, he got sterner and more traditional as he grew older, particularly so after his wife Rebekah's death, which had nearly broken his spirit. Like the others in the community, he had declared his forgiveness of the man who had killed her and five little girls, in a shooting at the West Nickel Mines School seven years before. But he had wrestled with his own sense of peace about it ever since.

Lillibet had been seventeen when her mother was killed and had graduated from the school four years before the shooting. Her mother frequently helped the teacher at the one-room schoolhouse, which went through eighth grade, and Rebekah happened to be there that day when a crazed gunman entered the building, took several hostages, shot ten little girls, five of whom had ultimately survived, and then killed himself. The school had been torn down ten days later, and the New Hope School replaced it six months after, in a nearby location, constructed to look entirely different from the building where the tragedy had occurred. The entire surrounding community of non-Amish people had been deeply sympathetic and supportive, having experienced the kindness and observed the decency of their Amish neighbors for many years. It had been the first and only act of violence against their community in history.

Lillibet and her family were members of the Old Order Amish Community of Nickel Mines, in Bart Township of Lancaster County, Pennsylvania. They lived almost exactly as their forefathers had when they established the community over three hundred years before, with no modern conveniences, no electricity, no telephones, and they drove no vehicles. Their transportation was by horse and buggy, and they cultivated the land with the help of tools and implements that had been used for centuries. The only change that occurred after the shooting was that there were two phones in the community now, kept in boxes at the edge of the farms, to be accessed only in emergency, in case another tragedy should happen.

They wore somber clothes in the same style as their ancestors, with no zippers or buttons. Lillibet's gray apron, as she milked the cows, was held to her black cotton dress, which covered her to her ankles and wrists, with straight pins. And her black bonnet, tied loosely beneath her chin in the heat, was identical to what her female ancestors had worn. Her only accessories were high laced-up boots and heavy black cotton stockings. Her father and the men in the community wore strict black Amish garb, long coats on Sundays, and the flat black wide-brimmed beaver or felt hats that were traditional, and straw hats in summer. Young men were clean-shaven until they married, and then they wore beards. Mustaches were forbidden. Women never cut their hair, wearing it in braids, or buns, with their bonnets.

Observing the Amish in her community, and the way they lived, there was no hint that they existed in a modern century. They were untouched by the modern world, lived in seclusion on their farms, and kept to themselves.

They were a devout, upstanding people, attached to their families. They took no charity from government agencies, no welfare, Social Security, or unemployment, and they were helpful to the communities around them. Several of the younger men in the Old Order served as volunteers in local fire departments. But other than that, the Amish stayed among themselves and did not mingle outside their community. And Lillibet's father Henryk was a particularly staunch believer that the "English," as the Amish referred to outsiders, had their world, and the Amish had their own. There was no place for the English in their lives. They respected them, and did business with them when necessary, but always in a distant way. Their community was not open to English visitors or friends. History and their religious beliefs had taught them that the two worlds did not blend. The rare young people who left their Amish homes, under strong ostracism from their families, did not return and were not encouraged to do so. Once tainted by the outside world and the English, they became outcasts from their former homes, sometimes officially "shunned." They were governed by a strict set of rules called the Ordnung, which told them what they could and could not do, and which they lived by rigorously. Young people in the Amish community were expected to remain among their own kind, follow the traditions, and carry them forward to future generations, and most Amish did. They could not intermarry with the English, only Amish.

It was a very unusual occurrence for a young Amish person to leave. One could not live in the community or follow the rules by half-measures. There was no bending of the rules for anyone. Henryk was an elder in the Old Order, and one of the sternest members of the board of elders. Lillibet's mother Rebekah had softened him somewhat while she was alive, or tried to, but in the seven years since her death, he had grown more rigid in his beliefs. And more and more lately, he preferred to speak Pennsylvania Dutch, a derivative of German, rather than English. It was a symbol of his preference for the old ways. He spoke to his children most often in German.

Lillibet brushed the flies away as she emptied the pails of milk into the large metal containers they used to take the milk to the dairy. They were heavy as she carried them to the cold room, a job usually performed by her brother Willy, or Josiah and Markus when she could get them to help. But with all three of them sick with chicken pox, she had to manage on her own. When she went back to check on the boys at lunchtime, they were miserable and itching, and she made cold compresses for them for their fevers, and all three boys were suffering in the heat. Lillibet had been mother, daughter, cook, housekeeper, farmhand, and slave to the men in her family since her mother's death. She knew it was her duty, and never complained.

Her mother had died at the time when Lillibet should have been taking a husband. Several men approached her father shortly after, but Lillibet had had no interest in the men in their community and, since her mother's death, no time to spend with them. She was too busy cooking, cleaning, doing chores, and bringing up her three brothers, who had been so young when their mother died. And now at twenty-four, she felt as though she had had all the responsibilities and disadvantages of a married woman, and she had no desire to do it again, for any man. And no man they knew had even remotely touched her heart. Several older widowers, like her father when he married her mother, widowed with four grown boys, had approached Henryk, anxious to win her hand, and she had rebuffed them all.

Now, when they broached the subject with him, he told them honestly that she was beautiful, unquestionably, and capable, and a serious, intelligent girl, but she was not a friendly young woman and had no interest in men. He had come to believe that she preferred to stay with him, bring up her brothers, and remain unmarried for the rest of her days. Her only passion was reading and studying, both the Bible and the box of books her mother had left her, which Lillibet had read many times over the years, by candlelight, late at night, more even than her father suspected. She devoured everything she could read. And she begged the schoolteacher to lend her any books they had. Reading was the greatest pleasure in her life.

Her only male friend was a boy she had gone to school with, Friedrich, Freddie. Her mother had been hopeful she would fall in love with him, but they had been childhood friends forever, he was too young, and he had since married a sweet and docile young woman whom Lillibet had never really liked, and they had four children. Freddie's life was light-years from Lilli's now, although they still chatted from time to time after church meetings on Sundays, and he still worshipped Lillibet. They had had so much fun when they were young. His wife said Lilli had all the makings of a spinster now, but he felt sorry for her—he knew how hard she worked taking care of her father and brothers, and working on their farm. She had had too serious an existence for such a young girl, catapulted into her mother's shoes by tragedy at seventeen. And he knew what a dreamer she was, lost in the books she kept hidden from her father. Freddie was sorry her life had turned out the way it had. And her little brothers were hellions, always into mischief and keeping her busy. And her father was a robust man, who could live another twenty years. The only time Freddie saw Lillibet was at church meetings on Sundays, which rotated between houses every week and lasted three hours, with the men in one room and the women in another.

After tending to her brothers at lunchtime, Lillibet carried the heavy cans of milk out of the cold room. She shooed the chickens out of her way and had already fed them. She had left chicken broth on the stove for the boys to eat at dinner, with vegetables from their garden. And she had to bring the milk to Lattimer's Dairy, with no one else to do it. Her brother Willy had graduated from school the year before at thirteen and usually helped her with the heavy chores, but he was no use to her today.

She and her younger brothers spoke to one another in the modern form, using *you* instead of *thee* and *thou,* but with her father, and the elders in the community, they had to be more formal and follow tradition. She loved reading books where people spoke normally, and she could discover exotic places like Europe, Asia, Africa, New York, Paris, and London, all the worlds that she dreamed of and knew she would never see. Her mother had opened her mind and had given her everything she could lay hands on for Lillibet to read, after she read them herself. She had passed her passion for knowledge and literature on to Lillibet and no one else. The boys were content with the boundaries of their life in Nickel Mines, as was their father and everyone else she knew.

When Lillibet went back to the house to tell the boys she was leaving, Willy looked concerned about her. "They'll help you with the milk cans at the dairy," he said, showing rare solicitousness for his older sister. Most of the time he teased her mercilessly or gave her a hard time, arguing with her. The twins were easier to manage and were still in school, unlike Willy.

"I can carry them myself," Lillibet said firmly. She was tiny but strong and used to years of hard work on the farm, with no one to help her. She was expected to hold her own, and she did. Willy rolled over and went back to sleep then. She had set out lunch for her father when he came back from the fields. His four older sons worked the farm with him, and the younger boys were learning to do so. Having lost her younger sister, nine years before, and then her mother, there were no female companions in Lillibet's life. All her close friends were the characters in books.

Her favorites were the works of Jane Austen, she had read them all and had loved them since her childhood. They had just the sensitivity, frankness, and romantic style she loved and tried to use as inspiration in her own writing, without copying her directly. Lillibet wanted to develop her own style, and she had been working on it for years, in silence in the dark. She had begged stacks of books from the schoolteacher, who was a girl Lillibet had gone to school with, and who sneaked her a few empty notebooks whenever she could. She once asked what Lilli did with them, and she said she kept a journal, of her brothers' growing-up years, or memories of her mother, none of which was true. For three years Lillibet had been struggling to write a book, about a girl on a farm in the Midwest, not an Amish girl, and her adventures in New York, and then Europe, once she grew up and moved away. She had used everything she'd learned about New York and foreign cities from the books she'd read, and she had no idea if it was accurate, but she had studied it carefully. And the young woman's emotions in the book were her own, venturing into a brave new world, discovering new people, new places, and new feelings. In her writing, she tried to achieve the tenderness and depth of Jane Austen with a flavor all her own.

She had just finished the book only weeks before. There were twelve notebooks, carefully handwritten, which contained the manuscript of the story she'd written. And now she had no idea what to do with it, where to send it, who would read it. There was no one she could ask, no publisher she knew of. And if it had been discovered that she'd written a book, she would have been severely ostracized, so the notebooks were hidden under her mattress where no one would ever find them. She lived in a cell-like room with nothing more than a chest of drawers and a bed, and a candle to light the room at night. One of her younger brothers had discovered her writing in a notebook late one night, and she told him she was checking the farm accounts for her father, and he thought nothing of it. The book she had been writing was a dark secret.

If her mother had still been alive, she would have told her, and she knew her mother would have understood and maybe have been proud of her. But even her mother wouldn't have been able to help her get it published. And that was what Lillibet wanted now. She wanted her book to go out into the world, despite the fact that she herself couldn't. Her family could dominate her life and how she lived it, but they could not silence her voice. And she had a voice she wanted to be heard. But she had no idea how to do it, or if her book was any good. She had shown it to no one and would not be able to among the Amish. Hers was a lone voice in the darkness, a single bird fluttering its wings and singing softly. She had called her book *When the Swallow Sings*. And she wondered now if it would remain under her mattress forever. The thought of that filled her with despair and made her sad. She already had an idea for another book and could hardly wait to get started. The characters in her books populated her otherwise lonely life, with no one to confide in.

Her mother had had a dear friend, who had been like an aunt to Lillibet as she grew up and after her mother died. Margarethe wasn't as adventuresome as Lilli's mother, nor as creative, but she was a kind woman who had deep affection for Lilli and her brothers. She was a widow with ten children, the same age as Lillibet's mother would be now, at forty-one, although Margarethe seemed much older and looked it. Rebekah had been much like Lillibet, a tiny, slight woman who looked younger than she was. Until one looked more closely, or spoke to her, Lillibet seemed more like sixteen than twenty-four. She had the face of a child, until she became animated, and then one saw the beautiful young woman she was and the light in her eyes. Lillibet came alive when she became excited by her ideas, or had a chance to talk to someone about them, which was almost never. In the old days, she and Freddie had spoken of many things, and he had been curious about life. Now he only talked about his wife, his farm, and his children, and Lillibet would never have dared tell him about her book. Nor did she confide in Margarethe, who was a warm, cozy, affectionate woman. But she didn't have an inquiring mind, and she respected all the old ways, and followed all the traditions without question, and encouraged Lillibet to do the same, to avoid arguments with her father. Lillibet no longer challenged him, as she had tried to when she was younger. Now she put all her heart and soul and thoughts into what she wrote. It was all in her book, in the notebooks under her mattress.

She had told her father that morning that she would take the milk to the dairy and would use the buggy to do so. He gave her permission and told her to stay off the main road, although there were no tourists in the area during the week. But he didn't want his children photographed or ridiculed by the English. She promised to take the back roads, and she was excited to go to the dairy. She had only been there once before, when she was much younger. Henryk didn't worry about her going to the dairy. She was old enough to handle it and a very capable girl. He had reminded her to bring back the cheese they processed for them, and she promised she would.

She set out half an hour later in the buggy, with the horse they used for errands. They had a finer one for their best buggy on Sundays, but the horse she harnessed to the buggy for the trip to the dairy was a serviceable one, who traveled on the roads frequented by cars and wasn't skittish. Lillibet had never been in a car in her entire life, only a horse and buggy. And her father had one of the finest carriages in the county, which he used only for church meetings and special days. It was a treat to ride in it with him on Sundays.

The milk cans she had put in the work buggy were heavy, but she managed to get them in herself, without help. She was stronger than she looked, even though she was tiny, and she was used to doing heavy jobs on her own. Her younger brothers didn't help her as often as they were supposed to.

As she rode along, on her way to the dairy, she thought about her book, wondering again what to do with it. She knew she had to rely on her own ingenuity and judgment, if there was any hope of publishing it at all.

It was a beautiful, hot day as she rode to the dairy. She wished she could take off her bonnet but didn't dare. She pushed it back on her head and loosened the ribbons she normally tied beneath her chin, and it fell gently backward, exposing her lovely face, green eyes, and pale blond hair, which she wore in a long braid down her back. Her father would have gotten angry if he could have seen her nearly without her bonnet. She was warm in her heavy black cotton dress to her ankles, which covered her arms to her wrists. She was wearing a gray apron, her high shoes that laced up her legs, and heavy black cotton stockings. She had never worn makeup in her life and had no idea what it would feel like or look like on her face. She had seen photographs of made-up women in books, and women with nail polish. There was no frivolity in Lillibet's life, only in her imagination, which was rich and her ideas abundant. Her family had no concept of the fertility of her mind, which was just as well. She kept it concealed, like brilliant plumage under a dark cloak.

She reached the dairy, half an hour after she left the farm, going at a slow pace, letting the horse dawdle so she could enjoy the ride, and as they approached, she pulled her bonnet back up on her head and tied the black ribbons under the chin. The bonnet concealed most of her face, and the sun had felt warm on it before that. Her eyes were bright as they got to the dairy farm. It was an adventure for her.

Two boys approached her, as she pulled the buggy up in front of Lattimer's Dairy.

"Would thee help me?" she asked, smiling at them, and they both nodded, happy to serve her. They weren't sure who she was, but they recognized the buggy. "It's from Petersens'," she explained. "My brothers are sick and couldn't come. And I'm meant to pick up our cheese." They looked blank as she said it. They were only there to help lift the heavy cans, which they did with greater ease than she had and took them inside.

Lillibet wandered into the barn then, to inquire about their cheese. She saw the cows and the milking machines in the huge barn, the milking parlor, and the enormous refrigeration units. It was the biggest dairy in the area, and her father had been doing business with them for thirty years. They were a solid, reliable account. Joe Lattimer liked doing business with the Amish, they were good people.

She was standing in the barn, looking around, appearing almost like a child, or a very young girl, and Joe Lattimer noticed her from his office window and came out, wondering who she was. She turned to him with a smile as he approached her. She had an open, interested face and intelligent eyes, and he saw instantly that the face somewhat concealed by the restrictive bonnet was lovely. He was aware as soon as he spoke to her that she was more grown up than she looked. He guessed her to be somewhere between twenty-two and twenty-five, which was close enough. And a chord of memory woke in him immediately, at the familiar Amish clothes.

She reminded him of a girl he hadn't seen in forty years, since he was eighteen. He had seen her a few times when she came to the dairy with her father and fallen in love with her. She had been forbidden to see him or speak to him, and he had heard that she'd gotten married six months later, and he never saw her again. But he had never forgotten her. She was like a dream he had cherished ever since, a symbol of his lost boyhood, the girl he had wanted desperately and couldn't have. He hadn't pursued her, out of respect for her. But he remembered her still, as though it were yesterday.

"Can I help you?" he asked kindly. He

was in his late fifties and had inherited the dairy from his grandfather and father, both of whom Henryk had known and liked. Joe Lattimer was staring at her as though he'd seen her before. And his eyes were gentle as he spoke to Lillibet.

"I brought the milk from Petersens'," she said, looking shy, but only for an instant. "My brothers are all sick, so I brought it in for my father. I'll bring the goat's milk tomorrow, and they told me to bring back the cheese," she explained. He nodded and then realized who she was. She looked like her brothers, but she was so pretty that it had distracted him for a moment. And she looked so much like the girl he had seen as a boy.

"Of course," he said, smiling at her. "You're Henryk's daughter?"

"Yes, his only one," she laughed, and it was a sound like bells in the wind. "Lillibet." He knew about the tragedy that had happened to her mother and the others and vaguely remembered that there had been a daughter. "My brothers have caught chicken pox, and they look quite awful," she said, laughing again, and then she cocked her head to one side, and smiled at him. "May I look around? I've only been here once before."

"Of course." He knew that the women rarely left the farms, and in all the years he had known Henryk, he had never seen her, she had had no reason to come there until now. And he had never met her mother either, although he had heard that she was beautiful, and had been only thirty-five when she died, a young woman. He noticed that Lillibet appeared to be filled with curiosity and spirit, and with his permission, she left the barn to explore the farm. It was an enormous dairy, and smiling at the encounter, he went back to his office. She was a lovely girl. He very seldom met Amish women, and she was an exceptionally nice one and seemed very bright.

Lillibet took her time looking around and wandered toward the main building half an hour later. She noticed a bench under a tree, where people sat while waiting for deliveries, or to take a break during the workday, and she noticed a book sitting on the bench. She walked

toward the bench, sat down, and picked
up the book, wondering if it was one
she had read, but it wasn't. She flipped
through it, reading passages that she
liked. She was tempted to take it but
didn't want to steal someone's book
that they might return for—she saw that
it was dog-eared and a page was
marked, so perhaps someone loved it
and would be unhappy to lose it. Instead, she looked at who the publisher
was and saw a name she didn't recognize in New York.

But suddenly she felt as though destiny had taken a hand and she had been
given the opportunity she was so desperate for. It seemed like the answer to
her prayers. She grabbed a pencil stub
out of her pocket, and a little wisp of
paper she found with it, and jotted down
the name and address of the publisher.
She was sure this was a sign from
heaven, sent by her mother to help her.
She was going to send them her book.
She lay the book down on the bench
and went back to the main building,
seeking Mr. Lattimer, and found him in

his office. He was startled when he saw her hesitating in the doorway.

"May I come in?" she asked politely, and he nodded and gazed into her eyes. Her glance was honest and direct, and she was shy but not frightened. He was just unfamiliar to her, as she saw so few English in her life. Mostly county officials who came to see the elders, for the census or other things. And she had seen quite a lot of them, press and police, after the shooting, but none since, until now.

"What can I do for you, Lillibet?" He had remembered her name. It would have been hard to forget her, even if she didn't look like his boyhood love.

"If I give you a package, will you mail it for me? To New York?" It seemed like another planet to her, although she had read so much about it.

"Of course. That's not a problem. We send packages out every day." He tried to sound matter-of-fact about it and didn't question her about what she was sending and why.

"I have no money to pay you," she said, looking embarrassed. She knew her father had a bank account, and the dairy deposited money into it to pay him, but she had no right to invade it and didn't want to.

Joe Lattimer smiled broadly as he stood up and towered over her. "I think we can pay for a package to New York, as long as you're not planning to send a horse or a piano." She laughed at what he said.

"Just some notebooks. I can bring them tomorrow," she said, with an excited look. Her eyes were blazing, which made her even more beautiful.

"Just bring them in. We'll take care of it for you. And give my best to your father," he said, and walked her outside. The two boys had just put her father's cheese in the buggy. Lilli knew it was wonderful goat cheese they made at the dairy from her father's goat milk. Her father always said it sold very well. The English liked it. "See you tomorrow, then." Joe Lattimer waved and went back to his office, as Lillibet got back into her father's buggy, tapped the horse with the reins, and took off back down the road she had come. The horse was in a hurry to get home and trotted on the way back, as Lillibet sat beaming.

And in his office, Joe Lattimer sat lost in thought for a moment, remembering the girl he had loved so long ago.

And all Lillibet could think of on her way home was that she had found a way. It was fate for certain. Her book was going to New York!

Lillibet's brothers were just as sick the next day. In fact, the twins were worse, and Margarethe promised to come over and visit them that afternoon. They didn't need a doctor, it was only chicken pox, but they were feeling very sorry for themselves, and so was Willy, although he had a few less spots than the twins.

Lillibet milked the cows, as she always did, that morning, and two of her nephews came to help her, her oldest brother's sons. They were the same age as the twins. And they lifted the heavy cans into the buggy, along with the goat's milk she had promised to bring them. They brought the goat's milk on certain days, not every day like the cow's milk. And she set off toward Lattimer's Dairy after lunch. Just before she left, she had gone up to her room, taken the twelve notebooks from their hiding place under her mattress, and wrapped them in one of her aprons. And then at the last minute, she picked a different apron. She chose one of the fine ones in pale dove-gray linen that her mother had made her before she died. Lillibet kept them all out of sentiment, although some were frayed and worn now, but she selected one of the nicest ones, and bundled the notebooks carefully, and then pinned them into the linen. She thought the apron from her mother might bring her luck.

Carrying the bundle like schoolbooks in her arms, she ran lightly down the stairs and put it on the floor of the buggy, hopped in, and picked up the reins. No one had been watching, as she took off at a slow trot, and arrived at the dairy twenty minutes later after an uneventful trip. But all she could think of on the way were the notebooks she was bringing for Joe Lattimer to send to New York for her. It felt like the most exciting day of her life. She was sending her book out into the world. And little waves of terror seized her on the way. What if it got lost? If they hated it? If it was awful? If they laughed at her or said she couldn't write? But whatever happened now, she knew she had to take the chance. She had come this far and wasn't going to turn back. Providence had put that book in her path with the publisher's address. Now she had to send them her book and see what happened. And her mother's apron would protect it.

The farmhands took the canisters of milk out of the buggy for her, and she picked up her neatly wrapped bundle and walked into Joe Lattimer's office. He was working on his computer and looked up at her with a smile. She had never seen a computer before, but she could guess what it was. Some of the investigators who had come to talk to them after the shooting had used laptops. But she had never seen as large a computer as this one. He immediately saw the linen-wrapped notebooks in her arms.

"Is that the package you want me to send to New York?" She nodded, breathless with excitement and her eyes alight. "That doesn't look very difficult to me. I'll send it out for you tomorrow, first thing." She handed him the slip of paper with the name of the publishing house and the address in New York, in her neat lacy handwriting. "What address would you like me to use for the sender?" he asked her, suspecting what her answer would be. If she wanted to use her own, she would have asked her father to send it for her. Clearly, this was something she wanted to do herself, without her father's knowledge. It seemed harmless to him.

"Would you mind using the dairy as the return address?" Lillibet asked cautiously.

"Not at all. It's not a problem." And as he said it, he reached a hand out to take her package, and she handed it to him as though the Hope Diamond were hidden in it. "That must be a very important package," he said, teasing her a little, but he could see it was to her. She barely looked able to part with it and kept her eyes on her notebooks once he held the package. "We'll take good care of it for you, I promise."

"Thank you," she said breathlessly, and left his office again. She left the dairy a little while later, and she could feel her heart pounding all the way home. She felt as though she had put her baby in a box to be sent into outer space somewhere, with no idea when she would see it again, or if it would be well received. Sending her notebooks to New York was the most frightening thing she'd ever done. But she knew she had to. Her mother would have wanted her to do it. And would have been proud of her once she did, whatever happened next. It was almost too much to hope that her manuscript would be turned into a book one day, but perhaps with luck, if the gods smiled on her, it would. And for now, her book was on its way.

Chapter 14

Bob Bellagio swore when he saw that the elevator in his office building was out of order again. It had been shut down every other day for the past week. There was a heat wave in New York that had caused a brownout to occur. And the publishing house he had founded was in an ancient building in Tribeca on the fifth floor, just high enough to make you truly miserable on a hot day if you had to walk up the stairs. And it had been the hottest July on record so far in New York. His air conditioner had gone out that day too, and the fax machine. It was hardly worth coming to work, but he always did. He trudged up the five floors, and shoved open the fire door, into the offices he'd established five years before, when he was thirty-one.

Like everything else in his life, it had been a struggle to start the business and keep it afloat. They had published some very good young authors, some of them a little too edgy, but talented, he thought. The critics agreed, but the public didn't. They had had two moderate successes in the last two years, enough to keep their doors open and give him hope. Now they needed a major hit. He and his editors were always on the lookout for the book that was going to be their big breakthrough and put them on the map.

Sometimes he worried that the editors he'd hired were too smart and too literary to pick the right book that could appeal to the average reader. His staff included two Harvard graduates, one from Yale, another from Princeton, and a genius who had gone to a state school and was smarter than everyone else. All of them were offbeat and nontraditional and had brilliant ideas. But what Bob wanted was a big fat commercial success that was going to knock everyone off their feet, not a stroke of literary genius that would get brilliant reviews and sell a thousand copies to intellectuals at a Princeton reunion. He had explained that to his staff again and again. And he worried at times that their lofty ideals, or even his own, would put them out of business. They were hanging on by a thread. Their last two successes had given them a slightly better grip but not enough for him to relax yet. He was looking for that one book that would take off like a rocket, but so was everyone else. Every publisher in the business wanted the same thing he did. The competition was stiff. Strong commercial fiction usually went to bigger publishing houses. He was a small independent with high ideals but less cash to pay his authors.

He was breathless in the heat by the time he got upstairs. The weather was oppressive, and it would have been a relief if it rained. The building was baking, and his office was stifling. He had been invited to the Hamptons for the weekend but had decided to stay home and work instead. He had a new manuscript to read from one of their best authors, whom he'd been grooming for three years. And he wanted to look over some expense cuts he wanted to make. This publishing house was his baby, and he spent every moment he could nurturing it. He was determined to make it a big success and prove he could do it. He had gone to Harvard and to business school at Columbia; he had worked in the publishing business as an editor at Knopf for three years, and he'd decided to take the leap. Starting the business had been the most exciting decision in his life. Now he had to keep it alive until it became a resounding success. He knew he'd get there. He had just had lunch with an agent, trying to shake the trees and see what would fall out. He enjoyed what he was doing and had frequent meetings with his editors to try and come up with new ideas.

As he headed toward his office, he walked past Patrick Riley's desk. Pat was one of their Harvard graduates, had graduated summa cum laude in the English department, was twenty-nine years old, and was writing a book himself, on the decadent philosophies of ancient Greece and their impact on society today. Bob hadn't agreed to publish it, and he knew it would sell to Pat's mother, grandmother, eighteen cousins, Harvard lit professor, and no one else. Pat Riley was smart as hell, just a little too out there to be headed for commercial success, with his own book anyway. But he had found some very decent books so far for Bellagio Press. They hadn't set the world on fire, but they had done well. He was the junior editor and had worked for Bob for two years, after getting a master's in Renaissance literature. He was a brain. And as Bob's mother would have said, he looked like an unmade bed.

Pat had wild, curly, tangled, unkempt hair that wanted to become dreads but had never quite gotten there and looked like it hadn't been brushed in years, and possibly hadn't. He wore torn jeans to work every day that disintegrated before he bought new ones, and a collection of

torn, faded sweatshirts he wore in winter, and equally disreputable T-shirts for
the summer that he said were "vintage"
band shirts, some of them actually pre-
viously owned by rock stars, or so he
claimed, and Converse sneakers that
were in shreds. He said he hadn't owned
a pair of socks since high school. Bob
believed him, he came to work every
day looking like he'd been shipwrecked.
He had lunch with agents looking that
way. No one seemed to mind except
Bob himself. Pat was so funny and so
smart and so incisive and good at what
he did that no one gave a damn how he
looked. He had hired him for his talent
and his mind, not for his wardrobe, and
when Bob suggested he might want to
dress up a little occasionally, Pat just
looked at him blankly and shook his
head.

As head of the company, Bob tried to
look respectable when he came to work,
as though someone important might
come to see him at the office. They
never did, but he still felt obliged to show
up wearing khakis in the summer,
pressed jeans or gray flannels in the

winter, or maybe cords and a decent shirt, and he always had a blazer or a sport jacket lying around somewhere, and a tie in his pocket just in case. Pat liked to tell him he was hopelessly bourgeois, and the fact that he himself didn't care how he looked showed he was a true intellectual. Bob no longer argued the point with him.

Bob came from a traditional family of overachievers, and all of them had done well. His father was a neurosurgeon, his mother was a partner in a major Wall Street law firm, and his brother worked for Morgan Stanley, handling investments. Everyone had a respectable job. Only Bob had had the guts to try and start his own business, and he was trying to prove valiantly to himself that he could do it and make it a success. Some days he wondered, but he was willing to go down in flames trying. They had enough money in the bank to hold out for the next two years, if they were careful, and no one got a raise, and by then Bob hoped that they'd be off and running with some major hits. The business had become his baby, his girlfriend, his passion, his whole life since he started it. He had given up romance, relation- ships, sports, travel, and nearly sex to be there all the time and work most weekends. No woman wanted to put up with it, and lately he didn't care. The kind of women he'd been meeting for the last few years didn't make his heart pound, but his business always did. And the women he got fixed up with bored him. His brother gave him a hard time about it. Paul was married to a woman who was a lawyer like their mother, and had two kids. And Bob had gone from one woman to another, or sometimes none at all, for the past ten years.

"If it's meant to happen, it will," Bob always said to his brother whenever they had lunch.

"Not unless you make it happen," Paul reminded him. "Some sexy hot babe is not going to fall out of the sky and land on you as you walk through Tribeca. You've got to get out there and date." He felt that Bob should be married and have kids too. And at thirty-six, Paul thought he was late. He had gone beyond late bloomer to difficult and solitary and even reclusive in recent years.

"I don't have time to date. I'm too busy getting my business off the ground," Bob explained with a grin. He didn't really care.

"That's bullshit, you're just lazy," Paul insisted, and Bob laughed.

"Yeah, maybe I am," he admitted. "What's the point of going out with women I don't care about, and know in the first five minutes I never want to see again? Why bother?"

"Because you have to go out with ninety-nine duds before you meet the right one. That's the way it works."

"Wake me up at ninety-nine," Bob said, and changed the subject. He preferred talking business with his brother, and getting his advice about his investments, not his dating life. Besides, almost no one he had gone to school with had gotten married. Some had children, but few had wives. His brother was behind the times. And Bob took pride in saying he'd never been in love. He was in love with his business, and he hadn't met a woman yet who could make his heart race the way starting his own business had. He was a born entrepreneur. His brother was five years older, part of another generation, loved having a wife, two children, living in Connecticut, and commuting to work every day on the train. Bob said he would have died of boredom if he had to live that way. He had a loft in Tribeca, three blocks from his business, and he worked late at night and on weekends.

He stopped at Pat Riley's desk on his way to his office and nearly shuddered at the mess he saw there. It looked like Pat hadn't cleared his desk in years. Bob wondered how he could find anything on it. There were stacks of papers all over the place, notes, phone messages, business cards, empty Starbucks cups, and three stacks of manuscripts sitting on the edge.

"What is all that?" Bob asked, frowning. He had dark hair and brown eyes and was almost handsome in a crisp blue shirt and khaki slacks and loafers. And today he hadn't worn socks either in the heat, but on him it looked all right.

"It's the slush pile," Pat said vaguely,

digging for something on his desk. He looked like a cat searching for a mouse. He was referring to unsolicited manuscripts that came in from people without an agent. They were usually pretty bad. An agent provided a screening process so you knew you were getting decent material. These were mostly from untalented people who thought they could write. "I've been meaning to send them back. I just haven't gotten around to it."

"Do you read them?" Bob asked him. He would have been surprised if he did.

"Never," Pat said honestly. "I don't have time. I get enough stuff from agents to keep me busy for the next ten years. And nothing worthwhile ever comes in the unsolicited stuff. I used to try to read them, but I just can't." Bob nodded. He didn't disagree with him, but for some reason he started flipping through them and noticed a fat bundle halfway down the second stack, wrapped in a piece of fabric. He stopped and looked at it, surprised. The submissions he used to get at Knopf were in manila envelopes or boxes, not wrapped in fabric.

"What do they do? Wrap them up in their boxers before they send them to us?" How could you take something seriously from someone who wrapped a manuscript up in their clothes? Bob was mesmerized by that one.

"Yeah, I know, pathetic," Pat commented, and noticed what Bob was looking at. "She sent it in a blouse or something. Some farm girl in Iowa. I forget. I've got to send it back."

"How long do we take to return them?" Bob asked with interest, suddenly pondering the cruelty of the process. People poured their hearts out in books, sent them to publishers, praying they'd get published, and then they got them back with a form letter that basically told them to forget it or to try somewhere else.

"We take a couple of months," Pat said with a shrug. "I think I've had the one in the blouse for about a month. It struck me when it came in. I think she's young. She wrote the whole thing by hand."

"I hope she made a copy before she sent it to us, or put it on a disk," Bob said, feeling sympathetic again, and then pulled it out of the stack. He could see then that it was neatly wrapped in a piece of fine gray linen held together with straight pins. He nearly stuck himself on one of them, pulled it loose, and saw the stack of notebooks inside. He didn't know why, but he had been drawn to that package and was fascinated by it now. He saw that the fabric was beautifully stitched by hand, and when he held it up after he unpinned it, he saw that it was an apron of some kind, about the right size for a child. "How weird," he muttered, as he flipped open one of the notebooks and saw the lacy European handwriting inside. He could see that she had sent them the original, and he wondered again if she had copied it before she sent it off. What if they had lost it or thrown it out? He almost shuddered on her behalf. There was no cover note, he noticed, only the address of a dairy farm in Lancaster, Pennsylvania, and as he saw that, his eyes widened, and he looked at Pat. "Wait a minute, she's not from Iowa. She's from Pennsylvania, in the heart of Amish country."

He held up the apron again and suddenly realized what it was. It was the apron of a young Amish girl. "Shit, Pat, I'll bet this girl is Amish. Hell, we might have something here. She probably can't write for beans, but it might be worth a look. An exposé by an Amish girl on a farm in Pennsylvania could be interesting, even if she can't write."

"Don't count on it being anything," Pat muttered, still hunting for whatever he had lost in the rubble on his desk. "If she could, she wouldn't be sending us notebooks in the mail wrapped in her underwear."

"If she's real Amish, she doesn't have access to a computer, or even a phone. Or a copier. For all we know, this may be the only copy she has of her manuscript."

"That could be a blessing," Pat said unkindly, as Bob grabbed the stack of notebooks and the apron in one hand.

"I have no lunch date today. This could be fun. I'm going to read a few pages before you send it back."

"Have a ball," Pat said, and pulled a file out of a drawer, after he gave up trying to find the business card he had lost.

"I'll put it back in your stack if it's no good," Bob said. He walked into his office, dumped the pile of notebooks on his desk, and found himself with the pale gray apron in his hands. And for no reason he could understand, he held it, thinking of the woman who had worn it, wondering if she was young or old, and what she looked like. Suddenly the idea that she was Amish fascinated him, and he wanted to know who had written the book, and why. He set the apron down carefully on his desk and opened the first notebook. The handwriting was delicate and old-fashioned but strong, as though she were young. The only clue he had to her identity was her name. She had written "Lillibet Petersen" boldly under the title at the top of the first page.

Slowly, he began reading, falling into the pattern of her words. She had a strong cadence to the way she wrote, a powerful voice that he rapidly became accustomed to, and a way with words that he liked. She reminded him a little of Jane Austen, but in a fresher, stronger, newer way. Lillibet definitely had her own voice. And as he read through the handwritten pages, she captivated him with her characters as well. The main character of the book was a young woman who had left her family's farm and traveled far into the world, looking for new adventures, and her descriptions of people, places, and situations were mesmerizing. He moved on to the second notebook without stopping and was startled when he saw that it was after five o'clock. He hadn't put her notebooks down. And he smiled as he sat for a moment, staring into space. He had a strange feeling that she was sitting in the room with him, and as he glanced at the apron still on his desk, he had a sense that a powerful force was with him, and fate had taken a hand.

He closed the notebook where he'd stopped reading, signed some papers on his desk, and left his office at six o'clock, with the notebooks in a shopping bag, and at the last minute, he put the apron in with them. And he couldn't wait to get home to start reading again.

He picked up a salad at the deli where

he often bought dinner, and twenty minutes later he was at home in his apartment, sitting on the couch and reading
Lillibet's notebooks again. And suddenly
he stopped, as though he had to send
a message to her. The pull was so
strong, he felt like he could almost reach
out and touch her. Instead he ran the
delicate apron through his hands.

"Lillibet, I don't know who you are,
but I'm reading your story. I hear you,"
he said softly. He put the apron down
and began reading again. He sat there
until midnight, going through notebook
after notebook. He was normally a fast
reader, but he found himself wanting to
savor the story as he devoured it. He
didn't know how much of it was fact or
fiction, but it was so compelling, he continued reading through the night, and
finished just after four A.M. He hadn't
done that in ages. She had swept him
up in everything she'd written, and he
had fallen in love with her characters,
been fascinated by how she developed
the story, and needed to know what was
going to happen right until the end. He
was wide awake when he finished the

last pages. She had spun around expertly in a giant literary pirouette and landed on her feet in a remarkable tour de force at the end. He sat holding the last notebook in his hands, contemplating everything he had just read and bowled over by it. The farm girl from Pennsylvania, or woman, whoever she was, had knocked him squarely on his ass, and that didn't happen often.

"Holy shit, Lillibet Petersen! Who *are* you? You write like an angel, you think like a genius, and you are driving me insane!" He started laughing then. It was one of the best books he'd read in years, and he couldn't believe it was from their slush pile, sent to him longhand in notebooks, wrapped up in her apron. And he still wasn't sure if she was an Amish girl. She had never mentioned the Amish in the book, so maybe she wasn't. Undoubtedly not everyone in Lancaster, Pennsylvania, was Amish. Maybe she was just an ordinary farm girl, but in fact there was nothing ordinary about her. Whoever she was, she was a remarkable writer. And he felt as though fate had put a jewel in his hands. He had walked past Pat Riley's desk a thousand times on the way to his office, and the slush pile had never caught his eye. That day Lillibet's manuscript wrapped in her apron had mesmerized him. It could only be destiny at work.

He couldn't sleep that night, thinking about her notebooks, and on Saturday he read some of them again. He went for a walk then, stopped at his office, and everywhere he went, her story followed him. She was driving him crazy. He had already decided to call the dairy farm on Monday, to talk to her. But he still had to get through Sunday before he could. It was the longest weekend of his life. He felt as though she were waiting for him to respond, and he was keeping her on hold. He made the call from home on Monday morning and sat staring at her apron while he did.

He called the dairy and asked for Lillibet Petersen and was told that there was no one there by that name. He was suddenly panicked that she had used a nom de plume, but the return address on her manuscript had to be good.

Maybe someone at the dairy knew who she was.

"Is there a general manager or an owner on the premises?" Bob asked, with a nervous sensation in his stomach. He felt like he had the glass slipper in his hand and would have to look all through Lancaster County to find the woman it fit.

"That would be Joe Lattimer," the voice answered. She put Bob on hold, and three minutes later Joe was on the line.

"Joe Lattimer," he said crisply. And Bob felt tongue-tied as he tried to explain. He had no idea why this woman affected him that way, but he felt as though he was being swept away by a tidal wave.

"Hello. My name is Robert Bellagio. I'm a book publisher in New York. We received a manuscript a month or two ago, from a woman named Lillibet Petersen, if that's really her name. She used your dairy as her return address, but your operator doesn't know who she is. Do you?" Joe Lattimer was smiling as he listened. He had forgotten all about it until then. Bob had refreshed his memory immediately.

"Yes, I do know who she is," Joe Lattimer answered his question, as Bob let out a long slow breath. "I mailed that package for her myself. Quite a while ago, as I recall. You're right, a month or two, I think. She didn't tell me what it was. I think maybe there were some notebooks wrapped in an apron. So she's written a book." Joe sounded impressed. He hadn't seen her since a few days after he'd mailed the package for her. Her brother Willy had started delivering the milk to them again. And there was no reason for Lillibet to come back. She was busy at home.

"She certainly has written a book," Bob confirmed. "A humdinger of a book. Do you have a phone number for her? I'm sorry to bother you with all this. I just didn't know where to reach her. She didn't include a letter, just your return address."

"I don't mind your calling at all. She doesn't have a phone number. Her father doesn't have a phone."

There was a long pause at Bob's end

then, as he wondered if his first guess was right. "Is she Amish?" he asked Joe cautiously, wondering if it sounded strange.

"Yes, she is. They are Old Order Amish, and her father is one of the elders of the church. And my guess would be he has no idea she wrote a book. I'm sure that's not in keeping with their beliefs. Did she write an exposé about the Amish?" Joe asked, curious himself now about her book, especially after what Bob had said.

"No, she didn't. There's no mention of the Amish anywhere in it. Your address just caught my eye. That's the heart of Amish country, isn't it?"

"Indeed it is. I've done business with her father for thirty years. Or my family has. We buy his milk and make their cheese. Her father is about as serious Amish as you get. Good man."

Bob wasn't sure where to go from there. "I'd like to come down and talk to her. Do you suppose that would be possible?"

"I wouldn't want to try it. The Amish are very polite people, but they don't welcome English in their midst. They keep to themselves and expect us to do the same." Joe had had that experience with his first crush forty years before. It was what Bob had heard about them too, but he felt stonewalled here and had no idea how to reach Lillibet.

"English?" He had picked up on the word.

"Outsiders. Anyone who's not Amish. We're all 'English' to them. They've been living the same way since the seventeenth century. And for them, not much has changed. Many of them still speak German, or a form of it, just as their ancestors did when they came to this country. Even their clothes haven't changed, as I'm sure you know. I doubt that her father would let you see her if you just showed up at their farm. They're very protective of their women. I've only seen her a couple of times. She delivered the milk when her brothers were sick, when she had me send you the book. It must have seemed providential to her."

"And to me," Bob said, sounding pensive. "I wonder how she got my address."

"I have no idea. She gave it to me on a scrap of paper."

"How old is she?"

Joe thought about it for a minute, remembering her face that day. "Early twenties. She takes care of her father and brothers. Her mother died in a school shooting we had here. A crazed gunman got into the school and shot her mother and five little girls. A terrible tragedy. It happened seven years ago."

"I remember reading about it," Bob said in a hushed tone. It gave insight into the manuscript he had read, and the person behind it. But he wondered how she had known all the places she had described, and written about them so well, if she had never left her father's farm, and he was one of the elders of the church, which must have meant he was very strict. And then Bob had an idea. "If I send you an e-mail, do you suppose you could print it out and get it to her? I'm assuming they don't have a computer."

Joe laughed at the idea. "Not likely.

No electricity, no phone, no electronics, some Amish don't even have indoor plumbing. If there were no computers in the 1600s when they got here, they don't have one now. But yes, I could print up an e-mail for her. Her brothers come in every day. They're just young kids, so hopefully they won't forget to give it to her. The boys are around eleven or twelve. We can try. If they don't give it to their father first." Bob hadn't thought of that. He had a brilliant manuscript written by a girl who was completely inaccessible, and living in the seventeenth century. It was like contacting someone in a time machine. But it only made him want to reach her more. He was dying to go to Pennsylvania himself to see her. And he intended to. But he wanted to get in touch with her first. He didn't want to get her in trouble, or have her father forbid her to see him, which sounded entirely possible, particularly if she was young.

"I'll give it a try," Bob said about the e-mail. "And thank you so much for your help." It occurred to him that the owner of the dairy was being particularly cooperative as a go-between. He had no way of knowing that it was Joe's way of honoring his own distant past, and something about Lillibet had touched him in a tender place in his heart. And Joe felt for what she had gone through losing her mother. Maybe she needed a friend.

"Happy to oblige." He didn't want to anger Henryk Petersen either. But he had agreed to help Lillibet get her manuscript to New York, and now he wanted to help her get a response, particularly if the New York publisher liked the book. That would be exciting for her. "I'll put your e-mail in an envelope and give it to the boys when they come in."

"Thank you so much," Bob said, and hung up, thinking about everything he had heard from Joe Lattimer, who she was, how old, who her father was, how they lived, and even how her mother had been killed, which sounded tragic to him, and had obviously heavily impacted Lillibet's life. And with everything he learned about her, he wanted to know more. He had an unquenchable thirst for knowledge about her.

He sent a short e-mail from his home computer to the e-mail address Joe had given him. There was so much he wanted to say to her, but he didn't want to frighten her away, so he was extremely cautious and to the point.

"Miss Petersen, I have had the great pleasure of reading your very remarkable book. At your convenience, I would like to come to Lancaster to discuss it with you, and make an offer to publish it. Please let me know how, where, and when it would be easiest for you to meet. Congratulations on an extraordinary book! Respectfully, Robert Bellagio." And he added the phone numbers and e-mail where she could reach him. Given what Lattimer had said, Bob was sure she would be obliged to use the owner of the dairy farm to respond to him.

He sent the e-mail to Joe, and all he could do after that was wait to hear from her. It came through on Joe's office computer, and he printed it and put it in an envelope for her, to give to her brothers later. And he told the two dairy hands to let him know when the boys came by that day. He didn't have long to wait. They showed up just before noon, and Joe went outside and handed one of the twins the envelope, after inquiring about their father. The boys were identical, so he was never quite sure which one he was talking to. He had written Lillibet's name on the envelope and told her brother to be sure to give it to her, and he promised he would. And then they hopped in the buggy and drove home. Sometimes they came with Willy, but they hadn't that day, and they were perfectly capable of delivering the milk without him and had done so several times. Joe forgot about it after that, having accomplished his mission. But Bob Bellagio didn't. He went to the office and obsessed about her all day. He walked over to talk to Pat Riley about it. If possible, Pat's desk was a bigger mess than before and seemed to have gotten worse over the weekend.

"I read that manuscript that came wrapped in the apron," Bob commented. "The book is an incredible piece of work, written by a young Amish girl. I'm going to make her an offer. If I can get to her," Bob said, looking nervous.

"What does that mean? Is she in hiding?"

"Might as well be. Do you know anything about the Amish?"

"Not much," Pat admitted. "They dress funny, are conscientious objectors, I think, and live in Pennsylvania."

"They live in the seventeenth and eighteenth centuries. Whatever didn't exist then, they don't have now, including phones, cars, computers, televisions, and any electrical equipment. They're a very tight religious sect, run by the elders of the church, and unless I get her father's permission or she runs away, which is unlikely, I won't be able to get near her."

"Jesus, it sounds like jail." Pat looked impressed.

"Maybe. Supposedly they like it, and they're said to be very nice people. I just don't know how they feel about women publishing books. Something tells me they won't like it."

"It's like the Dark Ages," Pat commented. "How old is she? Twelve?"

"She's in her early twenties. They're not supposed to have contact with people outside their community. Not just the women, the men too. So this should be interesting. I sent her an e-mail this morning, to be hand-delivered by her brothers." And he told Pat about his conversation with Joe Lattimer.

"It sounds very cloak and dagger," Pat said with a grin, "and you're right, very seventeenth century. Maybe you could fight a duel for her, with her father, over the book. Or her boyfriend, if she has one."

"We'll see how it goes," Bob said cryptically. He didn't want to admit to his junior editor that he was fascinated by her and had thought about her all weekend. It sounded too crazy. It was wild enough that they had gotten a handwritten manuscript from an Amish girl that he wanted to publish. But the book was terrific, and he was sure it would be a smash hit, if they could get it, which remained to be seen. He certainly hoped so. And in the meantime, her apron lay on his desk at the office. He had brought it back with him. It was beginning to feel like a security blanket. He kept taking it with him, so he had a part of her or something familiar to her, like a talisman, near at hand.

Margarethe had come over to make ice cream with Lillibet that afternoon. It had been so hot, Lilli thought it would be a nice treat for the boys and her father when they finished working, and Margarethe had agreed to help her. They talked about nothing in particular. They had seen each other at the Sunday service the day before, which had gone on for the usual three hours. And Margarethe mentioned to Lilli that one of her daughters was having another baby, and the youngest who had just gotten married was pregnant as well. She was seventeen years old. And once in a while, when Lillibet heard about girls that age getting married and starting families, it made her feel ancient. She had led the life of a grown woman for so many years.

"Nathaniel Weiss is ready to start courting again," Margarethe said casually as they worked on the ice cream.

He had lost his wife the year before and was in his early thirties. His wife had died in childbirth, and he had five children.

"That's nice," Lilli said, clearly with no interest.

"He's a fine-looking man." Margarethe tried again, and Lilli smiled at her.

"No," she said simply. "I brought up three boys, and I take care of Papa. I don't need five more and a husband. In a few more years the boys will be married and on their own, and I'll only have Papa to take care of. Why would I want to start all over again? Would you want to, and have ten more children?"

"If that was what God wanted for me, I would. We're not meant to be idle, Lilli," she said gently.

"I haven't been. But I never get time to myself." She wanted hours to read and daydream and write, whenever she liked. Every moment of her day was filled now, with doing for someone else, and it had been since she was seventeen. Margarethe was forty-one years old, had married at sixteen, and had had twenty-five years of children and grandchildren, although her husband had died many years before and left her a great many acres. The community had helped her ever since and lent her a hand with her children. And now they were old enough to work her farm.

"Would you marry again?" Lilli asked her with interest, although she couldn't see why. She didn't need to and was never lonely. But Lilli knew that her father liked her, even though they were just friends. He had never really gotten over her mother and her shocking death.

"I might, if the right man turned up at my door."

"Like my father?" Lilli asked her bluntly.

"Maybe. He never asked. And I don't think he will. We're comfortable as friends. And he has you. He doesn't need a wife to run his house." And he was seventy, not in the first bloom of youth, but he was strong and energetic and looked younger than his years. Margarethe had always thought that if Lilli married, Henryk might want to marry again. And Margarethe was comfortable as she was. Living in the community they did, they enjoyed the company of other women, and the men were always near at hand to help. "He was so in love with your mother, I think it's taken him years to get over it, and maybe he never will." Lilli nodded at what she said. She still missed her mother too. She was so gentle and wise, so beautiful and so smart and funny. There was no one else like her. She had always known just what to do or say. And it was always the perfect answer. Lilli wished she could be like her one day.

Henryk and the boys were delighted with the ice cream when they got home, and Margarethe stayed for dinner. None of her children were at home anymore, so she had more free time than the younger women, like Lilli, whose chores and tasks with the boys were never done until bedtime. And in winter, she did homework with the twins.

Henryk and Margarethe sat and talked for a while, and then she went home, and Lilli had some sewing to do, and then she scolded the boys into bed. She had just said good night to the twins, when Markus remembered something and jumped out of bed. He grabbed an envelope out of the pocket of the trousers he had worn that day and handed it to her with a sheepish grin.

"I forgot to give this to you. It's from Mr. Lattimer at the dairy." She was surprised to get any letter, and opened it as she walked out of the boys' room. She stopped dead when she read it, and then hurried to her bedroom and sat down on her bed. Her legs were shaking so hard, she could hardly stand up. She had just read Bob Bellagio's e-mail to her about how much he liked her book. She folded the letter carefully and slipped it under her mattress without a sound. And a moment later she went back downstairs to check on her father. He was asleep in his chair, after a long day at the plow. He was still as active as the younger men, but tired at night. She woke him gently and told him to go to bed. He smiled and patted her hand and went to his own room a few minutes later. She turned off the kerosene lamps and blew out the candles and then went upstairs herself. She took out the letter and read it again, and all she knew was that she had to get back to the dairy to answer him. But she had no idea how she would ever see him. She knew she had to find a way, and as she lay in bed that night, she prayed to her mother to help her. She was sure that writing the book had been her mother's idea, so now she had to take her the rest of the way.

Chapter 15

Willy worked in the fields with his father and older brothers again the next day, and the twins were going to the dairy with the milk alone, when Lillibet stopped them and surprised them by saying she would go with them. She had her bonnet on and was ready to leave.

"Why? You don't need to." Both boys looked annoyed. They liked getting away from her and delivering the milk alone. She was always scolding them for something or telling them what to do. And Willy shouted at them and boxed their ears. It was much more fun going to

Lattimer's on their own. And they looked glum when she hopped into the buggy at the last minute and tied her bonnet strings.

"It's fun to take a ride with you two, and all my chores are done." They weren't, but she had no other valid excuse. She had slipped the letter into her pocket and had all of Bob Bellagio's phone numbers with her. She was hoping that Joe Lattimer would let her use his phone. She felt guilty for the imposition, but he was her only conduit to the outside world, and she wanted to reach Bob Bellagio before he changed his mind about her book. She had no idea that there wasn't a chance of that in the world.

They got to the dairy quicker than usual when she was with them, and she sent the boys to get the goat cheese for their father, and then slipped into Joe Lattimer's office, praying he was there. She had no idea how to use a phone. And she wouldn't have done it anyway without his permission. But fortunately, he was at his desk when she walked in with an anxious look.

"Hello, Mr. Lattimer. I'm sorry to bother you again," she said softly. She wanted to call the publisher quickly before the boys finished their mission, but they were chatting with the two young workers behind the barn and were in no rush.

"I thought I might see you"—he smiled at her—"after that e-mail I sent you yesterday. That's a serious letter. It must be quite a book." He looked impressed, and she smiled nervously at him. "Would you like to send him an answer?" he volunteered.

"Could we call?" she asked breathlessly, and he nodded, as she slipped the letter out of her pocket and gave it to him for the numbers. He dialed for her a minute later and handed the phone to her. She waited while it rang, and a voice answered immediately. She wasn't sure what to say, as Joe Lattimer watched her. He could see her hand shaking as she held the phone.

"May I please speak to Mr. Bellagio," she said carefully, amazed by how clear the connection was. The woman on the phone sounded like she was in the same room. Lilli thought she might have to speak loudly, but she didn't.

"I'll see if he's in." The voice disappeared off the line, and she looked at Joe Lattimer in panic.

"I think she's gone."

"You're probably on hold," he explained. "Just wait. She'll be back." And a minute later she was.

"I'll put you through. Who shall I say is calling?"

"Lillibet Petersen," she said clearly, hoping he'd remember her name. She assumed he was an important, busy person, and maybe he'd forgotten.

The receptionist had located Bob in his office and told him Elizabeth Petersen was on the line, and he knew immediately who it was, despite the garbled name. He had been hoping she'd call if she got the e-mail. And it hadn't taken long.

"Miss Petersen?" He took the call immediately, and she was startled by his voice. She felt as though she'd heard it before. Something about it was so familiar.

"Yes," she almost whispered, she was so overwhelmed to hear him.

"I want to come and see you. I love your book. I want to publish it," he said in a strong tone, and she was silent for a moment, listening to his voice.

"Thank you." She wasn't used to having a conversation on the telephone and didn't know what to say. At his end, he heard the softness of her voice, and thought she might be scared. It didn't occur to him that she had never spoken on a phone before and wasn't sure how it worked. It seemed like magic to her.

"When can I come and see you?" he asked more gently, and she relaxed a little.

"I don't know." She didn't want to admit to him that she wasn't allowed to go anywhere and couldn't meet him. Then he wouldn't want her book. "I don't know if . . . when I can." Her eyes filled with tears as she said it. "My father is very strict," she said softly.

"I understand," he said, feeling an insane desire to put his arms around her. He had no idea what she looked like, and all he wanted to do was protect her from a man he didn't know. "Maybe we could meet at the dairy, with Mr. Lattimer. Would that be more comfortable for you?" He was trying to make it easier for her, but it would be hard for her, which he didn't know.

"Yes. I will try," she promised him. She would move heaven and earth to get there, but something could go wrong. She had no reason to go to the dairy with her brothers, so all the stars would have to line up right so she could go with them again.

"Would this Friday work for you?" He was thinking of driving down on Thursday night, to make sure he'd be there, and there would be no delays.

"Maybe. If I can get out," she said honestly. "It's not easy. I have chores to do on the farm. I take care of my father and brothers."

"Yes, of course." He didn't have the slightest inkling of what her life was like, but he was trying to imagine. It was a world beyond his ken. "What time would be best for you?"

"They usually come in the morning. Perhaps at eleven, but before noon."

"I'll be there from ten o'clock on," he promised her, "in case you arrive early. Come whenever you can. I'll be there. I'll see you on Friday . . . and Lillibet . . . thank you for your wonderful book, and for meeting me. It's going to be a big success."

"I hope so," she said softly, not really knowing what that meant to him or even to herself. "Thank you for coming to meet me. I'm sorry it's not easier." She didn't know why, but she trusted him and felt as though she knew him. And he felt the same way about her and had no idea why.

"Don't worry about it. We'll work it out."

"Thank you," she said again, and then they hung up. Bob sat at his desk, thinking about her for a long moment, shaken by the reality of her voice. She sounded so touching, so young, and so shy. All he wanted was to do this right for her and make it as easy as he could. And it made no sense to him, but he had the feeling that meeting her on Friday would change his life.

And as soon as Lillibet hung up, she

looked at Joe Lattimer as though she were in shock.

"He's coming on Friday. He wants to publish my book."

Joe nodded. He had understood. "Are you going to tell your father?" He had become her co-conspirator and ally, but somehow it felt right to him too, and it was exciting to be part of it. What if her book was a big hit?

"Yes, but not yet," Lillibet said about telling her father. "I don't want him to stop me. He won't understand at first." And maybe never. But she couldn't imagine that he would shun her for something like this. She wasn't going anywhere. She wasn't leaving. They were just going to publish her book. That was all. But her father wouldn't be pleased. She had no illusions about that.

"I think this is very thrilling," Joe Lattimer said seriously. "You should be very proud."

"I'm very scared," she said honestly, and he smiled at her.

"Don't be. I think it will be fine. Your father may be upset at first, but he'll get over it. You haven't done anything wrong." She nodded, wishing that were true. "I guess I'll see you on Friday then."

"If I can get out," she whispered. But she knew she had to now.

She thanked Joe Lattimer then, and went to find her brothers. They were just coming from behind the barn. She waited for them to get the cheese for their father, and then they got back in the buggy. They didn't even know she'd gone to see Joe Lattimer, they'd been having too much fun on their own. And she was silent on the ride home. Her heart was pounding as she thought of the call to New York. She had to find an excuse to go with them on Friday, whatever it took.

Bob Bellagio had lunch with his brother Paul on Wednesday at a restaurant on Wall Street that both brothers liked. They talked about a big deal Paul was doing, and a killing he had made in the stock market for one of his clients, and how well his son was doing in school. Everything was always perfect in his life, or seemed that way to his younger brother,

who had been struggling with his business, had no love life, had never been
married, and had no kids. He didn't even
have a dog, and Paul had two. And Paul
was married to the perfect woman, who
entertained his clients, had brought up
their children impeccably, including piano lessons, Mandarin, and windsurf-
ing, did volunteer work for the Junior
League, and ran their home like a Swiss
clock. Bob always felt like a lesser being whenever he was with him, as though
somehow he had failed. Paul's wife had
a law degree but no longer used it. All
Bob wanted to do was publish books. It
seemed so meager compared to their
accomplishments. And all he wanted
now was one number-one best seller to
justify what he'd been doing for the last
five years.

"I think I may have found a winner this
week," Bob said, sounding excited, at
the end of lunch. They'd been talking
about Paul since they sat down. They
usually did, unless Paul told him the
many things he was doing wrong in his
life and should be doing differently. It

was the relationship they'd had all their lives, since they were kids. Paul was perfect. Bob fell short. Their parents saw them that way too, or at least that was Bob's impression. "It's a knockout book, written by an Amish girl. I found it totally by accident. I'm going down to meet with her day after tomorrow and buy her book."

"That's terrific." Paul sounded genuinely pleased for him. He always did. The disappointment always crept in later, and the comparisons. "What kind of book can an Amish girl write?"

"A damn good one. Like modern-day Jane Austen. Only better."

"Will that sell?" He looked concerned for his brother. He had been working so hard for so long, with nothing much to show for it yet.

"It will, like hotcakes," Bob assured him, and for once he felt strangely confident as he said it. As though he'd found the holy grail. He felt as though he had magic in his pocket. He was absolutely certain Lillibet's book was going to be a major hit.

"Who's the girl?"

"All I know is that she's Amish, in her early twenties, and talented as hell."

"Ex-Amish, or Amish now?"

"Amish now."

"Wow, that should be interesting. You can teach her to use indoor plumbing and have her milk a cow on the *Today* show. How the hell are you going to use her to promote? It's a little *Heidi,* no?" Bob hated how clever his brother was with words. Just like their mother, who could still reduce them all to rubble with tongue or pen.

"I haven't met her yet. We've only spoken on the phone."

"At least she has one. You had me worried for a minute."

"She doesn't." Bob was smiling at him, and for once he wasn't worried, and his brother didn't have him scared. He had a secret weapon. Her name was Lillibet Petersen, and she wrote like a dream. "She called me from a dairy farm. I'm meeting her there, if her father lets her." He was actually enjoying torturing his brother with the image, although he was nervous about it himself. He was determined to work it out.

"And if her father doesn't?" Paul said, looking intrigued.

"I'll find her. I'm not going to lose this book. I discovered it totally by accident, in our slush pile. I can't tell you why, but I think it's fate."

"Oh God," Paul said, looking at his younger brother. "Don't tell me you're in love with her. You wait thirty-six years to fall in love, and you fall in love with an Amish girl. Please tell me I'm wrong."

"I'm in love with her book. You will be too when you read it. She writes like an angel."

"All right, I'll grant you that. You're a great judge of contemporary literature. Just don't bring her home."

"Why not?" Bob said, intrigued by the idea. He was fascinated with her, and her voice on the phone had gone straight to his heart. He had been fantasizing about her for days.

"Mom would have a nervous break-down. I don't think she's ready for Amish." Their mother was one of the toughest lawyers in the city, and the thought of introducing an Amish girl to her made Bob laugh.

"It might do her good."

"Just get the book. Leave the girl on the farm. Besides, she may not be cute. And she's young."

"I can always adopt her," he laughed at his brother and picked up the check. It was his turn. "I'll let you know how it goes."

"Yeah, do that. And remember, we're supposed to marry women like our mothers." It was exactly what Paul had done, to a frightening degree.

"I've been trying not to do that for the past thirty-six years," Bob said in a rare moment of total honesty with his brother. "I don't think that would work for me."

"Amish might be a little extreme," Paul said as they left the restaurant. "Have fun at the dairy farm," he said with a rueful grin as they parted, and Bob walked back to his office, lost in thought. He could hardly wait to meet Lillibet on Friday. He had a strange feeling it was going to be extraordinary. He already felt as though he knew her. And her voice in the book was so strong. He wondered if you could actually fall in love with someone from reading their work. Maybe it was possible. Stranger things had happened.

Chapter 16

On Friday morning, Markus woke with a bad cold. Lillibet brought him some of the herbal medicine she made, and a cup of tea with honey, and made him stay in bed. She sent Josiah to do the chores and helped him milk the cows, and she noticed with dismay that they were falling behind and it was getting late. Willy had left with their father at the crack of dawn. She helped Josiah put the milk containers in the buggy. And then as though she'd just thought of it, she told him she'd go with him.

"I can go by myself," he said, looking annoyed to go with his big sister again.

"So can I," she suggested, "if you'd rather stay here with Markus." He looked suddenly intrigued by the idea. He got tired of going to the dairy every day. He liked the prospect of a day off, to stay at the house and play. "I don't mind going. I went alone when you had chicken pox, and I was fine. Papa won't mind."

"Okay," he said, hopping down and grinning at her. He scampered off without looking back, and she silently thanked her mother, for making it all work. She had worn a fresh black dress and clean pale blue apron and her black bonnet. She didn't dare wear her best Sunday dress for fear someone would notice. She gave the horse the reins and trotted off toward the dairy at nearly eleven, with her heart pounding all the way. She kept the horse at a good pace and was there in fifteen minutes. She saw Joe Lattimer talking to a tall man with dark hair, in a navy jacket and khaki slacks. They both watched her as she reined in the horse, and she hopped down, motioning to the boys at the dairy to take the milk cans out of the back. She walked toward the two men, and she knew it wasn't possible, but she had the strong sense that she had seen the man in the blue jacket somewhere before, and he was looking at her intently and smiling as she walked toward him. She didn't even feel shy—when she reached them, she felt like she was meeting a friend.

"Miss Petersen," he said, holding out a hand to shake hers, and she took it in her own, as their eyes met. Hers were huge and green in her honey-colored face, and her blond hair was peeking out from under her bonnet. "Lillibet," he said as though he knew her, and she smiled.

"Mr. Bellagio, hello. Thank you for coming. I'm sorry to be late. We had a busy morning."

"You came alone," Joe Lattimer said with a look of surprise.

"Markus is sick, and Josiah decided he'd rather stay home and play. I was lucky." She looked relieved. "And my father is having lunch at my older brother's farm today. It worked out perfectly."

Joe left them then, and she followed Bob to the bench where she had found the book that had his address in it. And nearly two months later, they were sitting on the bench together. It was like a dream.

He was looking at her, stunned by how young she was, and how lively. She had a determined step in her laced-up black boots, and fire in her eyes. She was different than he had expected. She was younger and prettier and not quite as shy. They talked about her book for a few minutes, and he could see her relax slowly, and she looked mischievous as she peeked at him around her bonnet, and then she untied the ribbons and took it off, and he was struck by how beautiful her hair was.

"I'm sorry, I shouldn't do that. But it's so hot today." Her hair looked like spun gold, as she smiled into his eyes. She was everything he had hoped she'd be and more, and she seemed fascinated by him too. "I don't meet many English," she said softly after a few minutes. "That's what we call people who aren't Amish. Except Mr. Lattimer and the police when my mother died. I very seldom leave our farm."

"Yes, I know." He was listening to the timbre of her voice and knew he had heard it before. He had no idea where, but he had the same impression he'd had on the phone. That they had met somewhere, although it wasn't possible. She was an enchanting creature, and the clothes she wore suited her. She looked like a doll from another century. "Would you like to see the contract?" he asked, getting down to business, and she nodded. He explained it to her in detail, and it was very straightforward. They were offering to pay her a twenty-five-thousand-dollar advance, and a fifteen percent royalty, which he said was reasonable for a first book by an unknown author. It sounded like a fortune to her. He had brought the check with him in case she signed. And he held it out to her. She stared at it in amazement.

"What will I do with all that money?" she whispered.

"Put it in the bank, I hope," he said with a smile. It was touching sharing the

moment with her. She had been catapulted into this century, and he was
there to lead her through it. He had the
same feeling of wanting to protect her
that he had had after reading her book.
She was so brand new and vulnerable,
and yet so strong and wise at the same
time. She was an odd combination of
gentle and brave, old and new.

"I don't have a bank account," she
said to him, and he nodded. It didn't
surprise him.

"We could open one for you, here in
Lancaster. So you'd have the money at
your disposal. I'm sure Mr. Lattimer
could tell us where to go." She nodded.
It sounded like a good idea to her. He
handed her a pen then, and she signed
the contract and handed it back to him.
There were two copies, and he gave
one to her. It was the simplest deal he'd
ever made for the best book he'd ever
bought.

"Thank you," she said softly, as she
gave him his pen back and put her copy
of the contract in her pocket with the
check.

"You'll have to do a little editing. One

of our editors is looking at it now. I can help you with that, if you like. I could come back here, or you could come to New York." Her eyes flew open wide as he said that.

"How would I do that?"

"Would you like me to speak to your father, Lillibet?"

"No. I'll have to speak to him first. He'll be very angry about the book. And he won't want me to go to New York. I have to find the right time to tell him and explain it to him. I don't want to be shunned." She sounded very serious as she said it, and she looked scared.

"Shunned?"

"We have something called the Ordnung, which tells us all the rules. The elders decide what they are. And if you do something very bad, they can send you away, and you can't come back again. I don't want that to happen. I want to live here." And then she looked at him with a twinkle in her eye, and her soft halo of blond hair around her face. "But I would like to see New York. Perhaps Papa would let me one day, if he

understands that I have not said anything wrong in the book."

"You didn't," Bob reassured her. "You
wrote a beautiful book." He was certain
of that, and he wanted this to go right
for her. He couldn't imagine the elders
of her community shunning her or sending her away. And what would become
of her if they did? She would be lost in
the modern world. "We would handle
everything for you in New York if you
come up. I can send a car to pick you
up here. And I would take care of you in
New York myself." She nodded. She
was sure he would, and she could see
that he was a nice person and a good
man. Explaining it to her father and making him understand would be the hard
part.

And as he looked at her, Bob remembered about the bank.

"Would you like to go now? We could
deposit the check today." That way if
anything happened, she would have
money to draw on. At least she would
have that.

"Do you suppose we could?" She
looked intrigued.

They walked to Joe Lattimer's office, and he suggested they go to a different bank than her father's. He said there was one two miles away, and he told Bob where it was.

"I could drive you," Bob offered. "We'd be back here in a few minutes." She looked at him and nodded and followed him outside. He had left his car parked under a tree, and she looked at it and then at him.

"I've never been in a car before," she said quietly.

"I promise, I'll bring you back as soon as we deposit the check." She had no idea why, but she trusted him completely. She nodded, and he opened the car door for her, and she got in. He told her how to fasten the seat belt, and she started to giggle when he turned the key in the ignition and they drove away. Bob glanced at her, and he started to laugh too.

"This is the craziest thing I've ever done," she said, and couldn't stop laughing, and he was glad she wasn't afraid. She looked like she was having a good time, and so was he.

They found the bank easily and he parked in front as she looked at everyone with fascination, and he waited for her to open the door and get out, but she didn't. She just looked at him. "I don't know what you do now," she said, mystified by how everything worked. He smiled again and leaned over her to open the door for her. It was like landing on another planet with her.

"Now you get out," he said simply. "You undo the seat belt first." He showed her how. Then they walked into the bank together, as though it were perfectly normal. The tall man in the blazer and slacks and the Amish girl. He helped her through the process. And fortunately they were used to Amish customers. With Bob as guarantor, the bank manager signed off on her not having a driver's license or ID and said they would apply for a Social Security number for her. They opened a simple checking account and said they would change it into a savings account later, if she wished. It took them ten minutes to open the account in her name and deposit the check. They gave her a book of temporary checks and told her they would send the permanent ones in the mail, and she gave them the dairy address.

"My father would have a heart attack if they came to the house," she explained to Bob in a whisper.

"Yes, I think that's correct," he agreed. Five minutes later they were back outside the bank, and she noticed an ice-cream store down the street. She looked at Bob with the same childlike expression she'd had when she first met him. It was confusing being with her. One minute she was a child, and the next a woman.

"Can I write a check for an ice-cream cone?" she asked him seriously. The woman at the bank had explained to her how they worked.

"You could, but it's not necessary. I would be happy to treat you, as a celebration of our new contract."

"That would be very nice of you," she said, and followed him to the ice-cream store, where she ordered a cone with one scoop of chocolate and another of banana ice cream. And he had a double scoop of rocky road. They walked out of the store together, eating their ice cream, and wandered slowly back to the car. She was a woman with a bank account now, twenty-five thousand dollars in it, and a book contract. She had grown up in about five minutes.

"I would get in a lot of trouble for this," she explained on the way back. But he had figured that out all by himself. "Riding in a car with you. The contract, the book, the money. Maybe even the ice cream."

"I think they might let you off the hook for the ice cream—the rest I'm not so sure," he said as he drove her back to the dairy, and he was worried about her. "Will you be all right, Lillibet? I don't want you to get into trouble."

"I don't either," she said, finishing the last of her ice-cream cone. "I think I can handle it. I'm not going to tell anyone for a while. And my mother will protect me." She looked at him with sad, serious eyes, and she felt as though they had been friends for a long time, and she sensed that he would protect her too.

"You have my phone numbers. I want

you to call me if anything happens. Just go to the dairy and have someone call me. I can drive down here anytime if you need me. You didn't do anything wrong today. You did something wonderful. You wrote a very, very good book. And it's going to be published."

"I wish I could tell my mother about it. But she knows. She helped me find you, and made all of this happen," Lillibet said seriously as they pulled up at the dairy, and he turned off the car. "I wanted you to publish my book. That's why I sent it to you."

"And I was meant to find you. I know that too. Things happen the way they're supposed to." She nodded and got out of the car herself this time. She was looking seriously at him, as he stood next to her.

"Thank you for everything," she said, and he walked her back to her buggy.

"I'll let you know when we're ready to do the editing." Her book was coming out in a year, so there was time. He wished he could call her directly, but he knew he couldn't. "I'll send you an e-mail

at Lattimer's. Call me if you need me,"
he said again, and she nodded and got
into her buggy and picked up the reins.
And then she leaned over gently and
kissed his cheek, like a child.

"Thank you. I had a very good time."
She smiled at him. She had put her bonnet back on by then, and he could see
her big green eyes peeking at him, and
her fuzz of pale blond hair. He thought
his heart would break as she drove
away, and he wanted to run after her.
But she was disappearing back into her
world, to another century where he
couldn't follow her. She looked over her
shoulder at him and waved as the buggy
turned, and then she vanished from
view, and he went to thank Joe Lattimer
and tell him he was leaving.

"She's a nice girl," Lattimer said, looking at him wistfully. "I knew a girl who
looked like her a long time ago. Lillibet
is courageous to do this. It won't be
easy for her with her father." They both
knew that, but sometimes things turned
out right, and this had. Joe was glad for
her. Bob looked like an honest man to

him. "The Amish are very decent people." Bob nodded, still too overwhelmed by her to know what to say. And he knew he had just bought the best book of his career. It would be a blessing for them both.

"How tough is her father?" Bob asked him, looking worried.

"Very. But fair. But they all live by the Ordnung, the rules they follow, even the elders. He won't be happy about a book. I don't think that's part of their culture. And they keep their women close to home. She's brave to have done this with you. I hope it works out for both of you," Joe said sincerely. "I won't say anything." And Bob knew he wouldn't, for Lilli's sake. The two men shook hands then, and Bob wondered if Joe had been in love with the girl who looked like her. A few minutes later Bob got back in his car and drove away. It had been the strangest, best, and most moving day of his life. And all he could think of, as he drove home, was Lilli back on the farm with her father and brothers. He wondered what she was doing, but it would have been hard for him to imagine. She came from another world. He thought of her eating her ice cream, and he smiled. Meeting her had been the best gift in his life. And so was her book.

Chapter 17

Everything went smoothly when Lilli got back to the farm that afternoon. And in all, she had only been gone for two hours, but her whole life had changed when she signed the contract and put the money in the bank. She put the checkbook, papers from the bank, and contract under her mattress and went to take care of Markus and brought him some soup. And as she went about her chores, she thought about what a nice man Bob was.

She did some sewing for her father, Willy had gone off with friends from the neighboring farm to fish in a nearby stream, and Margarethe dropped by to see her that afternoon. And when her father came home, he was in a good mood. Everything seemed normal until Sunday afternoon, when they got back from their Sunday service at one of their neighbors' homes.

Lillibet was setting the table for dinner, when her father asked to speak to her and sent the boys outside.

"You went to the dairy twice this week, Lillibet," he said quietly, and she felt panic rise in her throat, wondering if someone had seen her with Bob, or getting into his car, which would be impossible to explain.

"Yes, I did, Papa. I kept the boys company one day, because I had finished my work in the house. And Josiah wanted some time to play when Markus was sick, so I went by myself. I did it when they had the chicken pox too."

"Are you meeting an English boy at the dairy, Lilli? One of Lattimer's boys? You've been old enough to court for a long time. I never pressed you about it after your mother died, because I needed your help here with the boys. But if you are ready now, I will find you a husband. Many men have asked about you, and you never looked kindly at them, so I thought you wanted to stay here. Some women don't want to marry, and you can stay at home with me if you wish." And in fact he hoped she would. "But I will not have you courting with an English, Lilli, if that's what you're doing. You know what the Ordnung says. You must marry in our community. You can't go outside."

"I wasn't trying to go outside, Papa," she said, looking nervous, thinking of the money she had in the bank. "I wasn't courting with anyone at the dairy. I just wanted to go for a ride in the buggy."

"I think it's time you had a husband and children of your own. The boys are growing up. The twins will be finished with school in another year."

"I don't want to start taking care of children all over again," she said honestly. "I've done that for seven years, since Mama died."

"You need your own," he said firmly. He had never said that to her before.

"I don't want any, Papa. Or a husband. I'm happy as I am."

"It's not natural for you to only have brothers and a father to take care of. You should have a husband and children of your own," he insisted. He didn't understand that she had used up any desire to have children on the family she had raised for him. "Klaus Mueller is a good man. He would be a good husband for you. He's ready to marry again." Her heart sank when her father said it.

"Papa, he's fifty years old."

"I was almost thirty years older than your mother. We were very happy. You need an older man. You're too wise for a young man."

"And too wise to marry a man I don't love," she said simply. But she had never been in love and didn't expect to be now.

"You can learn to love him. Your mother hardly knew me when we married. Her father thought I was a good choice for her, and he was right. She was barely more than a child. And you're a grown woman. You will learn to love a good man. If you're going off on buggy rides with your brothers because you have nothing to do, you need something more."

"Yes, I do," she said softly. Listening to him, she realized that she couldn't lie to him anymore. She had been wrong to try. "I want to do something else. It's something Mama would have understood. I think she would want me to do this. And I can stay here with you." She could see that he didn't understand. But how could he? What she wanted was so far beyond his wildest imagination. "I wrote a book, Papa. It took me three years. It's a good book, like the ones Mama used to give me. It's not about us. I didn't say anything about the Amish in it. It's just a story about a young girl who grows up on a farm and travels to see the world."

"Is that what you want to do? Travel to see the world?" He looked shocked.

"No, I'm happy here. I just want to write. There is nothing in the Ordnung that says I can't write." She wanted to travel too but didn't dare say so.

"I know the Ordnung better than you do. You need a home and children, and

then you won't have time to write stories and read books. If you want to read,
read the Bible. There's no need to read
other books. And I want you to put your
book away."

"I can't, Papa," Lilli said in barely more
than a whisper. "I sent it to a publisher
in New York, and they liked it. They're
going to publish it next year."

"I forbid it!" he said, slamming his fist
on the table. "How dare you do that behind my back!"

"I'm sorry, Papa. I know it was wrong.
I prayed about it. And I think Mama
would have wanted me to do it." It was
a brave thing for her to say, and foolish
at the same time.

"Your mother would never have allowed it, without my permission. She
was an obedient woman. I will not allow
you to publish a book, Lillibet. You must
tell them immediately that you won't."

"I won't do that," she said softly. "I
want to publish it. I did nothing wrong."

"It is wrong to disobey me. I forbid
you to publish a book. And to write anymore. You will study the Bible, and marry
when I find you a husband. It's time."

"You can't force me to marry, or to stop writing. You can't make a prisoner of me, Papa."

"Do you want to live with the English? Is that what you want?" He was threatening her, and she knew it, but she wouldn't give in.

"No, I don't. I want to stay here, in your house, with you and my brothers. I will stay until I'm an old woman if you want me. But I won't stop writing. I need that for my soul."

"You need God for your soul, and nothing else. I will not allow you to publish a book and live under my roof. Now go to your room. Your brothers and I will cook dinner tonight. I don't want to hear about your book again. Have you made an agreement with them to have it published?"

"I signed a contract," she said quietly, her voice growing stronger.

"Then write to them and tell them you changed your mind. They can't force you to publish a book."

"And you can't force me not to," she said, with fire in her eyes. "I'm being honest with you. I told you about it. I don't want to lie to you."

"You will not leave this house until you cancel that contract. Is that clear? I will shun you if you disobey."

"You can't force me to leave. I won't go." None of his children had ever dared to defy him, and he was shaking with rage as Lilli left the room and went upstairs. The others had all heard him pounding the table, and they were waiting outside for the storm to subside. They knew that something terrible must have happened, but none of them could have guessed that she had written a book. Lillibet went to her room without a word. She did not come down to dinner. And she lay awake for hours that night thinking about her book and her contract, and nothing was going to make her cancel it. Not even her father. She was more determined than ever to have it published. And she came downstairs in the morning and went about her chores.

Her father didn't mention it again for several days, and then he asked her if she had written to the publishers to withdraw the book.

"No, I haven't," she said quietly. "And I won't." It had become a war of wills. For the next two weeks her father wouldn't speak to her, and she finally went to see Margarethe in despair. She knew all about it, Henryk had been ranting to her about it since Lilli told him. And he was determined now to get her married and was sorry he hadn't done it before.

"He'll get over it. Your mother would have been proud of you," Margarethe said softly. Lillibet was stunned by what she said. Margarethe was a far more docile woman than Rebekah had been, but in this instance she thought Lillibet was doing the right thing. It was a big step for her, and she needed something in her life if she didn't want a husband and children.

But Henryk wouldn't relent. It went on for two more weeks, with her father alternately berating and threatening her, and not speaking to her, and his threats to shun her were getting stronger and more vehement, which meant she would be expelled from their community if he followed up on his threats. Being sent away forever was the one thing she feared, so in September Lillibet wrote a letter to Bob Bellagio, explaining what was happening and that she couldn't allow him to publish the book. She offered to return the money to him and enclosed one of the temporary checks the bank had given her, for the full amount. She walked to the dairy to give Joe Lattimer the letter and asked him to mail it. And when she got home, she told her father what she had done and looked at him with hatred in her eyes. He didn't care. And she told him that she would leave the community on her own if he forced her to marry. She went to her room then and didn't come out for three days. And then she went back to her chores, and her life of slavery, with a dead look in her eyes. Margarethe told Henryk that she was seriously worried about her, and that she thought he was wrong. And he told Margarethe she was no longer welcome in their house.

*   *   *

When Bob got her letter, he could see by her erratic handwriting how upset she was, and he hated to think of the pressure she had been under, and the threats from her father. She had told him all of it, and that she couldn't go forward with the book. Feeling ill after he read her letter and sensing how distraught she was, he tore the check she sent him in half and was at Lattimer's Dairy the next day and asked Joe for her address.

"Did something happen?" Joe asked him. There was a desperate look in Bob's eyes.

"Her father won't let her publish the book. I want to talk to him myself." Joe nodded, although he didn't think it would help. Henryk Petersen was a stubborn man, rooted in the old ways. But he told Bob where they lived and hoped he was doing the right thing.

It was late afternoon, and Lillibet was cooking dinner when Bob knocked on the kitchen door. She opened it and stared at him as though she had seen a ghost.

"What are you doing here?" He

thought she looked thinner than when he'd last seen her, and very sad.

"I came to talk to your father and try to reason with him about the book. Maybe he should read it himself."

"He won't," she said miserably. "He threatened to shun me and send me away." Bob took the torn check out of his pocket then and put it in her hand. And then he looked at her with a serious expression.

"Lilli, do you want to publish the book?" He wouldn't force her, in spite of the contract. She had too much at stake.

"Yes," she said softly. "I do. But I don't want to get sent away. I have nowhere to go. This is the only life I've ever known." As he looked around the kitchen, Bob felt as though he had traveled back in time, to the seventeenth century, where they lived.

"Let me talk to him." She didn't think it would do any good, but she let him wait in the parlor and gave him a cup of tea. And she went back to cooking dinner, so her father wouldn't see them together when he walked in.

Henryk came home half an hour later,

and Lilli told him he had a guest waiting for him in the parlor. He was surprised and walked in, as Lilli followed him. Bob stood up immediately, looking solemn and respectful, and extended a hand. Henryk shook it, not knowing who he was.

"Mr. Petersen, I'm Robert Bellagio. I'm the publisher who would like to publish your daughter's book. It's an extraordinarily good book. It in no way embarrasses your community, it says nothing about the Amish. And people who read it will admire her enormously, and the education of your young women. I think you'd be very proud of her if you read it. I came here to tell you that myself. I am deeply respectful of the way you live, but I would like to see Lillibet able to publish her book too. I think it's important to her."

"It should be important to her to obey her father," he said, "and I will be proud of her when she does. We live by rules here, and laws. It's important that she respect those laws." He looked at Bob with a fierce expression, and then relaxed a little and invited him to sit down.

He didn't want to be rude. "It was very kind of you to come here and speak to me." Lilli could see that he appreciated the gesture of respect. "But I will not allow Lilli to publish her book."

"Is there anything that I can do to make you more comfortable about it, sir?" Bob asked him quietly, and Lilli could see both men taking each other's measure. Each had met his match, but she could already sense that Bob would not win. Her father was stronger, and they were playing by his rules.

"Only if you agree not to publish it. She's my daughter and she must respect me." He said it man to man.

"It's an enormous sacrifice to ask her to make," Bob said seriously. "I believe she worked on it for three years, writing it in longhand at night."

"She shouldn't have. She has more important things to do here, taking care of her brothers and me." He sounded like a selfish old man to Bob, but he nodded respectfully. He didn't want to make things worse for Lillibet. "Will you join us for dinner?" Henryk asked unexpectedly. "You've come a long way to see me. This book must be important to you."

"It is." Bob purposely didn't look at Lilli as he said it. He didn't want to anger her father, only to talk to him and see if he could sway him at all. So far he hadn't, not an inch.

"I'm sorry then, to disappoint you. You couldn't know how we'd feel about it when she agreed to let you publish it. It was dishonest of her. Will you stay?" he asked again, and Bob didn't want to refuse. And he liked being near Lillibet, and gaining a better understanding of how she lived. He was shocked at what he saw. Not at the archaic simplicity of it, but at her father's total jurisdiction over her. Henryk thought a life of servitude was enough to satisfy his daughter and all she deserved. Lattimer had hinted he would be like this, stubborn and difficult and steeped in the old ways.

"I'd be honored to have dinner here," Bob said quietly. Her father nodded then and invited him to come into the other room, and then asked if he'd like to see something of the farm, and Bob said he would. The two men went outside and disappeared, as Lilli sat down at the kitchen table with shaking knees and Willy came downstairs.

"What's happening now?" The battle between her and their father had been raging for a month, and they were all tired of it, Lilli most of all.

"The publisher who wants to publish my book is here. He came to see Papa to explain it to him," she said with a look of despair, and Willy laughed.

"Did Papa take him outside to shoot him?" Willy guffawed at his own joke.

"Probably," she said with a smile, and went to check on dinner and slow it down. And as she did, Bob was following her father around the barn, asking intelligent questions about how they ran the farm without electricity or modern farm implements or even a tractor, while her father explained to him the simple principles of their life and how they lived, and why they felt it was a better choice. Bob found it fascinating, but not for Lilli, who had none of the freedoms she wanted and Bob thought she deserved.

Women had a role in their society, but it was an ancient, traditional one, and all the important decisions were made by the men. They had final say on everything, on any subject, and total rule over the women. Henryk said the women were happy that way, and Bob was sure Henryk believed that was true. He was an honest, sincere man, with deep convictions and beliefs.

Henryk found he actually liked Bob, and the interest and respect he showed. Both men looked entirely comfortable when they came back to the house an hour later. Lilli had dinner ready by then, and called to the boys to come downstairs.

They spent a surprisingly pleasant evening, and Bob was nice to the boys and they enjoyed talking to him. It was an exchange of information between his world and theirs. He asked serious questions about the Amish life, and the boys asked Bob a thousand questions about the things he did and places he'd been. It was a lively evening, and as Bob prepared to leave, Henryk thanked him for coming and looked as though he meant it. All Bob could hope was that he had planted a seed somewhere that would cause Henryk to relent, but there was no sign of it yet.

"Thank you for coming. You were brave to come," Lilli said softly, as she walked him to the car. Her father had allowed her to do that. He trusted Bob. "I wish I were leaving with you," she said miserably. It was the first time she had ever said anything like it, and meant it.

"So do I," he said, searching her eyes. "He's a tough guy," he commented about her father.

"Yes, he is."

"Lilli, honestly, if you ask me to, I won't publish your book. I don't want to ruin your life to publish a book."

"No, I still want you to publish it." There was determination in her eyes.

"What if they shun you?"

"I don't think they can. I'll go live with Margarethe if I have to, my mother's friend. She might take me in." But she wasn't sure. If her father convinced the elders to shun her, no one could help, nor would they dare, for fear of being shunned themselves. But she told herself her father wouldn't do that. He was hard, but she knew he loved her. Enough to punish her, but not shun her.

"You can come to New York," he said with a wry smile. "You might like it."

"I'd like to see it one day. Just for a visit," she said.

"You will." He squeezed her hand then—he didn't want to kiss her cheek in case someone was watching. "And we still have to edit it." She nodded, not sure how they would do it. Especially now.

"Thank you for coming," she said again, as he slid into the car and started it. He looked at her for a long moment and pulled away. She waved as he drove off, and he felt as though he were abandoning her. He hated to leave her there in her medieval life, in her father's control, with no one to talk to her who understood her, or protect her from the rigors of her world. It was a strange feeling, and she felt as though she had watched a ship sail away. The ship she wanted to be on, with the only friend she had in the world. There were tears

running down her cheeks as she went
back into the house and walked upstairs. It no longer felt like a home to
her—it felt like a prison.

Chapter 18

The day after Bob's unexpected visit, Henryk seemed slightly mollified, and kinder when he spoke to Lillibet. Bob's gesture of respect had not been lost on him, and he thought he was a good man, although he thought it was strange that he wasn't married at his age, but the English were like that. And he wasn't worried that he was going to try and court Lillibet. He seemed too sensible and too respectful of the Amish to do that, and Bob's interest was clearly business, not romance. But however much Henryk liked him, he was not going to allow Lillibet to publish the book, now or at any later date. As the head of the family, he had decided and he knew that Lillibet would accede to his wishes. She had no choice, and no wish to be shunned. Henryk had made himself clear. And he was a very determined man. Bob had understood that too.

Lillibet didn't argue with him again after Bob's visit. But her decision had been made too. She wouldn't stop the book from being published, and she was counting on her father having too much heart to shun her. She knew he loved her, and she loved him. He would be angry with her, but she felt sure he would get over it. He and the boys needed her too much. So she did her chores and said nothing to him about it. There was no need to confront him. The book was a year away. And discretion seemed to be the better course, rather than full-on confrontation, which only fanned the flames of their anger, both his and hers.

She was waiting to hear from Bob about what she needed to do to edit the book, and they hadn't figured out where to do it, or how. She thought it best if he sent the material to Lancaster for her to work on alone, and she could mail it back to him from the dairy. Bob thought she would need guidance and conversation about it, and for this first time at least, he thought that she needed to work with an editor face to face, either the one currently editing the book or himself.

Mary Paxton had been working on the manuscript since Lilli signed the contract, and she came back to Bob with it at the end of September. There was less work to do on it than she thought there would be, but it still needed some polishing and a few changes. She was surprised by how clean the manuscript was, from a novice writer, but Lillibet had been meticulous in her work.

"It won't take more than a few days," Mary reassured him after she sat down in his office, using considerable effort to lower herself into a chair. She looked like Agnes Gooch in *Auntie Mame,* and was expecting twins in two weeks. She felt like she was about to pop. She had been miserable in the heat all summer

and could hardly wait. Mary was the
Yalie he had hired when he started his
business, and he thought she'd be perfect to work with Lillibet. "How soon can
she be here?" Mary asked with a look
of concern. "Would tomorrow be too
soon?" She was kidding, but not by
much. "I'm planning to run around the
block until I drop tonight, so I can get
these guys moving." And she was planning to take three months off to be with
her babies. They were her first and she
had no idea what to expect, times two.

"I'm not sure she can," Bob said, looking worried. "How much do you think
you can get across to her in an e-mail?"
He had mentioned to Mary that Lillibet
was Amish but not how violently her father objected to the book. They didn't
need to know. And Mary had been impressed by how smoothly Lillibet described things that she had never seen
and didn't know, like air travel, other cities and countries, what people looked
like, how they thought, the way they
dressed, and the choices they made in
life. She had amazing insight for such a
young woman and seemed to be able

to channel herself into other people's heads, in situations she'd never been in. She was a true writer to her core, and clearly had an immense gift, just as Bob had thought.

"I don't think we should do it by e-mail the first time," Mary said, looking pensive. "Maybe after we're used to working together, but I really want to get this right. The book is too good not to. Can she come to New York?" Bob sighed in answer and thought about it.

"It'll be tough. Her family needs her on the farm. And realistically, she's never traveled out of Lancaster. They'll be nervous about it." That was a major understatement of her father's reaction—"atomic explosion" was more like it. "And it will be like taking her to another planet. I hoped for a gentler introduction to the process and the modern world. She's never been off the farm, or used a telephone. I took her for her first ride in a car. Bringing her here will be pretty extreme for her."

"Well, unless she's trained as a midwife, I can't go there," Mary said ruefully. "And I really think we should meet."

He did too, he just didn't know how to pull it off. He wrote her a letter, not wanting to rely on her young brothers to get an e-mail to her, now that he'd met them. He just hoped that she'd get the mail before her father did. And two days later she called him from Joe Lattimer's office at the dairy, with panic in her voice. Fortunately, Bob was in when she phoned him first thing in the morning. He took the call the minute he heard it was she.

"How can I come to New York?" she asked him. It would have been hard enough if he came to Lancaster, and she couldn't have explained his visit to her father, especially for several days. But disappearing for a week to go to New York was even worse. The logistics of it seemed impossible to her, and almost equally so to him. "I'm too old for *rumspringa*," she said, sounding anxious about it, and using a term he'd never heard.

"*Rumspringa?*" And then she laughed and relaxed a little.

"Sorry, it's an Amish term. We are baptized as adults, not children, when we're old enough to make a choice about the way we live and embrace the Amish ways. Some families allow young people and teenagers to kick up their heels a little before they're baptized. Some even smoke and drink a little, have English friends, ride in cars. It's a very liberal way to look at things, so they know what they're giving up. But no one in my family has ever done that, and my father would probably have killed us if we did. And I don't think a week in New York would qualify as *rumspringa* to him—more like Sodom and Gomorrah." They both laughed, and what she had described sounded like an interesting concept to him. So many things they did were sensible and carefully thought out—it was the extreme position and the rigidity of the old guard like Henryk that made her life so difficult, but she had accepted it till now and planned to for the rest of her life. As long as Henryk was alive, nothing would ever change for her.

"My parents weren't so keen on *rumspringa* either," Bob said, laughing. "I was picked up for drunk driving once in

college, and joined a traditional freshman jogging event at Princeton with a
friend there, where all the freshman boys
ran around the campus naked at the
first snow. We got a little carried away,
jogged to a bar off campus, and got arrested. My father had to come down
from New York to bail me out. He cut
off my allowance for two months."

"That's a little racier than *rumspringa*
here." She was laughing at his story. "So
what are we going to do? Is it really important for me to be there in person to
work with this woman?"

"She thinks so, and she can't come
to you. She's having twins in two weeks,
or sooner, so that rules out her going to
you. And she's a better editor than I am
and has been working on the book."

"Then I'll have to come there. I'll find
a way," she said, sounding frightened
but sure.

"I'm sorry, Lillibet," he said sincerely.

"For what? Giving me the biggest opportunity of my life?" He was glad she
still felt that way.

"I'll send a car for you. And you can
stay at a hotel near the office. We'll pay

for everything, of course, and I'll drive you back myself if you want, or have a car take you back." He realized that it might look better if a car and driver took her home, so her father didn't think she had spent the week with him, shacked up in his apartment or at a hotel.

"Will I be safe at a hotel?" she asked, sounding as young as she was and brand new in the world.

"Of course. It will be a very nice hotel. And I'll get to show you New York." He sounded happy about it, and she was excited at the prospect. She just had to get through her father's fury and threats before that, whatever it took. "How soon can you come?"

"I don't know. This week? Next?" Her father would be livid whenever she went, and she wasn't going to lie to him. She had to tell him now that she was going forward with the book, and going to New York for several days to edit it.

"I think it should be sooner rather than later, given Mary's condition. She looks like she's going to explode any minute." He had never seen anyone so pregnant in his life.

"So did my mother when she had Markus and Josiah." She had been a tiny woman like Lilli. "All right. Let's say Friday then." It was Tuesday as they were speaking. "How long do you want me?" He wanted to say "forever," jokingly, but he didn't dare, because there would be more truth to it than she knew. But he didn't want to cloud the work issues with feelings he couldn't explain and might make no sense to her. He couldn't make sense of it himself.

"Why don't you plan to stay a week, and you can go back sooner if you finish? Give yourself a little time." She found herself thinking of the old saying "Might as well be hung for a sheep as a lamb." Going at all would infuriate her father, five days or a week wouldn't make much difference. The principle and the fact would enrage him, and her disobedience to him. She didn't want to push him so far that he shunned her, but she knew how much he loved her and even though she worried about it, she couldn't really imagine his doing that to her. "I'll have a car and driver at your house on Friday morning," Bob said simply, relieved that she was coming and had agreed, although he was worried for her too.

"Send him to the dairy. I'll have Willy drop me off. It's better than putting it in my father's face that I'm leaving in a car." She thought of her drive to the bank and the ice-cream store the day they met. Her father would have been horrified by that too, but she had enjoyed it, and still cherished the memory of being with him.

"I'll take care of it," Bob assured her, and then in a gentle tone, he took off his publisher's hat and donned that of a friend. He felt like both. "Good luck with your father. I promise I'll take good care of you while you're here." She knew he would. She hung up and thanked Joe Lattimer for the use of his phone. He had left her alone in his office, so she could talk freely. Her life seemed very complicated these days since she had sent her manuscript to New York and Bob had discovered her. Joe hoped he hadn't done anything wrong. He had just wanted to help her and still did. He didn't want her to get shunned as a re-

sult, and neither did Bob. It clearly wasn't
what Lilli wanted either.

She took the buggy back to the farm
then. She had come alone and brought
the milk in with her. She hadn't asked
for permission. She just did it, and her
father had been out when she left. She
stopped at Margarethe's on the way
back. Her father still wouldn't allow Margarethe at their house, since she had
tried to get him to let Lilli do the book.
Lilli missed seeing her but had gone to
visit several times. And she needed to
talk to someone now. She told Margarethe about Bob needing her to go to
New York to work on the book, and the
editor expecting twins and unable to
come to her.

"I have to go," Lilli said with a sigh
over a cup of mint tea that Margarethe
had made herself, with peppermint
leaves from her garden. And she had
baked hot buns with the peach jam she
was famous for. "Papa will kill me," Lilli
said, worried. She really had come to a
crossroads with the trip to New York.
Either she went, with all the potential
consequences from her father, or she

had to abandon the book now. She was almost sure that Margarethe would tell her the risk was too high and to stop while she still could. Lilli looked at her with big sad eyes, with her black bonnet in her lap, her long braid streaming down her back.

"You have a choice, of course," Margarethe said cautiously—she didn't want to influence her, only help. "And your father is a stubborn man. We all know that." She smiled ruefully. He hadn't spoken to her in weeks, and they had always been close. "He sincerely believes in his position and thinks it's best for you. And as an elder of the council, he has to stick to the principles of his beliefs and to the Ordnung. But I think there is more at stake here than your father and the council and the Ordnung, Lilli. There's your heart and your life and what you need to do. We don't get to make decisions very often, in our way of life. And certainly not once we're married. You're young and free, and you have to respect your father, but you have to honor yourself and God. I believe He gave you this opportunity and your talent, and you shouldn't waste it.

"I want to say what I think your mother would have, and she and I didn't always agree. She was much braver than I am, but this time I do agree. . . . Go, Lilli . . . follow your dreams . . . follow your heart. If this book is important to you, go to New York. See it through . . . don't waste it. You'll always regret it if you don't go. And you could become bitter about it. Your father will get over it. He has to. He needs you, and he loves you. I think you should go to New York." Lilli stared at her in amazement. For the second time recently, Margarethe had said the exact opposite of what Lilli had expected and told her to choose the path of freedom, whatever the consequences. And Lilli knew in her heart that it was exactly what her mother would have wanted her to do, and then she would have helped her pick up the pieces later. This time Lilli would have to do that herself, but she was willing to.

"Thank you," she said, throwing her arms around Margarethe's neck. "Thank you." She didn't want to waste the opportunity either. If she did, it might never come again. She knew she had to seize it while she could. And she believed that the chance to publish her book had been a gift from her mother, in heaven.

She went back to the house and began quietly making preparations that night. And the next day, when her father was at her brother's farm, with Willy, and the twins were in school, she took the buggy and went to the dairy to find a ride into town. After asking around, one of the farmhands took her. She bought a few simple things at a women's store. She was going to wear her Amish clothes, but she wanted a few English-style things for New York, so she didn't attract too much attention. She bought a black skirt, and some blouses, a dark blue dress, and a red one, and flat shoes that looked like ballerina slippers and felt like air on her feet. And she bought a pair of blue jeans. She was fascinated by the buttons and zippers, and she bought a small suitcase to put it all in. She would take her black Amish cape with her that she wore all winter, but she bought a dark blue coat too. It fit her

perfectly and would keep her warm if
the weather was chilly. And she bought
two pairs of sheer stockings, which she
had never even seen before. Her legs
looked naked when she had them on,
instead of the heavy black cotton stockings she had worn all her life. She paid
for all of it by check from her bank account.

And the woman who helped her was
very kind, and gave her good advice
when she said she was going to New
York on business. She packed it all in
the suitcase in the store and hid it under
her bed when she got home. No one
had seen her leave and return. She felt
dishonest, but she was certain she was
doing the right thing now. And she broke
the news to her father on Thursday night.
She waited until after dinner and told
him she needed to speak to him. She
sat quietly until the boys went upstairs,
and her father was stone-faced, before
he knew what she had to say. He thought
she had given up the idea of the book,
but he wasn't sure. Sometimes she was
as stubborn as he was.

At last, alone with him, she stood in

front of him, trembling, but he couldn't see it, as she held tightly to the edges of her apron. It was one of the ones her mother had made her. She had worn it on purpose to speak to him. It reminded her of her mother and gave her courage.

"Papa, I want to tell you two things. I am going to let them publish my book. I don't think it's wrong. And I think Mama would have approved. And I am going to New York to edit it with them, and make some corrections. I will be working with a woman Bob Bellagio has assigned to do it. She's having twins soon, so she can't come here. So I am going there to work on it with her. I'll be back in a week or less, as soon as I finish. Nothing will have changed. And I will go on as before. But I have to do this, Papa. And I love you very much." She added the last for good measure. And she said it to him in the German they often spoke at home, so he would know that she wasn't abandoning him or their traditions. And when she finished speaking, there was deafening silence in the room. His brows were knit, he said nothing, and he didn't move. It was almost a full five minutes before he said a word. He stood up then and spoke to her in English, in a strong clear voice that rang out in the room.

"If you go to New York, do not come back here, Lillibet. I will speak to the elders, and you will be shunned. You cannot disobey me and live like the English and stay in our community. You have no home here anymore, if you leave." They were powerful words that hit her like blows, but she did not believe him. In her mind, she loved him and their family too much for him to shun her. Her heart and mind would not allow her to accept that he could do it. The memory of her mother would not permit him to do it in the end. She was certain.

"I will be back, Papa. As soon as we finish. A week at most, maybe less," she said calmly, refusing to be frightened by him. He said nothing to her in response. He stormed past her, walked up the stairs to his room with a heavy step, and slammed the door. Lillibet went to her own room after that, after she put out the lamps. She took out her suitcase and put the rest of her things in it. She had taken two of her Amish dresses and was going to wear another, in a plain black wool, with her winter bonnet, and cape, and tall black shoes. And she knew that whatever she wore, her old clothes or the new, she would always be an Amish girl, and chose to be, just as she had promised at her baptism, and she would come home again. But first, no matter how angry her father was, or how much he threatened her, she was going to New York. And she could hardly wait.

Chapter 19

On Friday morning, Lillibet got up even earlier than usual, and she went to wake Willy. She hated to make him do it and didn't want to get him in trouble with their father, but she needed him to drive her to the dairy in the buggy. She had no other way to get there, and she had told Bob to have the car meet her there. It was too far for her to walk with her suitcase. She had discussed it with Willy the night before, and he said he was willing. He didn't want his sister on the road alone. Things happened to people, especially to girls late at night, and it would still be dark when she left.

"Are you coming back?" he asked her, looking worried. His eyes were huge when he asked.

"Yes. I promise. I'll only be gone a week."

"Do you think Papa will have you shunned?" He looked frightened, but she didn't.

"No, I don't. He loves me. He'll just be very angry, but I wrote a book, and now I want to get it published. I didn't do anything bad."

"Does the book talk about us?"

"No, it's just about a girl." It sounded dull to him and not worth making such a big fuss over, but their father had been furious at her for weeks. Willy hoped it would be over soon, and so did she.

She was dressed and downstairs long before sunup, and didn't even dare make herself a cup of tea. She didn't want to make any noise and wake her father or the twins. She and Willy were both carrying their shoes when they left and walked across the grass in the front yard, covered with morning dew. They walked to the stable, Willy hitched the horse to the buggy and put her suitcase in the back, and they took off as quietly as they could. Neither of them knew that their father was already awake and had been listening to them as they left. And when he heard the buggy take off down the road, with his only daughter in it, he sat on his bed and cried.

The car and driver were waiting for her at the dairy, as promised. And she hugged Willy fiercely when she said goodbye. Her little brothers were a nuisance, but she loved them, and she had never left them, or home, let alone for a week.

"I'll miss you. Be good, and take care of Papa and the boys. Tell Mr. Lattimer if anything happens—he knows where to find me in an emergency." But she didn't expect there to be one, and hoped there wouldn't. One tragedy had been enough in their lifetime. Lightning couldn't strike again.

"Bring me back something from New York," Willy said with a shy grin. He was caught between being a boy and a man. He was a gangly adolescent but expected to work on the farm among the men now, since he had finished school. Lillibet always wished, as their mother had, that they could stay in school longer, but that was not the Amish way.

"Okay, I will. Now go back, before Papa gets up," she urged him, and he took off a minute later, at a good trot on the way back. She knew he'd be home soon and hoped their father didn't make too big a fuss about it when he discovered that she had left for New York, just as she said she would.

The driver opened the car door for her, and she got in the backseat and remembered to put the seat belt on, as Bob had shown her when she had ridden in his car with him. She settled back to watch the countryside go by, as the sun came up over the farms of Lancaster County. She gazed wide-eyed, trying to imagine what New York would be like. She had written about it, but this would be so different. She would be there herself, and it was real.

*   *   *

Bob lay in bed before his alarm went off that morning, thinking about Lilli, and hoping everything had gone smoothly, and her father hadn't locked her in her room. He knew she wasn't a prisoner, but she was an Amish daughter, and her father was a stern old man. He knew they had started early, and he expected her to reach the city before noon.

It was going to be a long morning waiting for her, and when he got up, he went to his small office in his apartment and noticed her apron neatly folded on his desk. It had been there since he first read her book, and he had read it several times since, in order to help make editorial comments, and sometimes just because he enjoyed "hearing" her. Her work had such a distinctive voice, and he got fresh insights into her each time. He walked over and picked up the apron and realized again how small she was. It was comforting to him for some unknown reason just to touch something she had worn, as though a part of her spirit had infused it with some essence of her. He knew now that her mother had made the apron, and Lilli thought it had brought her luck. He wasn't sure, but he was still convinced that their meeting had been fated. The strange way she had heard about his publishing house when she found the book on the bench at the dairy—none of it seemed like an accident to him. And each time he'd seen her, he had an inexplicable sense of déjà vu, although he had never seen her before. And his newfound fascination with the Amish had been richly satisfied in the past two months. He had always thought them intriguing when he heard about them. And now, through Lilli, he had learned more about them than he had ever wanted to know.

He took his time getting to the office and was relieved to see Mary Paxton lumber toward him. She was waiting for Lilli too and excited to meet the young Amish woman who had written the book.

"I'm glad to see you're still here," he said with relief.

"Me too." She grinned at him. "I'll try not to have these guys before we get our work done." She had the manuscript on her desk, and her notes, and was ready to roll. They had had it typed and put on a disk. Bob was going to give Lillibet's notebooks back to her as a keepsake. She had told him she had an idea for a second book but hadn't had time to start it yet.

After that Bob sat in his office, looking out the window, sipping a mug of coffee, and thinking about her.

His brother Paul called that morning, just to say hello. "So how's your Amish girl? Anything new there?" Bob had told him that her father was upset about the book.

"She's on her way to New York, as we speak, to do some editing with one of my best editors."

"That should be interesting. Has she ever been off the farm?"

"Never," Bob said with a slow smile. He was excited to show her New York and knew what it meant to her. It was a lifetime dream come true.

"Let's hope she arrives wearing shoes," his brother said. He always made demeaning comments about her, which annoyed Bob. But that was what

Paul did, about everything and everyone. He thought he was clever, but he was just rude. Their mother did the same thing and had a razor-sharp tongue and equally bright mind. Their father was the gentler of the two, more like Bob, who always wondered why his mother's caustic remarks never bothered their father. Maybe after forty years, he didn't listen.

"She'll be wearing laced-up boots, a bonnet, and her apron, if you want to meet her," Bob suggested, and then regretted it immediately. He didn't want Paul being unkind to Lillibet, or hurting her feelings, or his own.

"I think I'll leave Heidi to you. Not my kind of woman." And his wife wasn't Bob's. The two brothers had nothing in common. He and Bob had always been different. Each one taking after the other parent, like chalk and cheese, as the Brits said.

Bob was sitting quietly at his desk, thinking about her, as Lilli crossed the George Washington Bridge into Manhattan, and caught her breath as she saw the skyline glistening in the sunlight.

She spotted the Empire State Building immediately and felt like Dorothy entering Oz as they crossed the bridge. It was the most beautiful sight she'd ever seen, and she had no idea why, but she felt as though she'd come home.

As he'd been instructed to do, the driver called Bob on his cell phone as they entered the city and headed downtown. They were on the West Side Highway, heading south, when he handed the phone to Lillibet. She looked at it and had no idea what to do.

"How do I use it?" she said to the driver, and he glanced at her as though she had landed from Mars. She was traveling in her Amish clothes, with her bonnet and cape, a fresh apron, and her high shoes and heavy black stockings.

"Just talk," he said to her.

"Where?" Bob could hear the exchange and knew there would be a lot of new discoveries in her life in the next week. The driver pointed then, and Lilli held the phone to her ear tentatively. "Hello," she said, wondering if he could hear her.

"Welcome to New York, Lillibet," he

said warmly, and sounded clear as a bell, which amazed her.

"It's so beautiful," she said, glancing at the buildings to their left, and the Jersey shore and Hudson River on her right. "It's better than I thought it would be." And the splendid fall weather helped.

"Just for you," he said, sounding happy. "You'll be here in a few minutes. How did it go when you left?"

"Fine. Everyone was asleep. Willy took me to the dairy in the buggy." Bob had feared a scene with her father as she walked out the door. He was relieved that hadn't happened.

Ten minutes later, they were at his office. Bob was waiting on the sidewalk, he couldn't contain himself anymore. He held out a hand to her, to help her, as she stepped out of the car. She looked up at him with the now-familiar sense of déjà vu she had every time she saw him. Bob had said he felt it too and suggested jokingly that maybe they had known each other in another lifetime. Lillibet said that this one was extraordinary enough.

"It is *quite* amazing," she said with

awe. Everything looked so tall to her, even in Tribeca, and she tucked her hand into his arm as they walked into the building. The driver was going to drop her valise off at the hotel. Lillibet peered into the elevator when it opened. "What's that?"

"This is magic." Bob was teasing her a little. "It's an elevator. In this case, sometimes it works and sometimes it doesn't. It will take us upstairs to my office. You get in, you press a button, and a trolley system pulls you upstairs."

"Is it solid?" She was wary of it, although she'd read about them, but the one in Bob's office building was ancient and looked it.

"Very." She walked in with him, and he looked at her seriously. "Say abracadabra." He seemed to mean it, and she laughed and did what he said. He pressed five as she said it, the door closed, and with a hideous rattling the elevator went up, and a moment later they were on five and the door opened into Bellagio Publishing. There were desks everywhere, fluorescent lights, and the first thing they saw was Pat Riley, looking worse than usual, with a stack of manuscripts on his desk—the slush pile, yet again. It had proven to be a treasure trove for Bob. He walked Lilli over to it, introduced her to Pat, and pointed to the manuscripts on his desk. There were even more than before.

"That's where I found you, Lilli," Bob said softly, as Pat stared at her with interest. He had never seen a woman in Amish dress before, and he was fascinated. She looked like someone in a movie. And as they talked, Mary Paxton came out of her office, belly first. She came over to Lillibet quickly and gave her a warm hug.

"Welcome to New York!" Lillibet looked overwhelmed, but she beamed when she saw Mary.

"It's hard to imagine, but my mother was bigger with our twins. They each weighed over nine pounds. Amish babies are huge!" The women ate well and lived a wholesome life.

"These two are big enough, thank you. I can't wait to have them—you came just in time. I hope I last the week."

"I'm sure you will," Lilli said reassuringly. "Ours were two weeks late."

"Don't even say it!" She followed Lillibet and Bob into his office, and the three of them sat down on his couch. He had ordered lunch from a nearby deli, and they were planning to get right to work. Every moment with Mary was precious. Lillibet looked around as she took off her cape and bonnet, and set them next to her on a chair, as the two New Yorkers watched, mesmerized by her. She looked like a Dutch portrait come to life, with her long blond braid hanging down her back. She had never cut her hair in her life. She turned to look at them, and she was smiling blissfully.

"I can't believe I'm here." She had had to endure weeks of her father's threats to get there. But it seemed worth it now, and it was only for a week. She wanted to soak up everything she could in the meantime, and do the work they wanted on the book. "It looks exactly the way I expected, only bigger and with more people."

"That's about right." Bob was planning to take her sightseeing, but not yet.

And as the lunch came from the deli, they got to work. Lilli ate little and worked hard and made all the changes Mary wanted to improve her book. They had made good headway by five o'clock. Both women were pleased, and Bob had left them alone to do other things and checked on them from time to time. He could see it was going well.

At five, Mary got up and stretched, and they agreed to call it a day. Bob said he would take Lilli to her hotel. They had put her up at the Mercer in SoHo. She put her bonnet and cape on again, and a few minutes later they went back down the elevator and walked through Tribeca toward SoHo, as Lillibet looked at everything on the way.

"It's just like the book!" She was delighted with all she saw, and seemed oblivious to the stares of passersby. She was so busy observing what was around her, that she didn't register their amazement at her antiquated garb. To them, she appeared to be wearing a costume. Few people realized that she was Amish, or what that meant. She looked like someone in a time warp. But Bob was proud to walk beside her. She was so bright and alive, and such a beautiful girl. He felt giddy being with her.

They walked into the lobby of the Mercer, after a brief stroll through SoHo, as she glanced at all the shops. She had never heard of any of them before, which he found refreshing. Prada, Chanel, Miu Miu, she was more intrigued by the people than by their wares. And she found the street vendors interesting too. They went to check in at the desk—the hotel was expecting her and her room was ready. He had taken a suite for her, in case she and Mary preferred to work there. This time she recognized the elevator and felt very worldly as she got into it, and they followed the bellman to her room. He unlocked the door and handed her the key, Bob tipped him, and the bellman disappeared. She noticed that the key was actually a card of some kind that he had slipped into a slot in the door, a green light went on, and it opened.

"That looks complicated," she said to Bob in a whisper, and he grinned.

"It isn't." But she was staring at the

room by then, and he had sent her flowers, a big bouquet of pink roses. And
the suite was very handsome, with a
nice view. She walked from the living
room to the bedroom, thinking of her
small cell-like room at home. And here
everything was lit by electricity. Bob
showed her how to work the lights, the
TV, and the bathroom. She stood staring at the bathtub and shower.

"We had to bathe in the barn until I
was eleven. And then Papa built a bathroom. We all share it. But we have hot
water now from the propane tanks." He
showed her how the hot and cold water
worked, flushed the toilet for her, and
skipped an explanation of the bidet. Everything was new to her, and she loved
the TV, although she jumped when he
turned it on. She had never watched
television in her life, and had only read
about it.

"Are you exhausted, Lilli?" He knew
that new information and stimuli were
coming at her fast and furiously. There
was so much to absorb.

"No," she said honestly, although she
had worked hard on the book that day,

"just a little overwhelmed. There's so much to see and learn and discover. I must seem very stupid to you." She looked embarrassed. "Everything is so new to me. Even if I wrote about it, I've never seen it." Bob had expected that, and he found it touching, not stupid. They discovered the minibar then, and Lilli helped herself to some candy with delight. There was a disposable camera too, and Bob explained it to her. It seemed like a fantastic idea to her. "Can I take a picture of you before I go home?" she asked him shyly, and he grinned at her.

"I want one of you too," he said, and she grew instantly serious and shook her head.

"I can't. It's in the Ordnung. You can't photograph the Amish. It's not allowed."

"I'm sorry," he said, looking contrite. He had as much to learn as she did, about her customs in his case. And he had already learned a lot in the past two months, the expressions, the rules, the German words they used. "Would you like to go out to dinner?"

She nodded, looking intrigued. "Could

we look around New York a little afterward? I want to see everything before I go home."

"You just got here. I promise, we'll see it all." He looked at his watch then. It was almost six o'clock. "Why don't I come back in an hour? We'll go to dinner and drive around afterward. That'll give you an hour to relax, lie down, do whatever you want." She wanted to try the bathtub, but she didn't say it. It looked fantastic. And she wanted to change.

She thanked him for the roses after she read the card, and he left a few minutes later. And then she opened her suitcase and took out the clothes she had brought with her. She thought about it and decided to wear the black skirt and white blouse, the dark blue coat, the little black ballerina shoes, and the sheer stockings.

She attacked the bathtub first. The hand shower sprang out of control the moment she turned on the taps, and leaped at her like a snake, spraying everything with water, as she laughed and caught it, turned some knobs, got it under control, and got the water coming out of the faucet. She got in and tried all the body wash and scented soap, and she was smiling when she got out of the tub. She looked at herself in the mirror and brushed her hair and braided it again. And then she got dressed and stared at herself in amazement. She looked like a different person.

She felt shy when Bob came to pick her up, and she opened the door to him. He was shocked by what she was wearing—you could no longer tell she was Amish, she was a beautiful young girl.

"I feel very English," she whispered, suddenly worried about the outfit. She felt very strange and had never worn such a short skirt or even seen one. It reached her knee, as did the coat, but she felt naked in it, particularly in the sheer stockings. She looked up at Bob and seemed about to cry. "Do I look stupid?" She trusted his opinion in all things, and he was her guide to modern times.

"No, you look beautiful, Lillibet. I just didn't expect to see you in—in 'normal' clothes." He could see how odd it felt to her.

"I love the zippers," she giggled conspiratorially, showing him how the one on her skirt worked, as though he had never seen one before, and he laughed as she did it. "They're so efficient. I wish we had them. Even buttons would be an improvement. I'm always sticking myself on pins and bleeding on my apron when I prick my finger." He couldn't imagine living like that, but she had done so all her life and intended to continue. She never made any mention of leaving her community, and he didn't ask her. And she still thought being shunned and forced to leave was the worst fate of all, which told him she planned to stay. But would her father take her back? Lillibet believed he would never shun her and Bob hoped she was right. She was convinced her father would forgive her disobedience when she got home.

Bob took her to a nearby Italian restaurant, and she ordered pizza. She said some of the teenagers brought pizzas in during *rumspringa,* and she confessed that she loved them. He had pasta, and a glass of wine, which she declined. She had never tasted alcohol and didn't want to try it. She wasn't trying to break all the rules and go wild. She had come here to edit a book and didn't want to take advantage of it. She was an honorable person.

Bob had rented a town car after dinner so he could show her around. He took her to the Empire State Building, and they went upstairs and looked at the view. All of New York was below them, and they talked about the tragedy at the World Trade Center. He pointed out the tall buildings all around them and where the Twin Towers had been.

They drove to Broadway and Times Square and saw all the theaters sparkling brightly, and then they headed uptown and then through the park. He had no idea why, but he wanted to show her Central Park, and they drove down Fifth Avenue until he told the driver to stop at the Plaza. When they got out of the car, they looked up at the enormous hotel, and then she noticed the hansom cabs and the horses parked along the street.

"Almost like home," she said, smiling, except she thought the horses looked tired and old, and the buggies were more ornate with plastic flowers and little decorations, as young couples got in, for romantic rides in the park. It was a little more commonplace to Lilli, as she rode in horse-drawn buggies and carriages every day. There were none as fine as her father's Sunday carriage, she noticed. "Do you ever ride in them?"

"No," he said with a terrified look. "I hate horses. I'm afraid of them."

"Really? Why? Did you fall as a child?" Horses were part of her daily life, like buggies, and always had been.

"No, I'm just afraid of them. I always have been. I mean really terrified. They scare me to death." He looked anxious as he said it.

"Something must have frightened you about them," she said gently, and he shook his head again.

"I've been frightened of them as long as I can remember. I feel like I'm going to die if a horse comes near me."

"Well then, we won't offer you a ride in my father's Sunday carriage," she said gently, as they walked away from the carriages and horses, crossed the street, and stood in front of the fountain outside the Plaza, as Bob looked pensive, as though remembering something.

"What are you thinking?" He had a faraway look in his eyes as she asked.

"I don't know. I had one of those crazy déjà vu moments again, as though we'd been here before." She was smiling at him, and as he looked at her, he could see a scene of a woman in the snow, but it wasn't Lilli, and then the feeling was gone. For a moment he had felt as though they had both been there before.

"Where are we going next?" she asked, looking like a child at Christmas. His moment of déjà vu outside the Plaza had rung no bells with her. She was having too much fun being a tourist.

They drove down Fifth Avenue then, toward Washington Square in the Village. He told her about the big Christmas tree at Rockefeller Center every year, and she glanced at St. Patrick's Cathedral as they drove past. And then he took her to a coffeehouse in the Village, where they had dessert and cappuccino, which she thought was delicious. Their tour of Manhattan had been perfect, and there was more he wanted to show her in the coming days, historical parts of New York that he thought would interest her, between her editing sessions with Mary.

He brought her back to her hotel at eleven-thirty, and took her to her room to make sure she could open the door with the electronic system, and she was beaming when she thanked him.

"I had the best time of my life," she said with dancing eyes.

"So did I," he said, and meant it, still haunted by the brief déjà vu he'd had at the Plaza, which appeared to have nothing to do with her. He felt foolish about it, especially after admitting his fear of horses, and didn't mention it again.

He promised to pick her up in the morning and walk her to the office the next day. He didn't want her getting lost. He had promised to take care of her while she was in New York, and he had every intention of doing so. And he was enjoying every minute of it.

After he left, Lilli took off her English

clothes and hung them up in the closet that was bigger than her room at home, put on her heavy flannel nightgown that she and Margarethe had made the year before, and lay down on the bed. The nightgown was comfortable and faded. She lay there, thinking of her father and brothers at home, and even though she was having a wonderful time, she missed them. She had never been away from them before. And as she thought about it, the phone rang. Bob had shown her how to answer it, and she did with a tentative "hello." It was Bob.

"I just wanted to make sure you're okay and didn't get attacked by any strange machines in the room." She had told him about the hand shower going wild when she tried to run a bath before dinner.

"No, all the machines are behaving." He loved the lilt in her voice. She always sounded excited and happy, particularly now. "Thank you for a wonderful evening. I'll never forget it."

"We're not through yet," he said, sounding wistful. He wanted it to go on forever, but they only had days, and then she'd turn back into a pumpkin, and so would he. He wanted to maximize every minute. "By the way, if you get hungry, you can call room service, order anything you want, and they'll bring you food. Like an ice cream cone maybe," he teased her, remembering the day they met.

"I couldn't eat a thing," she said, still overwhelmed.

"You can order breakfast in the morning." She sighed as he said it.

"It's going to be awfully hard to go home after this. *I'm* room service there." She caught on quickly, and he laughed.

"See you in the morning, Lilli. Sleep tight."

"Thank you, sweet dreams." She turned off the lights after that, lying in the bed, and looking at the moonlight spilling across the room. And all she could think of was how perfect the evening had been, as she fell asleep.

Chapter 20

Bob showed up at the hotel at nine o'clock the next morning and knocked on the door of her room. She opened it wearing a plain Amish dress again and a clean apron. She was dressed for work. It was a striking transition after the night before.

They talked easily on the way to his office and stopped at Starbucks to pick up coffee. They bought Danish pastry since neither of them had had breakfast, and as soon as they arrived, Lillibet went back to work with Mary, editing the book. It was going well, and both of them were pleased. Mary told Bob later that she took direction perfectly. The three of them were working on Saturday when it was quiet in the office.

They had lunch together at a restaurant nearby, and went back to work on the book afterward for an hour. Mary was exhausted by then and said she had to go home, and as soon as she left, Bob told Lilli to get her coat. He took her to see the Statue of Liberty, and then they went to the museum at Ellis Island, which she found fascinating, although they couldn't stay long. She pored over the exhibits with intense concentration, and he saw tears in her eyes a few times. And when they got back to the hotel, they both admitted they were exhausted and had a burger downstairs at the bar. They talked about a thousand things, and he told her about his family.

"I've always been something of a misfit. They're all very intellectual and very driven and career oriented. My career plans were a little 'softer,' and I've wanted to be in publishing all my life, unlike my doctor-lawyer-banker parents and brother. Even my sister-in-law is an attorney, although she never practiced. She became a professional homemaker instead, like Martha Stewart, and their kids are like robots. They've had every kind of dance, music, language, and computer lesson on the planet." It was all foreign to Lillibet, in a community where children stopped going to school in eighth grade and their upbringing was more informal, and no one took tap dancing or Mandarin in school, although the boys loved to play baseball, and the girls learned to cook and sew. "I just thought life should be a little less uptight, and warmer. You shouldn't have to try so hard," he said, trying to explain it to her. But she seemed to understand.

"And I was the reverse. I always wanted more. I wanted to stay in school and try harder. My mother gave me so many books, it opened up whole new worlds, and I wanted to see more and do more than they expect of Amish women. My mother taught me that. She taught me to love what I read, and she encouraged me to try writing, although I never did until after she died. And then

I felt like she was pushing me, or I owed it to her or something. But it doesn't fit with our way of life. If I married, no man in our community would let me do it. And we can't marry outside," she said simply, and she didn't seem to mind. "Marriage seems so restrictive," she added, looking pensive, "in our way of life anyway. You give up all the decisions, and the man decides everything. I couldn't do that." Although her father made the decisions for her now.

"You shouldn't have to, if you marry the right person. It should be about teamwork." Then he laughed. "What do I know? I haven't had a steady girlfriend since college, and she dumped me for my best friend, and she was right. I was a jerk then. All I cared about were my lit classes and reading books, which were a lot more interesting than she was." They talked about their taste in books then and found they had read many of the same things, and had had a lot of the same favorites when they were young, although in some cases, their interpretation was slightly different. And they sat discussing that for hours, and then he told her about starting his business and how challenging it had been. She envied him that, working with writers and discovering books.

"Like yours," he said, teasing her, still amazed that he had found her in the slush pile. She realized now that she could easily have gotten her manuscript back with a form letter, and he would never have known. "Your apron caught my eye."

"That's why I sent it. I thought it might bring me luck."

"It brought us both luck," he said gently, and then he paid the check and walked her back to her room. The next day was Sunday, and Mary had begged for a day off. She needed to put her feet up and relax, and Bob felt guilty about pushing her so hard. They were playing beat the clock, before she had the twins.

"What do you want to do tomorrow?" Bob asked her, as they stood in the living room of her suite.

"Whatever you like, a walk in the park, a drive, nothing in particular."

"We can decide tomorrow. Maybe

you'd like to sleep late," he offered, and Lillibet laughed.

"For me, six o'clock is a late morning. I get up and feed my father and Willy before they go to work." She had a hard life, and he admired her for it, but she didn't seem to mind. It was the restrictions she objected to now, the rules, not the demands or the work.

They agreed to meet at ten o'clock, and he found her in the lobby in blue jeans and a sweater and the blue coat. He took her to Café Cluny for a delicious breakfast and then they took a cab to Central Park, walked for hours, went to the model boat pond, and sat on a bench. They talked constantly, as though they had a lifetime to catch up on. They went to the Village again for dinner that night, and Bob checked in with Mary and was relieved to hear that she hadn't had the twins yet. So they were going to work on the book again the next day. It had been nice having a day off together. They both looked relaxed and happy when he took her back to the hotel. And after he did, Bob walked to his apartment, thinking about her. He couldn't imagine what life would be like when she left again. He loved having her nearby, and their endless conversations, confidences, and shared views of life. He felt as though he had been starving for her and hadn't known it, but the clock was ticking and soon she would go home. And he could visit her in Pennsylvania, but he could never do more than that, and he knew it. She was completely comfortable and resigned to her Amish life, which was light-years from his own.

Lilli didn't say anything to him, but by Monday she was seriously missing her father and brothers. She had been gone for three days, and it felt strange not to talk to them and see them. She couldn't call them, or tell them any of the things she'd done. She even missed Margarethe. And she looked wistful when they got back to work on Monday morning, and she noticed that Mary looked more tired. But they were making good progress with the book. They worked a full day and never left the office, and Bob came in and out of the room periodically to check on them. They were work-

ing well. Mary estimated they would finish with another day's work.

Bob took Lilli to a baseball game that
night, and Lilli loved it. They ate hot dogs
and popcorn and pretzels and ice cream,
and the Yankees won the game. She
couldn't wait to tell her brothers. They
loved playing baseball at home with their
friends. It was a game that was allowed.
And every day she spent with Bob was
better than the last one. He was a nice
man, and a kind one, and he had made
every effort for her to have a good time,
and she was totally at ease with him. It
seemed as though he had always been
part of her life, and she felt safe with
him. She said something about it when
they went back to the hotel that night.

"I've never felt that way with anyone
before," she admitted, "like you're my
brother and my best friend, and I have
fun with you and can tell you anything."

"I feel the same way about you, Lilli. I
don't know what I'll do when you're
gone." He felt closer to her than ever.

"It's strange, isn't it?" she said, thinking about it. "It's like we've always been
together, and we haven't known each

other that long. Maybe my mother introduced us, with the book." She was only
half-joking. She didn't understand why
she felt so close to him, but she did.
And she couldn't imagine her life without him now either, but he was from a
different world, and there was no room
in hers for him. Her father might let him
visit occasionally, if he ever forgave him
for the book, but he could do no more
than that. There was no place for English in their community. He had to be
Amish or he didn't fit. "I'm going to miss
you when I go back," she said sadly.
And now she missed her family so much.
With each passing day, she was a little
bit more homesick, in a way she never
thought she would be. But also with
each passing day, she grew closer to
Bob. She felt torn either way.

And he was respectful of her and
never crossed any lines he shouldn't.
He was well aware by then that he was
deeply in love with her. But she was
young, and he didn't want to confuse
her with his feelings for her. Being Amish,
and what it meant, was no small thing.
And he would never take advantage of

her. He didn't even dare kiss her, although every time he said goodbye to her, he wanted to kiss her and tell her how much he loved her. But he knew that once they let the genie out of the bottle, nothing would ever be the same again. He preferred to remain silent and hide his feelings from her, but they were strong. And she was so innocent. She really was like a child, discovering a whole new world with him, but he knew she couldn't stay, and so did she. And he wasn't even sure she wanted to. She admitted to being homesick a few times. She had seen so many new things, and had so many new adventures with him. She never said that she didn't want to go back to Pennsylvania. She had every intention of taking her place in her father's home again.

She and Mary finished their editing on Tuesday night. Mary stayed late, and they both looked relieved when it was finished. Mary handed the edited manuscript to Bob, and she looked like she could hardly move when they put her in a cab a little while later. She said she was going straight to bed. It was a beau-

tiful night, and Lilli and Bob walked for a
while, stopped to have something to eat
at a deli, and then went to the living
room of her suite and talked for a long
time. Lilli felt good about the book and
the work they had done. She had a
sense of completion about it and said
she was ready to start a new book when
she went home. She had discussed her
new story idea with Mary, and she liked
it and thought Bob would too. Lillibet
had real talent.

And after a while, Lilli and Bob fell silent, and he looked at her with eyes full
of love. He didn't want to tell her and
spoil everything, but it was getting
harder and harder not to.

"Why are you looking at me like that?"
she asked gently. She had the gaze of a
woman in the face of a child and the
elfin body of a wood sprite. He wanted
to hold her in his arms, but he was afraid
he would break her, and he didn't dare.
And he didn't want to frighten her and
ruin what they had. She was so un-
spoiled and innocent, and he cherished
that about her.

"I don't know, I feel funny things when

we're together sometimes," he said with a sigh, "like I know you to your soul and I don't know why. Maybe it doesn't matter."

"I feel that way too. Like our souls know each other, or our hearts. Maybe that's what love is," she said with a pensive look and undid her braid. They were both tired, and their guard was down, and it was late. "I've never been in love," she said simply, and almost said "until now," but she stopped herself. She didn't know if she was in love with him or not, and she didn't want to damage anything they shared or shock him.

He wanted to ask her if she was in love now, but he didn't dare. He was afraid to ask. They sat quietly together in silence on the couch for a time, and he gently stroked her long hair. It was well past her waist and still white blond at twenty-four.

He finally got up to leave her, before he did something he knew he'd regret or she would. She followed him to the door in her stocking feet. She was wearing blue jeans and a sweater, and she reached up gently and touched his face.

"Thank you, Bob," she said softly. "I care about you so much. I don't know what that means, but I love being here with you."

"I know. Me too." He sounded sad as he said it. He was already thinking of her leaving. They had finished the work, and she had to go back. His life would be empty without her. He felt as though he had traveled through his whole life looking for her, and now he couldn't have her.

"Will you visit me when I go back?" she asked, sad as well. Even though her place was at home, she couldn't bear the idea of leaving him now.

"If your father will let me visit, I will." She nodded. She thought he would in time, but it might take a while for Henryk to forgive them for the book. But it was the link that had brought them together and bonded them now, so Lilli didn't regret it. She was sure her father would come to understand about the book, if only because he loved her.

Bob kissed the top of her head then and left. "See you tomorrow. Sleep tight." The words "I love you" had almost slipped out, but he stopped them in time. He walked all the way home, thinking about her. She was staring out the window of her hotel room, wondering what had just happened. She felt as though she belonged to him now. And she wasn't frightened at all. It felt right.

Bob came to have breakfast with her at the hotel the next morning, and Mary called him on his cell phone while he was with Lilli. She had had the twins at two o'clock that morning. She sounded tired but elated. Lilli talked to her too and congratulated her, and asked if they could come to see her.

They visited her that afternoon at the hospital. Lilli held the babies one by one, and as Bob watched her, he knew he wanted to have children with her. He had never wanted children before in his life. It was frightening what being with her was doing to him. He was falling apart, but it didn't show.

They had brought Mary flowers and two little blue teddy bears, and the babies were adorable. She was naming

them Trevor and Tyler. It reminded Lilli
of when her little brothers were born
when she was thirteen and she had
been so excited. Her mother had had
them at home, and Lilli had been there
when they came into the world.

She admitted to Bob as they walked
to the hotel that she didn't want children, and he looked surprised.

"Why not?" She had been so good
with the babies he just saw, and looked
completely at ease with them in her
arms, more so than their mother, who
seemed overwhelmed.

"I've done all that, for my mom when
she died. I brought up my little brothers.
I don't need to do it again."

"Maybe if you fell in love with someone, you'd want kids of your own."

She shook her head in answer. "I don't
think so. My father thinks I should marry
one of the widowers in the community
and have children. I won't marry someone I don't love." He was relieved to
hear it. And then she laughed her mischievous giggle. "I like the idea of me
being a grumpy old spinster, doing what
I want." But she couldn't do what she

wanted, only what her father wanted, and they both knew it.

"Well, invite me to the wedding, if you get married," he said, with an aching heart.

"Don't worry, I won't," she said, drawing closer to him and tucking her hand into the crook of his arm. He loved it when she did that, and he could feel her close to him, walking along at his side. And then she said what neither of them wanted to hear or think about. But the work she had come to do was finished. "I should go home soon," she whispered. He had dreaded hearing those words all week.

"I know." It was Wednesday.

"Maybe Friday?" she said hesitantly. It was the week she had promised her father and no more, which was fair.

He nodded. "I'll order the car. What would you like to do tomorrow, for your last day?" he asked her.

"Just be with you," she said simply, as though she knew what he was feeling. He wanted to spend the day making love to her and keep her with him forever, and thinking it, he knew he was insane and hoped she didn't know it too. He wanted to beg her not to leave him, but he couldn't. "Maybe go back to Central Park?"

They did just as she requested. They rowed on the lake, and lay on the grass on a blanket he had brought, and talked. They had a picnic, and walked through the zoo. It was like a day in the country while being in the city. They listened to a steel band and watched children and jugglers, and at the end of the day, they stopped outside the Plaza again, and Bob had that same odd feeling that they had been there together before, and then they hailed a cab and went back downtown.

They went out for pizza again, and Lillibet smilingly said that her *rumspringa* was about to be over, and she would have to be a grown-up now, forever.

"Will you come back to New York?" His heart was in his mouth when he asked her.

"I'll try." But she didn't want to push her father too far. Maybe for the next book, when he forgave her for this one.

And until then they would have to be content with Bob's visits to Pennsylvania, if her father allowed them. It was entirely up to her father.

And then he said something that sounded strange, even to him. "If anything ever happens, I want you to call me, or just call the limo company, and come back . . . come home . . . I'll be waiting for you here. Or I'll come to get you if you want. You're not trapped there if you don't want to be. I'll be here for you anytime you need me." He had never meant anything more in his life.

"I'm not trapped, Bob. I belong there. I'm Amish like they are." She said it proudly, with a straight back, and he realized that she meant it.

"Just know that I'm here, and you're never alone, if you have a problem." She smiled, and hoped she wouldn't need it, but was grateful to hear it. And he reminded himself to give her the card of the limo company when she left. You never knew. Her father was a difficult man, perhaps more than even she realized, Bob thought to himself. She was used to his dictatorial ways.

Bob had to tear himself away when he left her at the hotel that night, and he said he'd come back in the morning when she left. She wanted to come by the office to say goodbye to everyone and thank them, and Bob was with her when she did. It was noon when she got in the limo outside his office, and she thanked him again for everything with grateful eyes. He had done so much and been so kind to her. She threw her arms around his neck, standing on tip-toe, and hugged him like a child. And he wanted to keep his arms around her for-ever.

"Take care of yourself, Lilli," he said in a gruff voice. "You have all my numbers if you need me." She nodded with tears in her eyes and then pulled away from him and looked into his eyes and won-dered why she was leaving.

"You take care too. Come to see me." He nodded, and she got in the car and put her seat belt on. She waved as the car drove away, and Bob stood looking after her on the sidewalk. He had never felt lonelier in his life.

Chapter 21

The drive to Lancaster took longer than she'd expected in Friday afternoon traffic. Bob called her in the car twice, and they both tried to sound lighthearted, but she felt like she was in a spaceship going back to another planet, and she was. She was going back four hundred years to where she lived, as far away from Bob as if she lived on Mars. And he knew it too.

They stopped to get gas, and the driver gave her his card as Bob had asked him to, so that she would have it if she needed it in an emergency. And

they didn't enter Bart Township till after
six o'clock. He couldn't leave her at the
dairy, because she couldn't call her
brother, and there was no one to pick
her up or drive her home. The dairy was
closed by then. So she told the driver to
take her to the house. She gave him directions, and she wanted to call Bob to
say goodbye again, but she didn't. She
was home now, and she had to face it.
It felt familiar and safe as they drove
toward her father's farm. And no matter
how much she had liked New York, this
was home, and she belonged here.
Nothing had changed. She knew her father would probably still be angry at her
for the next few weeks, or maybe he
had missed her enough in the past week
to forgive her and be glad she was back.
She was ready to take her place and do
the work in his home now. And she intended to write her new book by candlelight at night, just as she had done
the first one.

She thanked the driver when he
dropped her off, and he handed her her
valise. She stood there looking at the
house for a minute, as he drove off, and

then she walked inside, happy to be home again. She was wearing her bonnet and cape and full Amish garb. She had worn it in New York much of the time too. But the English clothes had been fun for a change, along with all her other adventures in New York, and the time she had spent with Bob. They had formed a deep friendship, which she was grateful for, but her place was here.

The house was quiet when she walked in, which surprised her, since it was almost seven o'clock. They should have been eating dinner then, unless they had gone to one of her older brothers'. And she had had no way of warning them she was coming home. She thought the house was empty, and then she jumped as her father walked out of the parlor and stood looking at her in the kitchen. There was no sound from the boys, so she knew they were out.

"Hello, Papa," she said, smiling at him. "I'm back. I missed you all so much. Where are the boys?" He had sent them to their brother's, thinking she might come home that night. He wanted to see her alone.

His face was like granite as he approached her, pointing at her and then at the door. He spoke to her in German with fury in his voice.

"Be gone from my house. You are no longer my daughter. You don't live here anymore. We don't know you. Do not come here ever again." Lilli looked at him in shock and tried to go to him and put her arms around him, and he pushed her away. She had never thought he would do this to her. He loved her, how could he shun her? But obedience and the Ordnung were more important to him than she was. Lilli couldn't understand it. Everything about it was so wrong. "You want to live among the English in New York? Go to them then," he shouted at her. "You cannot leave as you did, and come back here when you want, and disobey me. Lillibet Petersen, you are shunned!" He strode to the door then, yanked it open, and pointed to the outside. "Go! Now!" She couldn't believe it and tried to run past him up the stairs to her room, and he stopped her and dragged her to the front door, with her suitcase in his other hand. He threw the suitcase out and flung her out the door. She fell onto the dirt outside, sobbing, looking up at him.

"Papa, no!" she said. And with that he slammed the door and slid the bar across it from inside. It was why he had sent the boys to their brother's. They all knew she had been shunned. He'd been waiting to tell her. She lay there sobbing for a few minutes, and then picked herself up. Her knees were scraped from where she'd fallen, and her heavy wool stockings were torn. And then, not knowing what else to do, she walked to Margarethe's, crying. And when she got there, she found the door barred there as well, but Lilli could hear her inside. Lilli kept pounding on the door and shouted that she knew she was there. She was sobbing, and finally Margarethe took pity on her and came to the door but didn't open it and spoke to her from the other side.

"I can't let you in," she said softly. "You are shunned."

"Did the elders shun me or just Papa?" she asked through her tears.

"I don't know. But he forbade me to

let you in. He knew you would come here. He won't take you back, Lilli. You must go. You have money. Go back to New York. You can't stay here."

"Oh my God," Lilli said in despair, "he can't do this."

"Yes, he can," Margarethe said firmly. "No one will help you. Go now." She was crying on the other side of the door, and Lilli was sobbing. He had meant what he had said and done the unimaginable. She was shunned.

"I love you, goodbye," she said, as both women cried, and then, stumbling, in shock, Lilli walked toward the dairy. She sat down several times by the side of the road to cry, feeling sick. She had never thought he'd do this. He was crueler than she'd thought. He had done it because of the book and because she'd gone to New York and defied him. Obedience was all.

It took her an hour to get to the dairy, and it was eight o'clock by then. She had some coins in her pockets, and the card the limo driver had given her. She didn't want to call Bob in the condition she was in and admit how cruel her father had been to her and that she'd been shunned. It was her worst nightmare come true, and she was terrified and deeply ashamed, of herself and of her father. And she wanted to regain her composure before she talked to him. She felt pathetic, and she'd never been so frightened in her life. And as she walked into the phone booth, she prayed silently to her mother to help her.

She called the limo driver and asked him to come back. He said he was on the New Jersey Turnpike by then, and it would take him an hour to get back to her, but he agreed.

She waited on the bench at the dairy where she had sat with Bob that summer, and had found the book before that. She had no idea what would become of her now. She didn't want to live in New York, she wanted to be here, where she belonged. She was Amish.

She thought of her mother. She would never have let him shun her. He was so much harder now, since her mother's death, and with age.

The driver came back for her at nine-thirty, and she was still crying when he got there. Her face was streaked with tears and dirt, and her apron was filthy and torn. She pulled her cape around herself and got into the car. He had put some bags of food on the backseat and told her to get in the front, if she didn't mind. And when he got a good look at her in the car, he saw the condition she was in. She was a mess.

"Are you all right? What happened?"

"I fell," she said, not wanting to explain it to him. Nor to Bob. She didn't know where to go, except back to New York. She had Bob's address and cell phone number. She would call him when they arrived. The driver headed back to New York then, and Lilli said nothing, she just sobbed a few times and blew her nose on the tissues he had on the front seat. They got back on the turnpike and headed north. And she noticed that the driver was weaving a couple of times. "Are you okay?" she asked him.

"I'm fine."

"Are you tired?"

"No, I'm fine," he insisted, and drove on, as Lilli stared out the window, and thought about the scene at the house when her father had literally flung her out the door and she had landed on her knees. She had flown through the air like a rag doll with his full force. He meant what he had said.

They had been on the road for two hours, and she was still gazing numbly out the window when they swerved again. She turned sharply to look at the driver. He had dozed off, then jerked awake, and at the same moment she realized it, she saw bright lights coming toward them at full speed. He had gone over the divider, and a truck was coming toward them. Lilli saw it and screamed, and the driver noticed too late and turned sharply as the car flipped and rolled, and the truck hit them with its full force. There was the sound of grinding metal as the town car literally flew through the air, and the truck crushed it, and a horn was shrieking in her ear as Lilli passed out, and she smiled as she went to sleep.

It took the highway patrol three hours to pull the tangled mass apart. They closed the highway, and traffic came to a dead stop, but it was after midnight, so there were few cars. There were fire trucks and several ambulances, and they used the jaws of life and a crane to lift the truck and pry the car from under it. The driver of the town car was dead and so was the truck driver and a man in the cab with him. There was one sole survivor, a young woman who had been in the car. She carried no identification, and she was rushed to the hospital in New Brunswick in critical condition. She was listed as a Jane Doe, and no one expected her to live. She had severe head injuries, and her arms were broken. The nurses made note, when they cut her clothes off, that she was Amish, judging from what she wore.

The police called Jack Williams, the owner of the limo company, the next morning and told him that the car had been totaled and the driver was dead. An autopsy was being performed to check for drugs and alcohol. They mentioned a passenger, but the owner said he had had none, so maybe he had picked up a hitchhiker on the way.

"Great," Jack Williams said unhappily to his secretary when he hung up, "Grayson died, and they're checking him for alcohol. Thank God he didn't have a passenger of ours with him. He picked someone up, I guess, but we didn't dispatch it."

"Poor guy," she said. He had no wife or family, or children that they knew of, and they had no idea who to notify. And the next day, they were told he'd been drunk. There had been 0.10 alcohol in his blood.

The highway patrol called the local police to visit several Amish communities within a radius of a hundred miles to inquire about a missing girl. But no one reported a missing person. She was a mystery, as she lay in a coma. And six days later, the limo company received the contents of the totaled car, what was left. There were tools, a blanket, some paperwork, and a small suitcase, which the police had examined for ID, and there was none. They had nothing to go on. Jack Williams opened the suitcase himself, to go through it. It was filled with women's clothes in a very small size, and no ID. But as Jack dug through the valise, he found a small envelope with Lilli's name on it that had escaped the highway patrol's notice. It had a note from Bob Bellagio in it, and the envelope showed the address of the dairy. Jack recognized the dairy as the place where they'd picked up the girl for Bob Bellagio, and driven her to New York and then back to Lancaster a week later.

"That's the girl we were driving for Bob Bellagio last week," Jack said to his secretary with a troubled expression. "Grayson took her back to Lancaster on Friday." He looked puzzled. "Maybe she forgot her suitcase in the car." The police had told him that their driver had a passenger, but their dispatcher had confirmed that he had dropped the girl off at her home. So why did he still have her suitcase in the car? It made no sense, unless she forgot it. Or had the driver picked her up again and not reported it to dispatch? Was she the passenger in the front seat? Maybe she was it. Jack knew their driver had been on his way back to New York when he died, and he had called the dispatcher after he dropped Lilli off and headed back. But Jack had a strange feeling now, and he called the highway patrol to report the suitcase he'd found and the letter, and to inquire about the passenger they had mentioned earlier.

"She's still alive, in a coma," the highway patrol reported. "She's still a Jane Doe, we have no ID on her. The hospital thinks she's Amish, but none of the communities we were able to reach are missing anybody. We have no clues so far. All we know is that she's between twenty and twenty-five, five foot one, and weighs roughly ninety pounds, blond, green eyes." Jack Williams didn't know what Lilli looked like. He'd never seen her. Only their driver had. But with a strange queasy feeling, he called Bob Bellagio a few minutes later.

"We've had kind of an incident," Jack Williams began cautiously. "The driver who took Miss Petersen back to Lancaster last Friday had an accident on the way back. Head-on collision with an eighteen-wheeler on the New Jersey Turnpike. Drunk driving, I regret to say.

He died in the accident. He had called us after he dropped her off, so he had no passenger that we know of, but the highway patrol reported a passenger in the front seat. We assumed he'd picked up a hitchhiker on the way back. They're not supposed to, but they do some-times. The passenger is still unidenti-fied. I just got the contents of the car back, and there's a suitcase here. I found an envelope with Miss Petersen's name on it, with a letter from you in it. Either she forgot her suitcase, or he picked her up again and didn't tell us and was bringing her back to New York." Jack Williams sounded puzzled.

Bob had been sitting at his desk think-ing about her, as he had for the past week, assuming she was back at home with her family. He hadn't heard from her, and he hadn't written to her since she left.

"Was she killed?" Bob sounded like he was in shock.

"No, she's been in a coma since it happened, in critical condition. The hos-pital says she's an Amish girl. Blond, green eyes, twenty to twenty-five, five foot one, ninety pounds. Is that her?"

"Oh my God . . . oh my God . . . ," Bob said, instantly frantic. His heart was pounding so hard, he could hear it. "Where is she?" Williams told him the name of the hospital in New Brunswick, and Bob hung up and called them immediately, after thanking Jack Williams for the information. The hospital confirmed that she was still in a coma in critical condition, and the description matched. He told them he'd get there as soon as he could to see if it was Lilli. He didn't want to contact her family until he was sure. He assumed they would be frantic, wondering where she was, but no one had called him.

It was the worst two hours of Bob Bellagio's life. He drove at full speed and didn't care if he got picked up by the police, but miraculously he didn't. He parked outside the hospital and rushed into the emergency room, where they sent him upstairs to Intensive Care. It was a highly efficient state-of-the-art-hospital with an elaborate ICU and trauma unit, and they led him into the cubicle where the young woman was lying, with tubes and monitors everywhere. A nurse was observing her closely, and a doctor was checking her when Bob walked in.

"How is she?" he asked in a choked voice. It was Lilli, almost unrecognizable, with a bruised face, black eyes, two broken arms, and a bandage on her head. But it was Lilli. He was sure. He bent closer and touched her face. She was far, far away. Her face looked peaceful, and they said she still had brain waves, and she had survived for six days, but she was still at risk. The swelling in her brain had come down without surgery, but there had been no sign of her regaining consciousness since she'd been admitted.

Bob walked out of the cubicle with tears running down his cheeks. He thought of going to tell her father, but he didn't want to leave her. And for six days he had thought she was home, and she was here.

He called Joe Lattimer and told him what had happened, where Lilli was, and in what condition. "I don't know what happened," Bob said, sounding shaken, and feeling responsible somehow for what had occurred. The driver had been drunk. "The dispatcher says the driver dropped her off at home. But he must have picked her up again and didn't tell them."

"Her father shunned her," Joe said quietly, stunned by what he'd just heard from Bob. "He wouldn't let her come home. He threw her out for going to New York. Her brothers told me a few days ago. They're heartbroken over it. She must have called the driver back and left with him." Bob and Joe were piecing it together, the story was heartbreaking, and Bob was irate that her father had shunned her and as a result this had happened. It had been her worst fear. And now his fear was he would lose her forever and never get a chance to tell her how much he loved her. She was within a hair of dying now.

"You need to go and tell her father," Bob told Joe. "He should come to her here. He'll never forgive himself if she dies." Nor would he.

"Do you think she will die?" Joe sounded shocked.

"It's not looking good," Bob said honestly. "She's been in a coma for six days, with a severe head injury. Shunned or not, she's his child." Bob gave him the details of the hospital and then thought of something. "Maybe you can drive him. It's too far to come in a carriage— it'll take him forever."

"They move pretty fast," Joe said. "I don't know if he'll ride in a car. I'll ask him. It's all I can do."

"Thanks, Joe," Bob said, and hung up and went back to see Lilli. She had been alone in the cubicle for a few minutes as he sat down next to her and took her hand in his and talked to her.

"Please, baby, please . . . come back . . . I love you so much . . . I should have told you in New York, but I didn't want to scare you . . . please . . . it'll be all right. . . . I love you, Lilli. I love you." He kept repeating, "I love you!" He didn't realize he had said it out loud, as a nurse walked by and looked startled, and he kept looking at Lilli. "I waited my whole life to find you, and you can't leave me now . . . I love you until the end of time," he said clearly, and then realized he had never said that to anyone before. He had no idea where it had come from, or why he had said it, but as he thought about it, he knew it was true.

Chapter 22

Lilli had been wandering in a beautiful garden for many days. It was a peaceful place . . . she saw people in it once in a while, but she slept most of the time, under a green leafy tree. She was very tired, and she slept for a long time. And when she woke up, her mother was sitting with her, and she said she was happy about the book, and very proud of her.

"I knew you would be, Mama," Lilli said, feeling lighter than she ever had, and happy that her mother was pleased. And then she slept again, and something woke her up. All she wanted was to sleep.

Someone was calling her, and she wanted to stay in the garden and see her mother again. She had missed her so much. But when she woke up this time, there were two people with her, a man and a woman. The woman was very beautiful and had dark hair. Lilli thought it was her mother at first, but it wasn't. She was laughing and walking beside a man on a horse, and they stopped to talk to Lilli. She told them she wanted to go with them and find her mother.

"You can't," the woman said kindly. "You have to go back."

"I don't want to," Lilli said, feeling tired again. "It's too far away."

"You can't come with us," the woman said again. "You have to go back, Lilli," she repeated, ". . . for us . . ." She looked straight at Lilli and had beautiful blue eyes.

"Will you come too?" Lilli asked her. The woman only smiled and shook her head.

"Go back, Lilli," she said again, and

Lilli could hear the voice in the distance, calling her, as she watched them go. The man on the horse pulled the woman up behind him. They were laughing, and he kissed her, and then they rode away. They rode into the light Lilli wanted to get to, to be with them, but she couldn't see them anymore . . . all she heard was the echo of their words. "Go back, Lilli . . . go back . . ." and she heard her mother say it too, and then the voice changed and someone else was saying, "Come back . . . come back, Lilli," and she didn't want to. She was so tired, and it was so much harder walking away from the light than toward it. It was too far to walk. Much too far to walk, and she was so tired.

Bob was sitting next to her, holding her hand and talking to her, when she made a soft moaning sound and stirred. Bob called for the nurse immediately. It was midnight, and he had been there all day and night. Her father was in the room too, and Margarethe. Henryk looked stern but ravaged, and Margarethe was crying softly, as tears rolled down Bob's cheeks, and he held Lilli's hand in his own.

"Come back, Lilli," he said softly again, and she opened her eyes and saw them, and then closed her eyes again, as Bob choked on a sob of relief. She was waking up. She had come back, just as he had begged her to.

The doctor came in, and they checked her, and she opened her eyes again and looked straight at Bob, with a puzzled expression. She didn't understand why he was there, and her father. She had just seen her mother, and the couple on horseback. It was all so confusing.

"I have to go to the hospital," she said in a soft voice. ". . . Lucy is having a baby. . . ." She looked at Bob, as he smiled at her and stroked her cheek.

"Who's Lucy, sweetheart?"

"I don't know." A tear slid down her cheek, but she was so happy to see him.

"It's okay, you're okay. We're all here. We've been waiting for you."

"I know," she said, feeling confused, and drifted off again. She wanted to tell him about her mother and the couple on horseback, but she was too tired. She dozed for a while then, and opened her eyes again and looked at her father. "I'm sorry, Papa," she said.

He spoke to her in German and told her it was all right. His lip was trembling as he did, and Margarethe and Bob looked at each other, as tears rolled down their cheeks.

"We missed you," Bob said after her father spoke to her. "Thank you for coming back." She smiled again and squeezed his hand.

"They made me come back," she told him, and he didn't ask who.

"I'm glad they did. I was waiting for you. I've waited a long time for you, Lilli. I love you." It was all he had wanted to say to her in New York. He said it clearly, and he didn't care who heard him. He was never going to let anything bad happen to her again.

"I was waiting for you too," she said. "You took a long time."

"I'm sorry," he said, smiling at her. "I'll try to make up for it." And then she closed her eyes, and they left her for a little while to sleep.

Henryk looked hard at Bob as they stood in the hallway, with a mixture of relief and terror on their faces. They had almost lost her, and they knew it. Two hours before, her body had started to shut down and her blood pressure plummeted, and then she came back.

"You love my daughter?" he asked him directly, and Bob didn't waver.

"I do, sir. I have waited for her all my life. She's a strong-minded girl." Bob wanted to say "Like her father," but he didn't, and Margarethe smiled.

"Is she going back to New York with you?" Henryk asked.

"She wanted to come home to you. She never talked about staying in New York." Henryk nodded. "She is Amish above all. I'll bring her home to you when she leaves the hospital, if you like. She should be at home until she gets well."

"And you'll visit her?"

"With your permission. If she wants me to."

"I think she will. And she has my permission. You're a good man. Will you take her to New York when she's well?"

"If she wants to. When she's ready," Bob said respectfully. It was up to Lilli, not either of them.

"She should be with you," Henryk said quietly. He could see how much Bob loved her, and he had heard him begging her to come back.

"I hope she thinks so too," Bob said, grateful she was alive and had survived.

"I think she will. Bring her home to us when she's better," Henryk said to him. She was no longer shunned. Henryk and Margarethe left that night. The accident had brought them together. Joe Lattimer had driven them there and was waiting to take them home. He had been in the waiting room all night, not wanting to intrude.

Bob stayed with Lilli at the hospital for the next two weeks, until she was well enough to leave. He sat with her constantly, talked when she wanted to, and let her sleep. He never left her side and slept on a cot in her room. She talked to him about seeing her mother, and the couple on horseback. "They told me I had to come back," she explained to him while he listened. "I know it sounds crazy, but I had this strange feeling they were us. But they looked different."

"It wasn't me if he was on horseback," Bob said, smiling. "You know how I hate horses."

"Do you suppose it's true that people have past lives?" she asked him. "I never believed that before, but I knew that I knew them, and she felt like me even if she looked different."

"Anything is possible. I'm just happy you're here, in this life. I love you so much, Lilli." And she knew he did. She could feel it every time she looked at him.

"I love you too."

He drove her back to Lancaster when they discharged her from the hospital. She had made a remarkable recovery, although her broken arms hampered her. He and the nurses had to do everything for her. Margarethe was going to stay at the house to help her when she got home. They had been sending mes-

sages back and forth through Joe Lattimer at the dairy, who was more than
happy to be their messenger.

Henryk and the boys and Margarethe
were waiting for them when they arrived.
Her brothers hugged her and danced
around and told her how silly she looked
with the casts on her arms, "like Fran-
kenstein," Markus said, imitating her and
walking like a monster.

"Very funny, wait till I get them off,
then you'll be sorry," she said, laughing.
And her brothers had a surprise for her,
a beautiful golden Lab puppy.

Henryk invited Bob to spend the night,
or longer if he liked. They gave him Willy's room, and Willy offered to bunk with
the twins. Margarethe was going to
sleep on a cot they'd put in Lilli's room,
so she could help her at night. The doctors had told Lilli to rest for the next six
weeks. It would be Thanksgiving by
then.

Henryk invited Bob to take a walk after dinner. It had gotten chilly, as they
strolled to the barn.

"Do you have something to ask me?" Henryk looked at him with a smile.

"Yes, I do. I was thinking maybe around Christmas . . . if Lilli wants to . . . if you think . . ."

"Do you want to marry my daughter?" Henryk asked, laughing at him.

"Yes," Bob said, grinning, feeling younger than Willy. "I have to ask her first."

"No, you have to ask me first. You just did. You have my blessing. I never thought I would say that to an Englishman," Henryk said with a startled expression. "You can't marry her here. You'll have to marry her in an English church. But we'll give you the feast at the house. And then you can take her to New York. But you'd better bring her back to visit often. We won't come to New York to see you," he said sternly. And then in a gruff voice, he looked at his future son-in-law again. "Margarethe and I will be getting married soon. We'd like you to come to the wedding."

"Thank you," Bob said, grateful for the miracles in his life. At the moment there seemed to be many of them.

They walked slowly back to the house, talking about the farm then, as Lilli and the boys watched from the window, and she looked worried.

"What do you suppose Papa said to him?" Lilli asked Margarethe.

"I think he's trying to get rid of you again," Josiah said to her. "To the Englishman this time." He laughed out loud and Markus chuckled as Willy rolled his eyes.

The men looked satisfied when they returned, and Margarethe shooed the boys upstairs to bed, as Bob invited Lilli to sit outside with him for a while. Henryk and Margarethe exchanged a look and smiled, and he nodded slightly, and she looked relieved. Henryk had softened, she knew. He would never have welcomed an Englishman before this. It had taken Lilli nearly dying to open her father's heart.

Bob and Lilli sat outside in the cool autumn air, in an old swing, just as courting couples had done for hundreds of years.

"What did my father say?" she asked with a curious expression.

"That I'd better bring you back to visit often, because he and Margarethe won't come to New York," he said, smiling, and she laughed.

"They're getting married," Lilli told him, and he nodded.

"He just told me." And then he turned to her with a tender look. "What about us, Lilli? Are we?"

"I think we already were in another life," she said softly. She could still see the couple in her dream, on horseback, the handsome man and the beautiful woman with black hair riding behind him, who had sent her back.

"Maybe we should do it again, just for good measure, in this lifetime." But he didn't disagree with her. He had had the sense that he had known her before, since the beginning. And whenever she looked into Bob's eyes, she saw someone she already knew.

"I suppose we could get married," Lilli said with a slow smile. "What did my father say about it?" It was obvious from the look on Bob's face that they had discussed it.

"He said we have to get married in an English church, but they'll give the feast here at the house."

"I never thought my father would let any of us marry an English," she said in amazement.

"Neither did he." Bob laughed. "What will our wedding be like?" He loved the idea, and the thrill of being married to her.

"Loud, busy, happy, lots of children, tons of food. I'll wear a blue dress. And we'll have to spend our honeymoon night here, so we can help clean up the house in the morning." He had already decided to invite his parents and brother to a small celebration in New York. He didn't want them here. They would spoil it for him. And he didn't want anything to ruin the day for him and Lilli. He kissed her then, and they sat quietly rocking in the swing for a while, looking up at the stars.

"I used to think that when people die, they go up to the sky and become stars and that's where heaven is," Lilli said quietly. "I always think my mother is there, waiting for me." He put an arm around her and pulled her close, in spite of her awkward casts.

"I don't know where people go when they die," he answered her. "And I don't want either of us to find out for a long, long time. I don't want to have to drag you back again. And if we were together in a past life, I'll settle very happily for this one. I love you, Lilli, and I will until the end of time." She felt a deep sense of peace, and she nodded.

"I know. So will I." And just as she said the words, two bright stars drifted past them overhead and disappeared into the night sky together, as Bob and Lilli watched them and smiled.

About the Author

DANIELLE STEEL has been hailed as one of the world's most popular authors, with over 600 million copies of her novels sold. Her many international best sellers include *The Sins of the Mother, Friends Forever, Double Jeopardy, Hotel Vendôme, Happy Birthday, 44 Charles Street, Legacy, Family Ties, Big Girl,* and other highly acclaimed novels. She is also the author of *His Bright Light,* the story of her son Nick Traina's life and death, and *A Gift of Hope,* a memoir of her work with the homeless.

Visit the Danielle Steel website at daniellesteel.com.